**The intruder must have sensed the movement behind him for at that moment he began to turn. Kate didn't hesitate. She swung the pan, lifting as she did so, landing a heavy blow to the man's skull. To Kate's horror the intruder lurched toward her before collapsing into a heap.**

Petrified she had just killed someone, Kate hurried to the man's side. Carefully she put a tentative hand on his chest, her relief at finding it rising and falling cut short when a strong hand encircled her wrist and the man flipped her onto her back and pressed her body to the ground, pinning her there. Kate screamed, primal fear taking over.

"For pity's sake," he said in a deep, well-educated voice. "I'm not going to hurt you."

Kate stilled, taking the opportunity to look up at her assailant.

As she caught sight of his features in the darkness of the kitchen, she had a sinking sensation in the pit of her stomach.

"Lord Henderson," she murmured, her breath escaping her in one big gasp.

"Yes. Who are you?" He was still straddling her, his pelvis pressed against hers in a way that would be intimate if she hadn't just whacked him over the head with a heavy copper saucepan.

"Kate," she managed to stammer. "Kate Winters."

"Charmed to meet you, Miss Winters. What are you doing in my house?"

"I am your housekeeper."

## Author Note

A question authors are often asked is where they get their inspiration from. For some it is a conversation overheard or a relationship observed; for others it is a theme in a film or a television program. I find often it is a setting that catches my attention and sparks that first idea of a story. For *The Housekeeper's Forbidden Earl* it was during a long-overdue trip to the Lake District for a friend's wedding. Despite living in England my whole life, I had never been to the Northwest before, but last year we made the trip.

Picture the scene. It was November, pouring with rain and leaves flying everywhere. We arrived in the dark, struggling to find our way down the windy lanes and almost ending up nose first in a river. After retreating inside, I may have grumbled a little about English weather in the winter. The next morning, however, the sun was shining and I was in for a treat. As I stepped out the front door of our little cottage, the light bounced off the lake and there were trees with leaves every shade of yellow, red, brown and green. It was spectacular.

It was during that trip I decided I wanted to write something set in the Lake District. I was struck by how someone running from their past might find solace in the beauty of the area, and from there George and Kate, with all the pain in their pasts, evolved in my mind. I do not want to give too much of their journey away, but suffice it to say, they prove love flourishes and souls heal in beautiful places.

# LAURA MARTIN

---

## The Housekeeper's Forbidden Earl

**HARLEQUIN**
**HISTORICAL**

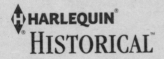

HARLEQUIN®
HISTORICAL™

Recycling programs
for this product may
not exist in your area.

ISBN-13: 978-1-335-72384-0

The Housekeeper's Forbidden Earl

For questions and comments about the quality of this book,
please contact us at CustomerService@Harlequin.com.

Harlequin Enterprises ULC
22 Adelaide St. West, 41st Floor
Toronto, Ontario M5H 4E3, Canada
www.Harlequin.com

Printed in U.S.A.

**Laura Martin** writes historical romances with an adventurous undercurrent. When not writing, she spends her time working as a doctor in Cambridgeshire, where she lives with her husband. In her spare moments Laura loves to lose herself in a book and has been known to read from cover to cover in a single day when the story is particularly gripping. She also loves to travel—especially to visit historical sites and far-flung shores.

## Books by Laura Martin

### Harlequin Historical

### Matchmade Marriages

### The Ashburton Reunion

Visit the Author Profile page at Harlequin.com for more titles.

For Sinead and Andrew,
thank you for introducing me to the
beauty of the Lake District

# Chapter One

With a sigh, Kate eased into the comfortable chair in the housekeeper's room and took a moment to enjoy the quiet of the house. It was late, a little after eleven in the evening, and she was the only one in residence. Even so, there wasn't complete silence. The old house creaked and groaned in the slightest breeze, and there was the ticking of the old grandfather clock in the hall. All these noises seemed familiar, comforting, and Kate revelled in the predictability of the routine here at Crosthwaite House. She might have been in her position for only six months, but every day was the same. Once she would have found that boring, but these last few months, it had been exactly what she had needed to heal her broken heart and bruised ego and start to discover what was important to her.

She took the cup of hot chocolate from the little table beside her and sipped at the warm liquid. It was her one indulgence of the day, something she looked forward to as the two young maids from the village said their farewells at seven o'clock. Sometimes she would take it curled up in the grand library upstairs, one of the thousands of books open on her lap, but most days she would retreat to the sanctuary of her room and enjoy the sweet drink just before bed.

The room was modest but comfortable. For thirty years, the previous housekeeper had kept the same furnishings, but when she had left, handing over the keys of the big house to Kate, she had told Kate to use pieces from around the house to make the room more homely, more to her taste. Now there was a rocking chair taken from a room on the very top floor, a set of bedsheets from a room that looked like it had once been allocated to a governess, and a footstool from a pile of furniture stored in the basement.

It was nothing like her bedroom at home, but it was functional and cosy, and Kate thought of it as a haven from the world outside.

With great effort, she stood and walked down the long passageway to the kitchen, taking her lone candle to light the way. She placed her cup next to the sink, happy to leave it until the morning to wash up, as she was always up and getting on with her day before the two maids arrived from the village.

Back in her rooms, Kate closed the door behind her and climbed into bed. There was something in the air here that meant she always slept well, especially if she took a long walk by the lake after dinner. Her eyelids were already drooping as she blew out the candle, and as the darkness surrounded her, she felt her body slip into that heavy state between waking and sleep.

The house was in complete darkness as he approached, but George could have found his way blindfolded with both arms tied behind his back. His childhood had been spent travelling between the various properties his father owned, but Crosthwaite House had always been his favourite. The grounds were filled with secret places to hide, and in the summer months, it had been a short run to the lake for a cooling dip. For a moment he allowed those happy memories to loop in his mind, knowing soon they would be pushed out by darker ones.

He hadn't set eyes on the house for two years, and even in the darkness, he was surprised at how well the grounds and building were maintained. On his departure to Italy, he had left the estate in the hands of Mrs Lemington, his elderly housekeeper, and her husband, who acted as groundskeeper. They were both into their eighth decade, and George felt a flicker of guilt that he had left them to cope for so long without any guidance. He did have a land steward who looked after some of his bigger properties in the south, but Crosthwaite House was a long way from London, and he doubted the steward had provided much input.

Tired from the long ride and ready for a good night's sleep in a soft bed, George found an empty stable and set about preparing his horse for the night. All the equipment he needed was on hand, including a small amount of fresh hay, and within fifteen minutes, Odysseus was settled in the stable with a shining coat and a hearty dinner.

Turning his attention to the house, George checked his watch. It was after midnight, and there had been no movement in all the time he had been rubbing down Odysseus. Mr and Mrs Lemington resided in a small set of rooms adjacent to the kitchen. He doubted there would be any other staff in the house. When he declared his intention to leave for good, his housekeeper had decided to hire maids and a gardener who lived in the village and who would go home each night. It reduced the cost of running the house and had allowed him more freedom to pursue his interests on his travels. Most of the rooms in the old place would be closed up, doors locked and furniture covered in dust sheets, waiting patiently for someone to return to Crosthwaite House who could love it again.

With a flicker of guilt for disturbing the elderly couple at such a late hour, George made his way to the front door and knocked loudly with the brass door knocker. Inside he heard the sound echo around the empty house, bouncing off the walls. Patiently he waited as a minute passed and then another. He wondered how long it would take the Lemingtons to get out of bed and make their way to the hallway. He reached for the door knocker again when a few minutes had ticked by.

He hadn't considered that he might not be able to wake the Lemingtons. When he'd set off on the ride north this morning, he had planned to be in the village of Thornthwaite much earlier than this, perhaps arriving around dinner time, but he'd been plagued by memories on this last bit of the journey and stopped for a drink in a local tavern to steel his nerves. For a couple of hours, he'd put off the inevitable, realising only when he stepped into the cool night how late it had become.

Cursing quietly, he took a step back and looked around, his gaze settling on one of the basement windows. It was slightly ajar, and from memory he thought it led into the kitchen, above the huge sink. He might get soapy knees from climbing in, but at least he would be inside the house for the night.

Deciding to abandon the idea of trying to wake the Lemingtons, he strode over to the window and began to prise it open, grazing his knuckles on the ground in the process. It took a minute to get it to stay fully open and allow enough space for him to slip inside.

The wiggle he had to do to make his way through the window was undignified, and George was glad he was unobserved. As he had suspected, it was a little drop to the sink, but in a couple of minutes he was standing on the kitchen floor, feeling quite pleased with himself.

Kate woke with a start, knowing immediately something was wrong. For a moment she lay completely still, listening intently, her whole body tense and on edge. Every muscle was poised, ready to move, and when she heard a clatter coming from the kitchen, she jumped out of bed, her heart hammering in her chest. Quietly she chastised her carelessness at not asking one of the lads from the village to come and fix the broken kitchen window today. It had been stiff for a while and now wouldn't close properly. She'd sent a message to the young man who would come and do odd jobs around Crosthwaite House when needed, and he had told her he would come up in a few days to fix the window. Now she wished she had insisted it be sooner.

They were remote here in Thornthwaite, with no neighbours save for the ducks for at least two miles. The new groundskeeper lived with his wife in the gatehouse at the end of the drive, but Kate knew he had gone to visit his daughter and her new baby for the week. There was no help, no one to notice a shadowy figure moving around. Kate stopped for a moment, weighing up her options. She could quietly turn the key in the lock of her door and wait for whoever it was to go away, or she could confront them. In the darkness, hopefully she would be able to trick the intruder into thinking there was more than just a twenty-four-year-old slightly built woman in the house.

Part of her wanted to hide away, but she felt a deep

responsibility for the house, and she knew that if the intruder was allowed to roam without challenge, thousands of pounds' worth of artwork and furniture could be stolen by morning.

Before she could talk herself out of it, Kate slipped out of her bedroom door and crept along the hall to the kitchen. The stone floor was freezing underfoot, and every step she took, she felt a pang of dread drive through her.

The kitchen had windows high in the walls that looked out at ground level, which meant it was a fraction brighter in here, and as Kate peeked around the door she was able to see a lone figure rising up from the floor. Her eyes flicked to the window, confirming it was the broken one that had allowed the intruder to get in.

At the moment the man's back was to her, and he hadn't noticed her at all. She knew her only advantage was that of surprise. He was tall with broad shoulders, and she didn't doubt he would easily best her in anything that required a physical show of strength.

Stepping slowly, she moved into the kitchen proper, her eyes focussed on the heavy copper pans that hung above the great fireplace. Some of those pans she could barely lift, and even the smaller ones would be a great weapon. Kate felt some relief as she lifted a medium-sized pan from its hook silently. At least now she was armed.

The intruder must have sensed the movement behind him, for at that moment he began to turn. Kate didn't hesitate, knowing this was her one chance. She swung the pan, lifting as she did so, landing a heavy blow to the man's skull. The clang of metal meeting skull echoed around the kitchen, and to Kate's horror, the intruder lurched towards her before collapsing into a heap.

Petrified that she had just killed someone, Kate dropped the pan and hurried to the man's side, crouching beside him. Carefully she put a tentative hand on the man's chest. Her relief at finding it rising and falling was cut short when strong fingers whipped up and encircled her wrist. He deftly flipped her onto her back and pressed her body to the ground, pinning her there. Kate screamed, primal fear taking over. The man loosened his grip a little, although he did not let go, and Kate was still pinned underneath him. She started to struggle, determined she would not give in to whatever fate this scoundrel had in store for her without fighting to the very end.

'For pity's sake,' the man said in a deep, well-educated voice. 'I'm not going to hurt you.'

Kate stilled, taking the opportunity to look up at her assailant.

As she caught sight of his features in the darkness of the kitchen, she had a sinking sensation in the pit of her stomach. He looked familiar, very familiar, probably because she spent ten minutes a day polishing the frame that surrounded his portrait in the great hall.

'Lord Henderson,' she murmured, her breath escaping her in one big gasp.

'Yes. Who are you?' He was still straddling her, his pelvis pressed against hers in a way which would be intimate if she hadn't just whacked him over the head with a heavy copper saucepan.

'Kate,' she managed to stammer, trying to slow her pounding heart and regain her composure. 'Kate Winters.'

'Charmed to meet you, Miss Winters. What the hell are you doing in my house?'

She bristled slightly, and this helped her to rally. With

a pointed expression, she looked down to where he was pinning her to the floor.

'Allow me up and I will be happy to tell you.'

He had the decency to look a little sheepish at the position he was holding her in and stood quickly, holding out a hand to pull her to her feet. She noticed he picked up the saucepan she had hit him with and placed it out of reach on the big wooden table.

'I'm hardly going to hit you again,' she murmured.

'I am a man who doesn't like to take chances.'

Kate took a moment to brush herself down, aware she was likely going to be out of a job after this debacle. The idea of being forced out of Crosthwaite House made her heart sink, and she knew she would have to fight for her position. There was no way she was ready to leave her sanctuary yet.

'Kate Winters,' she said in a brisk, no-nonsense manner, hoping introducing herself again would allow them to brush away the events of the last few minutes.

She saw the hint of an amused smile tug at the earl's lips and was delighted to find her master had at least a little sense of humour.

'I am your housekeeper.'

'No, you're not,' Lord Henderson said, frowning.

Kate blinked. She hadn't been prepared to stumble at this first obstacle.

'You are Lord Henderson?'

'I am.'

'And this is your house?'

'It is.'

'Then I am your housekeeper.'

'My housekeeper has decidedly more wrinkles and walks with a stoop. I may have been gone a few years, but I think I would remember if Mrs Lemington looked like you.'

'Ah,' Kate said, shifting from one foot to another. 'Perhaps the letter didn't reach you.'

'What letter?'

'Eight months ago, Mr Lemington passed away,' Kate said softly. There might have been a chasm between the two men in social status, but Mrs Lemington had told Kate the earl was fond of Mr Lemington. Now Kate saw the sorrow in the earl's eyes. 'A month later, Mrs Lemington fell ill. She realised she could not continue in her post here and advertised for a housekeeper. I applied. We worked alongside each other for a month. Then I took over.'

'Has she recovered?'

'No. Over the last few months she has deteriorated and does not have much strength now. The doctor says it is her heart.'

'Is she here?'

Kate shook her head. 'She went to stay with her daughter in Keswick.'

'And you became my housekeeper?'

'Yes.'

Lord Henderson pulled out one of the stools that surrounded the big table in the kitchen for the maids to perch on whilst they were preparing the food. He sat down heavily on it as if bone-weary. He was frowning deeply, his eyebrows almost touching, just a deep furrow in between.

'I am sorry for hitting you over the head. I thought you were a thief.'

The earl regarded her for a moment and then gave a dismissive wave of a hand. 'Understandable, I suppose.' He didn't sound all that understanding, growling out the words as if he were a wolf snapping at a lesser animal to keep away.

'Why didn't you knock on the door?' She realised once she had asked the question it was impertinent and not what a housekeeper would say to her master, and silently cursed. One of the reasons she had been so keen to take this job was the lack of interaction that would be needed with a mistress or master and their guests. Hard work she wasn't afraid of, but it would have been difficult to hide her true self all these months.

'I did,' Lord Henderson said. 'I would wager you are a deep sleeper, Miss Winters.'

'I am.'

For a long moment there was silence. Kate found herself spinning down a rabbit hole of possibilities, wondering what the elusive earl's return meant for her peaceful life.

'You must be tired,' she said, remembering her place in this house. 'I can have the master bedroom ready for you in a few minutes.'

'Good. I need to rest. There is much business to attend to these next few days.'

'Oh?' Kate tried to sound nonchalant, hoping he would give her some clue as to what he planned. She felt her heart sink, knowing instinctively nothing good could come out of Lord Henderson's return. 'Do you plan to stay long, my lord?'

'No,' he barked, as if the idea was repugnant to him. 'Three days, maybe four at the most.'

The news didn't allay Kate's fears this was the end of her pleasant sojourn at Crosthwaite House. There was an abruptness to his manner that made her feel he didn't want to be here, but something must have drawn him back, and it would likely mean change for her. Quickly she pushed away the sense of panic, trying to forget how lost she had felt before she had stumbled on this job and the kindness of the old housekeeper. She told herself she was a different woman now, more confident, more practical, more able to withstand being pushed out into the cold, unforgiving world.

'I have returned to find the deed to Crosthwaite House. Once I have that, I will be on my way.'

Kate tried to hide her devastation by turning away. Crosthwaite House was not hers—it was meant to be a temporary stop on her journey to find something of her own—but over these last six months it had become a sanctuary, and one she was loath to say goodbye to.

'Let me prepare your room,' she said, trying to disguise the lump in her throat.

Quickly she walked from the room, hurrying up the stairs to ensure the master bedroom was habitable. As she walked, she wondered why Lord Henderson was quite so keen to abandon his life in England, and if perhaps there was any chance he might change his mind.

## Chapter Two

There was nothing quite like a good night's sleep in your own bed. George had travelled much of the world and slept in hundreds of different rooms over the years, but nothing compared to his bed here at Crosthwaite House. Everything in the bedroom felt familiar, even though it had been two years since he had last visited.

Stretching, he felt the throb of the lump on the back of his head, and touched it gingerly. It was raised and tender, although he had sustained worse in racing injuries in his youth. He thought back to the events of the night before and shook his head, wondering about his new housekeeper. She'd looked like a petite warrior woman of old, ready to defend her castle armed only with a copper saucepan. The horror on her face when she had realised it was her master she had struck was almost worth the pain of the blow to his head.

George sat up in bed and sniffed. A wonderful smell was wafting into his room, making him want to spring from his bed and chase it down. A moment later there was a soft knock on the door. Before he could answer, the door opened, and Miss Winters slipped inside.

'Good, you're awake,' she said, smiling brightly.

George blinked in surprise as she bustled over with the self-assurance of a much older woman and began to pick up his discarded clothes from the night before. Normally he wasn't so messy, but the long journey and antics of his arrival had meant he'd thrown his shirt and trousers over the back of a chair and kicked his boots off somewhere near the fire.

'It's a beautiful morning today, my lord. The sunrise was sensational.' She smiled as she spoke. Once she was done tidying, she looked up and met his eyes, seemingly unperturbed by his naked body covered only by the bedclothes. He was used to having more of an effect on women.

'Good Lord, woman, do you need to be so cheery so early in the morning?' he murmured.

'I've got breakfast cooking. I assumed you would be hungry after your travels yesterday. Would you like it in bed or served in the dining room?'

He blinked, not used to being ignored. His diminutive new housekeeper was standing there watching him with a bland smile as if she had nothing better to do than wait for his answer.

'The dining room will be fine.'

'Wonderful.' She beamed at him and then spun and left the room, closing the door softly behind her.

For a moment, George did not move, then with a groan heaved himself out of bed. Tempting as it was to lie down and go back to sleep, the sooner he got on with the vital business of finding the deed to the house, the sooner he could leave England for good and never have to think about his past here again. It hurt him to be home, to be assailed on all fronts by the house that had once been such a special part of his life and now was just a shell filled with painful memories.

Once he was dressed, he started to make his way to the dining room, but as he descended the stairs to the hall, he heard the soft notes of a woman singing. He hesitated, knowing the proper thing for him to do would be keep away from the kitchen. When Mrs Lemington had been housekeeper, especially during his last few visits to the house, he had broken with tradition and taken breakfast in the kitchen with his elderly housekeeper and her husband, enjoying the warmth of the family atmosphere. They had known him his whole life and sensed the loneliness he was feeling after the death of his second wife. They folded him into their family.

Before he could stop himself, George turned and continued down the narrower set of stairs into the basement, following the delicious smells and the sound of singing to the kitchen. For a moment he stood in the doorway and watched Miss Winters work. Last night he had thought she was young, and although her self-assurance this morning had made him doubt his initial assessment, he saw now he hadn't been wrong at first. Miss Winters couldn't have been more than twenty-three or twenty-four. She moved lithely, as if with every step she was about to start dancing, and her voice was lilting and tuneful. If he didn't know better, he would have thought she'd had some singing lessons growing up as she hit every note perfectly, but women who went on to be housekeepers didn't normally have music in their timetables. Ten seconds passed and then twenty, and even though he knew it was wrong to stand there staring, he couldn't seem to stop himself.

As she sang, she flitted between the bacon sizzling in the pan and toast she was turning in front of the fire, arranging everything just so. Only as she took the pan with the bacon in it away from the fire did she turn enough to see him, exclaiming and tilting the handle a little. George saw the flecks of hot oil jump from the pan and splatter over the bare skin of her forearms before he heard her shriek, and in an instant he darted forward and relieved her of the pan, placing it carefully down on the side.

'Get some water on that or you'll scar,' he said gruffly.

Miss Winters nodded, not moving for a second as she looked at her arms. He grabbed a cloth from the side and dunked it in one of the buckets of water, dripping it over the floor towards her.

'Sit.' He directed her to one of the stools and then pressed the cool cloth against the creamy white skin of her forearms.

After a moment he looked up, seeing the tears she was desperately trying not to shed in her eyes. The skin on her arms was otherwise unmarked, and he wondered how this young woman had ended up as a housekeeper at such an age. Surreptitiously he looked at her hands, noting the reddening from manual labour and some cracking of the skin.

'Thank you,' she said quietly, looking up at him from under her dark lashes.

'Hold it on there for a few minutes,' he instructed her.

'I'm sure it is fine now,' she said, starting to get up as her eyes flicked to the plate she was serving his breakfast on.

'My breakfast will wait. Hold it on there a few more minutes.'

She looked as though she wanted to argue but had the good sense to sink back into her seat and press her lips together.

'Your toast will burn.'

'I like it well-done.' When he was sure she wasn't

going to disobey him, he stood and took the toast off the rack in front of the fire. He watched Miss Winters's eyes widen as he took a knife from the drawer and began to spread butter over the bread.

'I can do that,' she said.

'Sit there and hold the cloth on your arms,' He didn't look at her as he spoke, instead directing his words to the buttery toast on the plate.

'It really doesn't hurt now.'

'I am giving you a direct order, Miss Winters. Move and you lose your job.'

She watched him silently, her eyes following his every move, likely wary of another outburst. He took the bacon from the pan that was rapidly cooling on the side and shared it between two plates, then did the same with the eggs bubbling in the pot of simmering water.

'There,' he said, setting a plate in front of her and pulling out a stool on the opposite side of the table. 'Your arm should be fine now.'

'This is yours,' she said, motioning to the plate he had set in front of her.

'Have you eaten?'

'Not yet.'

'Then it is yours.'

'I can serve you upstairs in the dining room.'

'I do not need you to stand on ceremony with me, Miss Winters. I am here for a few days, and then I will be gone. Keep the dining room closed up for all I care with the dust sheets over the furniture.'

She blinked rapidly a few times and then pushed the plate away a fraction of an inch. 'I can't eat with you.'

'Why not?' He was getting tired of this discussion now and just wanted her to eat her breakfast so they could both get on with their day. She was petite in build, but more than that, she was very slim, and a good breakfast wouldn't go amiss.

'I'm your housekeeper.'

'I would wager you were raised with at least basic table manners.'

'Of course.'

'Then you will do as a breakfast companion.'

He tucked into the bacon, relishing the taste of the meat. Nowhere else in the world did bacon like England. It almost made him smile. A proper breakfast would be one thing he would miss.

Miss Winters nibbled on a corner of toast, and he wondered if she might refuse the rest of the breakfast, but after a moment she sighed and cut into the yolk of her perfectly poached egg.

'This really is quite irregular,' she murmured between mouthfuls.

'You have never sat down with your employer for breakfast in *all* your years of service.'

'Do you have a problem with my youth, Lord Henderson?'

For a long moment he looked her over, allowing his eyes to slip from her neatly pinned auburn hair to the unlined skin of her face. There was no denying she *was* young for the role she occupied. 'I do not care about age, Miss Winters. I care about efficiency.'

They lapsed into silence for a moment, and then Miss Winters smiled again, her visage sunny and bright. He wondered if she always managed to be this cheerful.

'What are your plans for today, my lord? Will you be reacquainting yourself with the estate? It is such a beautiful day to take a walk through the parkland.'

'No,' he said gruffly.

Miss Winters's smile only flickered for a second in response to his tone and then returned.

'I suppose you have much to do. Shall I prepare lunch for two o'clock and dinner for seven?'

'Yes, that will be fine, Miss Winters.'

'Is there anything else I can do for you today, my lord? Anything you require during your stay?'

'No. I expect to be here for three days, certainly no more than four. After that I am hoping my agent can sell the house quickly.' He paused, realising his selling the house would mean Miss Winters would be out of a job. 'There will be much to do, packing up and organising where everything needs to go after that, and I would like it if you stayed to oversee everything.' He cleared his throat, feeling a little uncomfortable at telling this young woman there wouldn't be a job in a few months.

'But after that, my services will no longer be required,' she finished quietly.

'I will provide you with good references.'

'That is good of you, my lord,' Miss Winters said, standing and starting to clear the plates away.

George had always thought of himself as being able to read people well, but Miss Winters was inscrutable as she took his plate. Her expression was serene, as if she had just been bathing in the clear waters of the Mediterranean Sea, but he sensed underneath that calm visage deeper emotions were hidden.

Knowing he could do no more than ensure she was well paid and had a set of good references to hand, George tried to let go of his guilt. Severing all ties with England and the life he had once lived here was not going to be easy, and he would need to get used to these difficult decisions. It would be worth it when he could sail away with no responsibilities to compel him to return to England ever again.

'What is he like?' Marigold said, voice low even though Lord Henderson was safely ensconced in his study with the door closed.

'Yes, tell us everything. Is he as devastatingly handsome as he looks in his portrait?' Mary said, her eyes shining.

Kate opened her mouth to answer, but as often happened with the chatty young maids, she didn't have chance to even start.

'Of course he's not,' Marigold said, rolling her eyes, 'They're never as attractive as they are in the paintings.'

'That's true,' Mary said, looking disappointed. 'What *is* he like, Miss Winters?'

Lowering her voice and checking he wasn't creeping up behind her, Kate smiled. 'He *is* handsome, in a dark, stern sort of way. I'm sure you've met people who look forbidding because they frown all the time, but actually when they smile, they're very attractive—well, he's like that.'

'I wonder why he's back?' Marigold pondered, furiously rubbing at a spot on a silver candlestick. 'My ma says it's been two years since he was last here. He left right after the funeral.'

Kate kept quiet. She couldn't tell these two young women they might be out of a job yet, not until everything was settled.

'My older sister used to work for him as a kitchen maid,' Mary said thoughtfully. 'This was before she got married and had a houseful of children. She said he was a different man after his second wife died, retreated into himself and didn't want to speak to anyone. Such a tragedy.'

'She died in childbirth, didn't she?' Kate asked.

Mrs Lemington had told Kate a short history of the family when she had taken up the position, but the old housekeeper had been very discreet, and it meant Kate knew only a little about the awful events that had plagued Lord Henderson's married life.

'Yes. Her and the baby. The doctor couldn't save either. Terrible for anyone, but he lost his first wife too.'

'How did she die?'

Mary sucked in her breath through her teeth and shook her head. 'She was only young, but dropped down dead suddenly one day a couple of weeks after finding out she was pregnant.'

Kate stopped what she was doing, her hand flying to her mouth. 'That's awful.'

'I know. Lord Henderson was young then, and his first wife even younger. My ma said he walked around in a daze for months, hardly knowing what to do with himself.'

'Did he marry his second wife soon after?'

'No, it was quite a long time. Maybe four years. He brought her here for their honeymoon, and they never really left. Lady Henderson, the second Lady Henderson, got pregnant quite quickly, and she liked to be up here in the fresh air rather than the crush of London.'

No wonder Lord Henderson had not returned to Crosthwaite House for so long, associating the death of both his wives with the place.

After Lord Henderson's announcement the night before that he was planning on emptying and selling Crosthwaite House, Kate had wondered if there was a way to make him change his mind. Her plan was to entice him to stay, to make his few weeks in the Lake District comfortable and enjoyable so that he would go back on his decision and decide to keep Crosthwaite House rather than sell it. His manner might be gruff, but she was well practised at holding her tongue and smiling demurely. Surely it couldn't be too hard a task to make him stay. At least, that was what she'd thought last night, but now, hearing what he had been through here, she wondered if perhaps she should allow him to mourn in the way he saw fit.

'Poor man,' she said quietly.

'It just goes to show money can't buy you everything,' Mary said.

'Oh, hush with that, Mary,' Marigold said, standing up and picking another piece of silverware to start polishing. 'Bad things happen to everyone, but I for one wouldn't mind a huge country estate or two to rest at whilst I drowned my sorrows.'

Kate stood, leaving the two maids to their friendly bickering. She had liked Mary and Marigold from the first moment she'd met them, both sloshing buckets of soapy water into one of the big sinks in the kitchen under Mrs Lemington's watchful eye. They were young and lively and gave Kate the company she hadn't even known she had needed when she arrived at Crosthwaite House.

Taking care to set the tray properly, Kate made a steaming cup of coffee and climbed the stairs to the ground floor. Lord Henderson had disappeared into his study after breakfast and hadn't yet emerged, although there were increasingly loud thumps coming from the room every so often.

Kate knocked on the door and waited to be asked to enter before opening it. Inside she paused. Yesterday the study had been immaculate. Everything had been in its place, and there hadn't been a speck of dust on anything. Today it looked as though a herd of angry bulls had crashed through the room, scattering furniture and making papers fly from the drawers and cabinets where they had been neatly stacked.

'Oh,' Kate said, unable to keep a neutral expression. In the midst of the chaos knelt Lord Henderson, rifling through a trunk of documents with a deep frown on his face.

'Miss Winters,' he said, standing up and regarding the room around him. He looked at it as if he saw the mess for the first time.

'I thought you might like a cup of coffee,' Kate said, bringing the tray in and setting it down on the low table in the middle of the room. 'You've been in here a while.' She paused, wondering whether to say any more or to leave him to his search.

Glancing over to the windows, Kate saw the curtains hadn't even been properly pulled. He must have been so eager to start his ransack of the trunks he just wrenched them back without securing them. After taking her time to pick her way over the piles of paper, Kate busied herself with tying back the heavy fabric, allowing more light into the room.

When she turned, she was surprised to find Lord Henderson's eyes still on her. His gaze was intense, and she felt as though he were scrutinising her every move and one day might stand in judgement. Over the last year, she had learned to hold her head up high and withstand the enquiring looks or probing questions of people when they found out a little of her circumstance. She had thought she was immune to anyone being able to unsettle her, but with Lord Henderson it was different.

She felt a ripple of nervousness run through her and quickly made her way back to the tray on the table, clearing space for the coffee cup to give herself something to do.

'My father always swore a cup of coffee mid-morning was the way to have a productive day,' Kate said. As soon as the words left her mouth, she realised her mistake and glanced up at Lord Henderson. He was regarding her with a frown and for a long moment didn't speak, as if deciding whether to let the comment go or probe further.

'Your father drank a cup of coffee a day?'

Kate nodded, knowing she couldn't claw the words back now.

'What did your father do, Miss Winters?'

She coughed, trying to buy herself some time. 'Land management,' she said with a smile, hoping he wouldn't question any further.

'Like a land steward?'

'Something like that.' She saw Lord Henderson frown again and knew he was the sort of person who wouldn't be happy until he got to the truth. Distraction was her only option.

'May I ask what you're looking for, my lord?'

'The deed to Crosthwaite House.' He grimaced, motioning to the papers. 'The house has been in the family for generations, so there is a lot of paperwork to look through.'

'Might I be of assistance?'

He started to shake his head and then hesitated. Kate sensed he did not like asking for help.

'I wouldn't want to take you away from the rest of your duties.'

'I can spare half an hour, my lord.' Kate wiggled her

fingers at the thought of getting her hands on the piles of papers in front of her. She loved to organise things and had often helped her father with the accounts at home. It was one of the aspects of the housekeeper job that she truly enjoyed, keeping a house this size running smoothly.

He nodded and moved over towards her, grabbing a blank sheet of paper from the desk and a pen with it. Roughly he sketched out what the document he was searching for might look like.

'There are a lot of places that could be hiding,' Kate said, blowing out her cheeks.

Ignoring the look he gave her, she regarded the piles.

'Which of these have you been through, and what have you still got to search?'

'I've looked carefully through these two here, but there's still a trunk filled with papers and the desk drawers.'

'I know it has been a while, but can you not remember where you put the deed, my lord?'

He gave her a withering look. 'This may be your idea of fun, Miss Winters, but I can assure you it is not mine. I have never seen the deed to this house before.'

'It could not be locked in a safe box somewhere with your family solicitor?'

'He tells me it is not.'

Kate nodded and then sank to her knees. 'Where would you like me to start?'

Motioning to the heavy trunk in front of her, Lord Henderson flipped open the lid, and Kate's eyes widened in surprise. Inside was a mountain of papers, all different sizes, shuffled together as if they had been stuffed there in a hurry.

'Someone in your family did not enjoy storing their

paperwork in a logical order,' Kate murmured. She took the top sheet and scrutinised it, unsurprised to see it dated from over a hundred years earlier. Her eyes flicked over the contents of the sheet as she put it to one side. 'Do you need records of the tenant incomes and expenditures for one hundred and five years ago?'

Lord Henderson looked at her as though she was the most infuriating person in the world.

'Obviously not,' he grumbled, 'but now isn't the time to sort through what can be destroyed and what needs to be kept.'

'That is what your ancestors have been saying for the past one hundred and five years.'

Lord Henderson gave a sigh loud enough to be heard by the maids down in the kitchens below. Kate pressed her lips together, reminding herself she was meant to be making him want to stay, not flee the country at the earliest opportunity.

For the next hour they searched, Kate patiently turning over page after page of ancient paperwork, long forgotten accounts and notes on disputes between villagers and what had been done to settle them.

'That's it,' Lord Henderson said, springing up into the air. 'I can't do this another minute.'

Kate sat back on her heels and stretched out her neck. So far there had been nothing that even vaguely resembled the deed for a house, but she had an inkling she might be getting close. The further she delved into the musty old trunk, the older the documents were becoming. It made her wonder if the deed might be sitting somewhere near the bottom.

'Why don't you go for a walk, my lord,' Kate said, smiling up at him. 'It is nearly lunchtime, and I could bring you your lunch outside if you would like to enjoy the views and fresh air. I am sure that would rejuvenate you.'

Lord Henderson looked at the piles of paperwork.

'They will all still be here after lunch,' Kate reminded him gently, 'and perhaps fresh eyes will not be a bad thing. You wouldn't want to miss something important and have to go through everything again.'

He nodded curtly. 'Thank you, Miss Winters. I will go for a stroll and take my lunch in half an hour on the terrace.'

'Very good, my lord.'

Kate waited for him to leave the room before she allowed her smile to drop. All her life she had been expected to exude an air of pleasant amiability, and it was something that on the whole she excelled at, but she had forgotten how exhausting it was to have someone else in the same house these last six months.

'Persuade him not to sell and see him on his way,' Kate murmured to herself. That was all she needed to do. Then she would have Crosthwaite House to herself again, just as she liked it. Kate closed her eyes and groaned, wondering if she could be so cold-hearted. The man was clearly in mourning, still consumed by the grief. She knew how long it took for wounds like that to heal. She had lost only her virtue and her trust in people in the debacle which led to her leaving home a year earlier, and she was still finding a way through her own pain.

Shaking her head, she told herself it did not need to be all or nothing. Two years Lord Henderson had been absent and the estate may not have thrived in that time, but it had survived. Were any decisions made in the throes of emotion wise ones? Lord Henderson did not have to live here if he found it too painful, but equally he did not have to sell Crosthwaite House either. He could hold on to it for future generations without ever needing to set foot on the property again.

She glanced down one last time into the trunk, meaning to pull the lid closed and start again after lunch if Lord Henderson still wanted her help. As she was lowering the lid, a piece of paper near the bottom caught her eye. She wasn't sure what made her want to take a closer look, but as she gripped the edge and felt the thickness and high quality of the paper, she knew this was what they had been searching for.

Kate drew it out of the trunk, her eyes flicking over it. There was no doubt it was the document Lord Henderson wanted. She almost called out, almost couldn't contain her excitement, but something made her pause. If she was going to persuade Lord Henderson not to sell the house, a few extra days whilst he continued searching for the deed might give her the time she needed. Perhaps if she could sit down and have a little heart-to-heart with him, remind him of all the people that relied on Crosthwaite House for their livelihoods, even explain a little about her own situation, he might see things differently.

Still she hesitated. He seemed so focussed, so intent in his purpose. It felt wrong to deceive him, especially when he was so on edge here. It pained her to see it, especially when she remembered Mrs Lemington's stories of Lord Henderson's childhood in this house. There must be some good memories buried under the bad.

Before she could talk herself out of it, Kate slipped the deed into the pocket of her apron. For now she was taking a few hours to think about things, nothing more. She would give herself the rest of the afternoon to decide whether she would keep the deed for longer and use the time to persuade Lord Henderson not to sell, or if she would slip it back in amongst the papers for him to find next time he looked.

# Chapter Three

It was late afternoon, that time of day when the sun starts to sink in the sky and there is an air of stillness about. George loved this time of day. In Italy, where he had spent the last year, he would often pause whatever he was doing, pour himself a small drink, and take a few minutes to sit on his terrace to watch the sun go down. It was quite a sight as it set the sky alight over the beautiful bright blue waters of the Mediterranean.

George checked the time, cursing as he realised it was later than he had thought. Hours spent bent over the papers in the study had made his back ache, and now he felt stiff.

'You need to move,' he muttered to himself.

Standing, he stretched, feeling better to be on his feet.

It was a relief to get out of the study, and he decided a few minutes in the fresh air would do him some good. Momentarily he wondered if he should tell anyone he was leaving. There were no footmen at Crosthwaite House, only Miss Winters and the two maids he had heard bustling about through the day. It meant if he left, there was no one to see him, no one to know he had gone. It must be close to dinner time and he didn't want anyone searching for him unnecessarily, but equally he liked the freedom of coming and going as he pleased.

In Italy he didn't have a house full of servants. The last place he'd settled was a small villa on the island of Ischia. It was on its own on a rocky outcrop with access directly to the sea. He lived there completely alone, revelling in the solitude, although a woman from the local village would come to clean and bring food three times a week with her two daughters. It was an arrangement that worked well for him. After a lifetime of having every aspect of his life attended to and scrutinised by servants, he liked no one knowing what he was doing.

Deciding he would only be gone for a few minutes, he slipped from the house.

The evening was warm, one of those late spring days where the sky was light and sunny and there was a hint of summer in the air. George paused as he closed the front door behind him, wondering which direction to take. He knew the grounds of Crosthwaite House better than any of his other properties, and there were a dozen paths leading to various corners. His favourite was probably a short walk skirting the edge of one of the wooded areas to the lake. It would only take five minutes and he would be in front of the shimmering water.

He set off on a brisk walk, shrugging off his jacket after a couple of minutes. It felt good to be out and active after a day of being cooped up inside.

As he approached the water, he saw a petite figure standing by the water's edge and was surprised to realise it was Miss Winters. Her back was to him, her sensible dark grey dress hitched up in one hand and her shoes discarded to one side. He paused, watching as she took a tentative step into the water. Lake Bassenthwaite was calm, its surface so smooth it looked like glass.

George imagined the gasp she would give at the cold of the water on her toes, and he smiled as she paused after the first tiny step to let her body adjust. He'd been swimming in the waters of the lake his whole life, and he knew how icy they could be, even on a hot day.

After a moment, she took another step and then another until the water was lapping at her ankles.

Continuing on the path he was on would take him down to where she was standing. He wondered whether to turn back, to allow his housekeeper some privacy, but he had a sudden hankering to feel the cool water between his toes.

'Good afternoon, Miss Winters,' he said as he approached. She jumped and stumbled a little on the soft ground but managed to right herself.

'Good afternoon, my lord.' She smiled at him brightly, and he realised what was different about Miss Winters. He'd known many housekeepers and upper servants over the years, and she wasn't quite like any of them. Most servants would hurry to assure him that they were working hard, that their short break by the water's edge was not a result of them neglecting their duties. Miss Winters did not even try to justify it. She was confident enough in herself to offer no explanation whatsoever. 'Did you find what you were looking for?'

'No. I needed a break.'

She smiled up at him, the light bouncing off her auburn hair. He was struck by how attractive she was, especially when she smiled. Her whole face was illuminated by the wide smile, and it pulled you in, making you want to smile too.

'You've chosen a lovely moment for it. I think this is my favourite time of day by the lake. Everything goes so peaceful, so still and serene.'

'How is the water?'

'Cold but marvelous.' She looked up at him, as if considering whether to say any more. 'I've dipped my toes in every day since I first arrived here.'

'Every day?'

'Without fail.' She grimaced. 'I arrived on a glorious day in early October, and recklessly I made a promise to myself I would paddle every day. Of course I did not think what it would be like in the middle of January when hail was raining down and the lake was half-frozen.'

'You didn't think to skip a day or two?'

She looked up at him, eyes wide.

'No. I don't break my promises, even to myself.'

'That's admirable.'

'Broken promises can ruin people's lives,' she said quietly, and George got the impression someone had broken a very serious promise to her. She brightened and looked up at him. 'Will you join me, my lord?'

He blinked, surprised by the question. Never had he imagined his housekeeper asking him to paddle with her. For a moment he wondered whether she had an ulterior motive, but there was no guile on her face, just the genuine question of whether he wanted to join her in something she found pleasurable.

'I shouldn't.'

For a long moment he looked out at the water, sorely tempted. He swam all the time in Ischia, often diving off the rocks before breakfast for a brisk swim along the coastline to invigorate him for the day. Here, though, it was different. As he looked out across the water, it wasn't the happy memories of splashing through the water in his childhood that assailed him, but the ones tinted with sadness. He remembered bringing Elizabeth, his first wife, to the lake for the first time and watching her face light up with wonder. He remembered taking out the small rowing boat from the jetty and her trailing her fingers along the water. And he remembered tearing out to the lake when he had been told she was dead, unable to believe his previously charmed life had changed so much in an instant.

Abruptly he turned away. He didn't want Miss Winters's sympathy or for her to see his sorrow. *This* was why he needed to sell Crosthwaite House. All the memories were tainted, all the happy times overshadowed by tragedy and melancholy.

'I will see you back at the house,' he said over his shoulder, his voice restrained.

Kate watched him go, her eyes fixed onto him long after he had become little more than a speck blending into the trees. She couldn't quite work out what sort of man he was. Mrs Lemington had always spoken of him fondly, reminiscing about the boy who had grown up here at Crosthwaite House, and the people in the local village thought of him as a fair if long absent lord.

Most of the time he seemed genial, if a little gruff, like when he had helped her after she'd burned her arm cooking breakfast. There were times, however, when she saw a darkness descend over him, as though he was being consumed by his grief, and he became cold, distant, and abrupt.

It had been a risk inviting him to paddle, but in the moment, Kate had thought he might genuinely enjoy it. She thought that once he had been very happy here in Thornthwaite, but understandably the memories of his late wives here made him feel lonely, raking up painful memories. She wondered if she might be able to spark some of that love for the house and grounds again, just enough that he wouldn't want to sell it yet.

With a sigh Kate, retreated from the water and sat on a flat rock to let her feet dry and pull on her boots. She hadn't been lying about coming to paddle in the lake every day. It was over a year since she had left home now, and most days she felt like a new person, but that hadn't come easily. She'd had to fight for her happiness. One thing that had drawn her to Crosthwaite House was how it was completely on its own, in the middle of nature. It reminded her to slow down, to appreciate the sound of the lake lapping at the shore and the glistening of the water in the sun. These little things made her remember she was only a small piece of the world, and her worries and woes did not stop the flowers from blooming and the trees from blossoming.

Her hand brushed over the stiff paper of the deed of Crosthwaite House that felt heavy in her apron pocket. Already she was consumed by guilt at taking it, and three times this afternoon she had tried to slip into the study to return it, but all three times Lord Henderson had been at his desk, frowning over some new pile of papers. Perhaps it was a sign to slow down, to consider her options. Kate felt a deep panic at the idea of having to leave this sanctuary, and even more fear at the prospect of having to return home. It wasn't an option for her, not one she could seriously consider after everything that had happened this past year.

Closing her eyes, she decided she would hold on to the deed for five days. That was only a few days longer than Lord Henderson had planned to stay anyway, so if she hadn't managed to change his mind in that time, he wouldn't have lost anything, not really. The five days would give her a chance to remind him of the beauty and wonder of Crosthwaite House, and hopefully persuade him against selling. If not, she would see out her time as housekeeper here and leave knowing she had done everything she could to fight the change.

She hurried back to the house, glancing at the setting sun. It would be time to light the candles soon, and it would be a much bigger job than usual with another person in the house.

'I'll finish your dinner and bring it up,' Kate said as she slipped into Lord Henderson's study. He was back to searching the papers again and acknowledged her only with a curt nod.

The rest of the evening passed quickly with all the normal routines of the house. Lord Henderson was so far not a demanding master, and Kate supposed she should be grateful that he hadn't arrived with a group of twenty guests and even more servants. It would have quickly become apparent that although she was a fast learner and had taken to her role as housekeeper, she had no experience with a large household.

It was approaching midnight when she slipped in between her bedsheets and took the book from her bedside table. At home she had often read long into the night, choosing to finish one more chapter and sleep in the next morning. She had to be more disciplined here, unable to justify so much use and expense of the household's candles and also aware it would be another early start in the morning. However, she liked to read a few pages to stop her mind thinking of anything else as she drifted off to sleep.

It was refreshing to be able to make her own decisions. Once she had left her father's house a year earlier, she had gradually come to realise how strictly he had dictated every aspect of her life. Even to rationing out how many candles she was allowed for her own personal use. The freedom of choice was something she cherished, and she knew whatever the future held, she would strive to protect that freedom at all costs.

She was about to blow out her candle when there was a loud noise from somewhere outside that made a shudder of dread run through her. It sounded other worldly, ghostly, and for a moment Kate had the urge to hide under her covers. The noise came again, this time a little closer. It was a mix between a bark and a howl, and she wondered if a dog had got loose from somewhere and injured itself.

The sound came again and again, each call a little more frantic, and she sensed it wasn't going to stop.

Slowly she rose, not wanting to investigate but knowing she would not sleep with the images of the possibilities running through her mind. She was wearing a long cotton nightgown that reached her ankles, and she pulled on her dressing gown that she had discarded on the chair next to her bed. Her hair was loose down her back, and she almost forgot to slip her shoes on before she left the room, having to pause in the doorway and turn back.

The noise was still occurring when she reached the main hall, a little fainter now, although she couldn't tell if that was because it was getting further away or if the creature was getting weaker.

Spinning around, she walked towards the back of the house, planning on looking out of the wide library windows to see if she could spot what was making the noise. She was taking little steps, creeping, even though she knew in here the creature couldn't see or hear her.

In the library she peered out of the window, wishing she had brought a candle to at least make her feel a little more brave. It was hard to see much, and she had to lean closer, all the time her heart pounding in her chest.

'What is it?' Lord Henderson's voice made her jump so much she screamed. Normally she wasn't someone who scared easily, but she had almost forgotten he was in the house with her, and considering all the nervous tension she had been carrying, it was an inevitable reaction. 'Forgive me for startling you,' he said.

Kate turned, and for a moment her body stilled. He was standing in the shadows, but still she could see the outline of his body. At first she thought he wasn't wearing any clothes, but after a moment she realised he must have hurriedly put on some trousers, and now he was pulling his shirt over his head, but not before she caught a glimpse of the toned muscles of his chest and abdomen. Distracted, she wondered how an earl, who would not have a job that required tough physical labour, built muscles like that.

'What is it?' Lord Henderson repeated, coming to stand beside her.

With difficulty, Kate managed to turn her attention back to the window and the dark lawn outside.

Unlike many grand houses, Crosthwaite House didn't have a parterre or formal garden. It made the most of the natural landscape, the gentle slope falling away to the lake below with trees dotted over the substantial lawn.

'I do not know, I can't see anything,' Kate said, feeling some of the dread ebb away now she wasn't completely alone.

'I'll take a look outside.'

'I need to fetch my keys.' She hesitated and then gave herself a silent but stern reprimand not to be a fool. She had walked through this house hundreds of times in the dark. A few spooky noises were not going to stop her from doing so again.

Before she could change her mind, she hurried out of the library and back downstairs, collecting the heavy ring of keys that normally sat at her waist throughout the day. On the way back up, she took the steps two at a time, eager for this ordeal to be over.

'It must be a wounded animal,' Lord Henderson said as she handed him the key for the door. 'I can't see it anywhere, but perhaps it is round the side of the house.'

'Be careful,' Kate said quietly, 'Even the most gentle of creatures might strike out when hurt and afraid.'

'You stay here,' he instructed her.

Kate balked at being told what to do. Even though she was employed by this man, she didn't like being given such a direct instruction that didn't pertain to her work. He stepped out of the library door and onto the terrace beyond. Kate waited for a few seconds. Then, with her heart hammering in her chest, she followed.

Lord Henderson turned and looked at her with a frown.

'Get back in the house.' He turned immediately as if it didn't cross his mind she might disobey him. With a flare of defiance, Kate continued following him quietly, noting how he stiffened when he realised she was behind him.

Focussing on putting one foot in front of the other, Kate breathed deeply. They were almost on the lawn now, and still there was nothing to see in the darkness, but the noise did sound like it was coming from a little further to the east.

'I see it,' Lord Henderson said. Kate stopped, squinting through the darkness to try and make out the shape where he was pointing.

'What is that?'

It was large, bigger than she had expected despite the volume of the cry when it had first started.

'I don't know.'

Kate took a step and then another so she was standing beside Lord Henderson. The creature had been silent for a minute or two, but now it raised its head and let out a cry. Despite her resolve to be brave, Kate felt her body freeze in fear, and she impulsively grasped hold of Lord Henderson's arm. She expected him to shrug her off, but he must have sensed her agitation, for instead he reached up and enfolded her hand in his own.

'I think it is a deer, Miss Winters, nothing more.'

'A deer?' She had seen plenty of deer since her arrival in the area months ago, sometimes the proud stags with the grand antlers, and more recently the occasional doe with a fawn alongside it.

'I'm going closer. You can come or stay here, but if you come, be ready to move quickly.'

Kate nodded, and with her hand still in Lord Henderson's, she matched his slow, careful steps.

As they approached, Kate saw he was right. The animal was a great stag, antlers branching high from its head and scarred and battered from clashes with the other local stags. It was lying on the ground, head raised and breathing hard. In its flank was a huge bloody wound, a mess of torn flesh and clotted blood.

The animal stiffened as they approached and after a moment tried to clamber to its feet, but it was too weak from the wound and subsequent blood loss than after a few stumbling attempts it sank back to the ground.

'What did that?' Kate asked, her voice hushed. 'A dog?' She peered in closer, trying to make out the shape of the matted area of blood on the deer's flank. She shuddered, wondering if there could be wolves in this part of the country, and glanced over her shoulder to check nothing was creeping up on them.

'A gun. Someone has shot this deer, but not cleanly, and they allowed it to get away, injured and in pain.' Lord Henderson's voice was tight and clipped, and Kate sensed the anger he felt for the person who had done this.

The stag gave another loud cry that cut through the quiet of the night and sent a shudder through Kate's body. It was horrific to watch an animal in that much pain and not to be able to do anything about it.

'Can we do something?'

Lord Henderson shook his head, crouching down so he was on the same level as the stag, but careful to keep out of striking distance of the huge antlers.

'The wound is too big, and there has been too much blood loss. I don't think even a skilled surgeon could save this animal now.' He paused, shaking his head, and Kate saw the sorrow in his eyes as he turned to her. 'I need you to get something from my study for me. There is a key in the little box on the top of the bookshelf. It opens the bottom drawer of the desk, and inside is a case with a pistol inside. Fetch it for me.'

Kate's eyes widened with surprise, but she nodded and headed off without hesitation. It took her a minute to locate the little box with the key in the darkness of the study, and her hands were shaking as she opened the desk drawer, but the case was inside exactly where Lord Henderson had said it would be. She grabbed it quickly, not wanting the deer to suffer more than was necessary.

Out on the lawn, at first she struggled to see where Lord Henderson was, but as she neared the wounded stag, she realised he had approached it and was crouching with one hand on its back, murmuring soothing words.

He looked up at her and shook his head, and as Kate watched, the great animal took a final shuddering breath before it stilled completely.

As she felt a rush of sorrow, tears spilled from Kate's eyes onto her cheeks. She let them sit there for a moment before brushing them away with the back of her hand.

'Has he gone?'

'Yes,' Lord Henderson said, not moving for a minute. When he did finally get up, Kate saw there was a long gash on his shirt, and the area around it was bloodied.

'The stag struck me with his antlers,' he said as he saw the direction of her gaze.

'Are you hurt?'

'A scratch, nothing more.'

Kate frowned. A scratch would hardly make a hole that size in his shirt.

'Come back to the kitchen and let me look.'

She saw the wince of pain he quickly tried to cover. As he fell into step beside her, she tried to peer at the wound he had sustained, but she was at the wrong angle to see.

# Chapter Four

George grimaced as he sat, the wound on his chest and shoulder smarting with every little movement. It had been foolish to get so close to an injured animal, but the stag had been in so much pain, he hadn't been able to leave it there suffering with no comfort. The stag had tossed its head, catching him with the end of one of its ragged antlers, before settling as George had laid a hand on its back.

They were inside now, and Miss Winters had disappeared upstairs to lock the door behind them. She looked pale as she re-entered the kitchen, and he recalled the trembling of her hand in his as she had reached out for him.

'Let me light a couple of candles, and then I will take a look,' she said. She might have been frightened by the events of the night, but he could not deny his young housekeeper was good in a crisis. In a matter of minutes the kitchen was illuminated, and she had set some water to boil to clean any blood from him. 'You will need to remove your shirt, my lord,' she said, as if she instructed earls to take off their shirts all the time.

With a grimace, he gripped the bottom of his shirt

and attempted to lift it over his head. A stab of pain ripped through his chest and shoulder, and he let out a grunt, wondering if he could remove the shirt with just one hand.

'Let me,' Miss Winters said, stepping to his side. Her body was close to his, too close for propriety's sake. He felt a ripple of anticipation as her fingers brushed against his skin and took hold of the bottom of his shirt.

Her touch was gentle, but she managed to manoeuvre his shirt over his head quickly, gasping as she caught sight of the torn skin below.

'I've never had anyone gasp in awe before as they undressed me,' he murmured, and looked up in time to see the colour flood to Miss Winters's cheeks. It was cruel to embarrass her like this, but the night had been so tense, so dramatic, he felt the need to lighten the mood.

She ignored his comment, instead peering at the wound with the expression of a doctor assessing a patient.

'That needs to be stitched,' she said after a moment.

'I'm sure it'll heal just fine.' He couldn't see it all that well, with the gash positioned just under his collarbone on the left side. It hurt, but that was to be expected.

'I'll clean it and then we can see,' Miss Winters said. He watched as she prepared the water and hurried in and out of the kitchen, collating a pile of cloths and towels before pulling up a seat in front of him.

As she began dabbing at the dried blood on his chest, he took the opportunity to observe her. She was a young woman who was always moving, always on the go, and it meant he hadn't had chance to *really* look at her before. He'd noticed the dark auburn of her hair, and her large green eyes were impossible to miss, but as she leaned in closer, he was able to see the tiny freckles that covered her nose and the creamy white softness of the skin underneath. Her lips were full and rosy in colour, and for a moment he imagined leaning in and kissing them, knowing instantly they would be sweet and soft.

George jerked back, shaking his head at the inappropriate thought. Thankfully Miss Winters assumed it was his wound that pained him and didn't notice anything else was amiss.

For the next few minutes, George tried his hardest *not* to look at his housekeeper, his eyes focussed on a spot on the kitchen wall straight ahead of him. It was as though she were torturing him with her presence. Every time she moved one way, her breast brushed against his arm, and when she moved another, her hip bumped gently into his back. She was petite, slender, but from this encounter he could tell she had ample curves hidden under the long nightdress and dressing gown.

'There,' she said eventually, standing back to admire her handiwork and then shaking her head. Glad of the distraction, George looked down and whistled through his teeth. She was right. The cut was deep, deeper than he had expected, the edges clean and straight but covering a large area of his upper chest. 'No arguing, you need that sewn up.'

'I will send for the doctor tomorrow,' George said brusquely, attempting to stand.

Miss Winters placed a small but firm hand on his shoulder, pressing him into his seat.

'It needs stitching tonight.' She bit her lip and then nodded decisively. 'Perhaps I may use your horse to get to the village. I think it will take too long to walk.'

'Absolutely not.'

'Oh.' She looked at him in surprise and then rallied,

but only after he had seen her suppress a roll of her eyes. 'Of course, my lord. I will walk.'

'Don't be ridiculous.'

Miss Winters turned away, eyebrows raised. 'What do you want me to do? Crawl?' she muttered, and George knew he wasn't meant to hear her words.

'You are not riding anywhere tonight. It is dark, the roads are treacherous around here, and there might be any number of dangers along the way.'

'You can hardly ride with that injury.'

'It will wait until morning.'

'My sister cut her leg when she was young. She fell from her horse onto a rotting log and ripped open the skin on her lower leg,' Miss Winters said slowly. 'Our father gathered her up and took her home and sent for the doctor straight away. He was able to stitch the wound and she recovered well, but I can remember the doctor saying these wounds need to be closed as soon as possible to stop them from festering. Even a few hours' delay can mean they do not heal as well.'

'You are not riding in the dark, Miss Winters.'

She opened her mouth to protest again.

'I understand the need to get the wound stitched, but I am not risking your safety for the sake of mine,' he said quietly. 'We have two options. Either you can stitch it with whatever sewing kit you use to mend your clothes, or we can wait until morning for the doctor.'

For a long moment, she didn't speak. Then she gave a sigh that sounded as though she had the weight of the world on her shoulders.

'Fine. I will dress it as best I can and ride for the doctor at first light.'

'Thank you,' he said and then muttered, 'Finally you see sense.'

Miss Winters jabbed at the wound with a piece of cloth, smiling sweetly at him.

'Sorry, my hand slipped,' she murmured, not looking sorry at all.

Carefully she began dressing the wound, the pressure firm. She was more concerned with ensuring it did not bleed further than with his comfort.

'Sit there for a moment whilst I prepare a bandage for you,' she instructed him.

For a minute they sat in silence, and George became aware of every movement his housekeeper made. Even if he fixed his eyes on a spot on the other side of the kitchen, he struggled to look away from her. Needing the distraction, he cast around for a topic of conversation. He wasn't well practised at polite chit-chat. These last few years, he'd done his best to avoid company. As such, it was an effort to follow the rules, so his next words were a little more pointed than he had planned.

'I'm curious, Miss Winters,' George said as she stepped back and looked with satisfaction at her handiwork. 'What has brought you here to Crosthwaite House, as a housekeeper?'

She looked up at him, eyes wide.

'You clearly are not from this area. Your accent shows you spent at least your formative years in the south. You speak of a sister who had her own horse, a father who drank coffee every day, yet you are comfortable running this house and doing the manual work of a servant. I am intrigued.'

He saw the housekeeper stiffen and realised he had stumbled on something she didn't like to talk about.

'Circumstances change,' she said eventually.

'Your family's circumstances changed?' It happened more often than people liked to talk about. Families of the gentry or upper middle classes would struggle to keep up with the demands of fitting in with their neighbours. Debts would accrue, and then suddenly it was all too much. Those who had been living comfortably were left to scrape a living somehow.

'Mine changed,' she said, turning away and gathering up the bowl of water and leftover pieces of cloth.

George frowned, even more intrigued than he had been but sensing she wasn't going to tell him any more right now. He knew about a need for privacy and normally respected that above anything else, but Miss Winters intrigued him.

As she bustled around the kitchen, George couldn't stop his eyes from following her and realised he felt an unexpected tug towards her.

He wanted to gather her up in his arms and pull her to him, to breathe in her sweet scent and kiss her until she spilled all her secrets. It was wholly inappropriate, and George felt his breath stick in his chest, making him feel like he was suffocating. He had lived a solitary life these past few years, and Miss Winters was a beautiful young woman. It might be natural to feel an attraction to her, but it was unwelcome. Closing his eyes, he tried to banish the thoughts. Of course there had been occasions over the last couple of years when he had noticed a pretty young woman, perhaps even admired her from afar, but he hadn't felt such a draw to someone. It felt like a betrayal, even though he was a widower of over two years, and even though he knew both his wives would urge him to chase any happiness he could.

'Might I help you up to bed, my lord?' Miss Winters asked, and although her intent was completely innocent, George almost groaned at the images her words evoked. He was stronger than this—stronger than base, primal attraction. He ruled his body with his head, rather than any other parts of his anatomy. Miss Winters was attractive, he couldn't help but notice that, but he would not allow himself to think any more about his housekeeper. He owed his memories that basic courtesy at the very least.

'I think I can manage, thank you. You've already done more than enough.'

Kate yawned as she tidied the last few things away in the kitchen. Lord Henderson had gone up to bed a few minutes earlier, and she was planning on getting a few hours' sleep before riding for the doctor once the sun had come up. She felt on edge and nervous and knew it would be hard to drop off to sleep, but she hoped that once her head hit the pillow, weariness would overcome her.

It had been an odd few hours, upsetting seeing the deer so badly injured and frightening in the darkness of the night. She thought of the anger Lord Henderson had shown at the careless act that had left the stag so hurt but had not killed it and shook her head at the compassion that had led to him getting too close to the injured animal.

She couldn't quite work him out, although she also couldn't deny she was drawn to him. There was something hypnotic about the man, but destructive too. When she was near him, she had the urge to get closer even though she knew any contact would leave her emotionally bruised. It was like the temptation to stick her hand in a fire; she knew it was bad for her yet couldn't quite get rid of the draw she felt for the flickering heat of the flames.

Telling herself she wanted nothing but a quiet life,

Kate grimaced. Surely she had learned to listen to the warning voice in her head.

Quickly she checked the kitchen one last time and was about to go along to her room when she heard a bump and a shout from upstairs. Stopping only to pick up a candle to light her way, she climbed to the ground floor and then up the main stairs to the first floor.

Lord Henderson's bedroom was at the end of the hallway, occupying the corner of the house overlooking the lake. A light still flickered under his door, and now it was quiet. Kate hesitated, wondering if she should leave him to it, but also knowing the cut on his chest would be starting to really hurt now and he might struggle to even take off his boots. She didn't want him pulling the wound apart even more and decided she would at least offer her help.

Softly she knocked on the door and was surprised to find it thrown open a second later.

'I heard a shout,' she said as Lord Henderson looked down at her.

'You should be in bed, Miss Winters.'

'I wanted to check you hadn't injured yourself further.'

He glared at her as if she had been the cause of his pain and then muttered, 'I am not normally such a clumsy oaf.'

'Would you like some help, my lord?'

For a long moment he was silent, staring at her with his dark eyes. She felt a shudder of anticipation run through her. Lord Henderson was a difficult man to predict, and it was impossible to know if he would throw her out of his room or accept her assistance.

'You are offering to help me undress, Miss Winters?'

Kate felt her pulse quicken at the thought, and her

eyes tracked involuntarily down to his naked torso. She swallowed and took a moment before speaking, hoping her voice would sound normal and composed rather than as flustered as she really felt.

'I am sure in this situation, Mrs Lemington would help you with your boots.'

'I am sure she would,' Lord Henderson said, his eyes not leaving hers.

'And your trousers I think you can probably manage.'

Again there was silence as he regarded her. She felt the intensity of his gaze and had to remind herself to stand tall, not to flinch. Kate was no longer a young, impressionable girl. She knew her own mind and what she wanted. No one could pressure her into something she didn't want to do. That is what she told herself again and again. All her decisions were her own, all her actions considered and consciously decided on.

It was one positive to come out of the ghastly affair that had caused her to leave home. These last few months, after rebuilding her self-confidence and her self-respect, she had determined that never again would she get swept away without stopping to consider the consequences. It didn't mean she would never make an unwise decision again, just that at least she would walk into it with her eyes wide open.

'Come in,' he said eventually, motioning for her to step into his bedroom. Kate let out a sharp exhalation as he closed the door behind her and took the candlestick from her hand, setting it on the desk to one side of the room.

Kate had been in this bedroom dozens of times, taking her turn to dust it or straighten out the bedcovers. Now it felt completely different with Lord Henderson's presence, and she wondered if it was too late to withdraw her offer and scurry from the room.

*He's just a man*, she told herself silently. He might be an attractive man who was already half-naked, but that didn't mean it had to faze her.

She made the mistake of looking up at him, and something cracked and fizzed in the air between them.

For a long moment he did not move, and then he slowly walked over to his bed. Kate followed, trying to keep her eyes off the huge four-poster bed that dominated the room and most of her vision. As he sat down, she paused and then dropped to her knees in front of him. Kate thought she heard a little groan leave Lord Henderson's lips, but as she looked up, he was silent. She put it down to his wound paining him.

'The boots are quite new,' he said as she placed a hand on one. 'The leather is still stiff, so they need a bit of strength to get them off.'

With one hand on the heel and the other further up, Kate pulled, the boot slipping off after a few seconds. She had expected it to be more difficult and as a result wasn't braced for the movement. She fell backwards for a moment before recovering.

'Thank you,' he said as she gripped hold of the second boot, pulling hard.

'Is there anything else you need help with, my lord?' Kate stood, placing the boots neatly by the side of the bed.

For a long moment he didn't answer, and then he shook his head. 'No,' he said curtly. He forced himself to continue in a clipped voice, 'Thank you for your help.'

Kate stood, and at exactly the same moment, Lord Henderson rose from the bed. Their bodies almost collided, only a fraction of an inch separating them. Kate must be the one to move. Lord Henderson had the edge of the bed right behind him and couldn't step back even a little, but for a second all she could do was look up at him, her heart pounding in her chest.

Finally she came to her senses, stumbling backwards and almost running for the hall.

'Sleep well,' she mumbled and threw open the door, rushing into the hallway so quickly she forgot to retrieve her candle.

There was no way she was going back into Lord Henderson's bedroom, so she felt her way through the dark house, only stopping when she was back in her room, the door closed and firmly locked behind her.

Resting her head against the cool wood of the door, Kate forced herself to breathe, not moving until the frantic pounding of her heart slowed enough and the pounding in her ears stopped.

'This is not happening,' she murmured to herself. All she wanted was a refuge, a place to call home for a while longer. Crosthwaite House had become that to her these past few months. She didn't need a completely ridiculous attraction to ruin everything.

Telling herself it was just the circumstance, the evening of heightened emotion that had led to the undeniable desire she felt as she looked up at Lord Henderson in his bedroom, Kate slipped into bed. An unwise decision with a man had ruined her life, forced her to leave her family and everything she knew and flee almost the entire length of the country. She wasn't about to make the same mistake again.

# Chapter Five

George clenched his teeth as the needle pierced through the skin of his chest, pulling at the wound. The doctor had offered him laudanum for the pain but he had refused, not wanting the heavy, muzzy feeling that inevitably accompanied the drug. It wouldn't have been so bad if the doctor had quickly stitched up the wound, but the man was no longer young, and despite the glasses he wore perched on his nose, it was clear his eyesight was poor. Each stitch was painstakingly placed, and it meant something that should have taken a few minutes was now approaching an hour.

'There, all done,' the doctor said eventually, cutting off the last of the thread and putting the needle away.

'Thank you.'

'I'll send the bill in the next couple of days, my lord. Send your maid if the wound looks like it is starting to fester and I will visit.'

George corrected him. 'Housekeeper,' he murmured, but the doctor gave a dismissive wave of the hand before gathering up his bags and moving to the door.

As the man left, Miss Winters knocked and entered,

her eyes immediately drawn to the now stitched wound on his chest.

'How do you feel?'

'Sore.' He watched as she paused where she was, peering forwards as if she wanted to get a closer look but after last night not wanting to be too near to him.

'You should rest, my lord.'

He grunted. He felt tired and grouchy, and the wound was throbbing. A few hours in bed would do him a world of good, but he didn't want to lie around when there was so much else to do.

'Some visitors have arrived,' Miss Winters said, her eyes flicking up to meet his. 'I've put them in the drawing room.'

'Who is it?'

'Mr Sorrell. He said he had some business to conduct with you. He tells me he is accompanied by Mr and Mrs Fariday. They were admiring the views outside, but I expect they have followed Mr Sorrell into the house now.'

'Ah, good, Mr Sorrell is here.' He frowned. 'But I don't know any Faridays.' He reached out and winced as the pain sliced through him. 'Would you pass me my shirt?

Miss Winters picked up the shirt from the chair where the doctor had helped him to discard it, hesitating before she handed it over, seeming to realise he wouldn't be able to pull it on over his head.

'Perhaps you should get a temporary valet to help you dress whilst your wound is healing,' she said as she took a tentative step closer.

'And deny myself the pleasure of having you do it?' He said the words sarcastically and immediately regretted it. He might be in a foul mood, but that didn't mean he needed to take it out on Miss Winters. She had done nothing except offer to help. It was his own traitorous mind that was being so troublesome.

The housekeeper paused with her hands outstretched, her eyes moving up to meet his.

'I will enquire in the village if there is anyone available for a few weeks.'

'I will not be staying a few weeks.'

'The doctor advised you not to travel. I heard him.'

'It is a flesh wound, nothing more. I will be back to normal activities within a day or two.'

'Unless the wound festers,' Miss Winters muttered, and for an instant he wondered if she was wishing that fate on him.

'It will not fester.'

'Wonderful. Shall we consult your crystal ball about any other matters of importance, my lord?'

With the air of a schoolteacher, she lifted the shirt over his head and helped him thread his arm through before stepping away, not meeting his eyes.

'What shall I do about the guests? I can give them tea and send them on their way if you need to rest.'

'No, tell them I will be through in a moment.'

He wondered if he imagined the disappointed expression on Miss Winters's face, but she was gone too quickly for him to be sure.

Knowing he looked disheveled, he decided not to check his appearance in the mirror before greeting his guests. He hadn't shaved, and although the shirt covered his wound, he couldn't manage a cravat or jacket. He reasoned it was his own home and if the Faridays wanted to be offended, whoever they were, then he didn't much care.

'Good morning,' he said as he entered the drawing

room. Mr Sorrell jumped up at once, his thick grey hair bobbing above his head as he bowed to George and then shifted from foot to foot.

'Good morning, my lord. I hope it is not too early for our business.'

'Not at all.'

'I have brought Mr and Mrs Fariday with me, I hope it is not too much of an imposition,' Mr Sorrell said as the young couple stood to be introduced. 'They are in the area on their honeymoon and are looking for a suitable property to make their home.'

'A pleasure to meet you both, and congratulations on your recent nuptials.'

Mr Sorrell took George to the side for a moment, lowering his voice. 'I am sorry to turn up with them unannounced, but they are heading south tomorrow, and given your eagerness to sell the property, I thought it would be unfortunate to miss an opportunity to have someone show them round. I can delay the viewing until you have vacated the house if you would prefer.'

George glanced over at the young couple, who were looking around the drawing room in delight.

'No, let them look. The sooner I get a buyer the better.'

'Very good sir. Normally I would offer to show them round, but I do not have any knowledge of this property yet. Is there someone else who might be able to oblige?'

With a nod, George went to the corner of the room and pulled the bell cord to summon Miss Winters from whatever she was doing. She might have been here for only a few months, but she knew the house well and was eloquent and likeable.

'This is my housekeeper, Miss Winters,' George said

as she entered the room. 'Miss Winters, this is Mr and Mrs Fariday. They have come to look round the house.'

'Good morning,' Miss Winters said, smiling warmly at the couple as she turned to them. George was watching her—he found it hard not to—and that meant he saw the exact moment the expression on her face froze, as if she had just seen a ghost.

'You're best placed to show them round. Please take them on a tour and show them whatever they would like. I will be in my study with Mr Sorrell.'

'Of course, my lord,' she said, her expression still stiff as if she had been frozen in that position. 'Might I have a moment of your time first?'

In the couple of days since he had arrived back at Crosthwaite House, Miss Winters had asked nothing of him, and he sensed the desperation in her voice, so he nodded, guiding her out of the room.

'Please make yourself at home,' he said over his shoulder.

Once they were outside in the hall, Miss Winters waited until the door was closed to say anything.

'Surely you would be better showing them round,' she said. There was a note of pleading in her voice, and George felt intrigued by why the housekeeper did not want to interact with these potential buyers. 'You know the house, the best parts of it. I just clean it.'

'You do more than that.'

'I don't live in it, though, not the part they want to live in. How would I be able to show them the best place to curl up with a book on a winter's evening or the perfect room for entertaining?'

'They are not going to want you to plan their life here Miss Winters, just show them around. Point out each room, let them have a look, and then move them on.'

'Maybe they would prefer having a wander round themselves without me impeding them.'

'*I* wouldn't prefer that.'

She fidgeted and down for a moment, and he could see she was weighing up whether to say anything else.

'Is there a reason you don't want to show them round?' he asked.

'Of course not, my lord.' She spoke a little too quickly. George shrugged. Perhaps if she told him the truth, he might be more inclined to indulge her, but if she wasn't going to explain her objections, she would just have to get on with it.

'Go on then, Miss Winters. Remember to show them all the best bits. I want to be rid of this place as soon as possible.'

He watched as she slipped back into the drawing room, squaring her shoulders.

'If you would like to follow me, Mr and Mrs Fariday, I will show you the house.' George frowned, wondering if he imagined the slightly northern lilt to the house-keeper's voice. Normally her voice was pure southerner. As they walked out of the drawing room, he noticed Miss Winters's head was bowed, and she had pulled free a few loose strands of hair to cover her face.

Intrigued, he watched them go through to the dining room. She was an unusual housekeeper, far too young for her position, although he could not fault her work. In the last six months, she had smoothly taken over the running of the house and did it seemingly effortlessly. She was eloquent and had the air of someone who had been at least partially formally educated, and she called him *my lord* all the time when the other servants would call him *sir*.

It was none of his business, the background of his

housekeeper. If she did a good job and kept the house in order, it didn't matter if she was the impoverished daughter of some second son of a baron or the illegitimate daughter of a *respectable* parish vicar, yet George found himself unable to walk away. He should use this time to meet with his solicitor, to discuss what was needed for him to proceed with the sale of all his English properties, but he found himself staring after the housekeeper and the couple walking after her. Telling himself it was a desire to see the house sold, he moved to follow them, suppressing the part of his mind that probed him to admit it was Miss Winters he wanted to follow, to garner some knowledge about her past if it was offered. He tried to forget the previous night, the images he'd been plagued with after she had come into his bedroom. George had always dreamed very vividly, and last night had been no exception. In the morning he'd woken in a mixture of desire and guilt.

'It was delirium,' he muttered as he followed Miss Winters into the hall. His wound had throbbed until he fell asleep, and no doubt that was to blame for the dreams he'd had.

'I'll be with you in a few minutes, Sorrell,' he said into the drawing room. Then, with a decisive stride, he hurried to catch up with the Faridays and Miss Winters.

They were coming out of the dining room and entering the library now, and he caught the housekeeper telling the young couple about the room in a sing-song northern accent.

'You're not very good at that,' he murmured in her ear as he came up behind her.

Miss Winters threw him a look most servants would never dream of giving their employer, pressing her lips together. For the first time that day he smiled, amused by her reaction. Normally he didn't like to get involved in other people's lives, but anything to distract him today was a good thing.

'Where did you say you were from, Mr Fariday?' George said, stepping further into the room.

'Sussex, although I spend most of my time in London. I met my dear Edwina in Sussex, though.'

'What brings you looking for a property so far north?'

'It's beautiful here.' Mrs Fariday answered this time, her eyes wide as they stepped into the impressive library.

He studied the newlywed couple, taking in how his housekeeper kept her face turned away from the young woman as much as possible. He supposed they were of an age and wondered if they perhaps knew one another somehow.

'Why don't you show them the terrace, Miss Winters?' he suggested, watching as she unlocked the door that led outside. The view from here was magnificent. In all the years he'd lived at Crosthwaite House, it never ceased to take his breath away. In the foreground were the lush green rolling gardens, dotted with trees and gently sloping to the banks of Lake Bassenthwaite. The lake itself was dark but not foreboding, and George always thought it looked different depending on how the clouds formed and moved above it. Further, often shrouded in the mist, were the hills and mountains that surrounded the lake.

'This is glorious.' Mrs Fariday turned to Miss Winters and smiled. 'I wonder you ever get any work done with views like this to marvel at.'

'The countryside is beautiful,' Miss Winters said, turning her face again, 'And it changes with the weather, so the view is never the same.'

Mrs Fariday glanced back at the housekeeper and frowned. 'Have we…' she began, but Miss Winters hurriedly began speaking.

'The terrace is a lovely place for taking meals on a sunny day, and it has views over the garden if you wanted to keep an eye on any children playing in the future.'

'You do look terribly like someone I used to know,' Mrs Fariday said quietly.

George saw the flicker of panic in his housekeeper's eyes and then marvelled as she rallied quickly.

'Perhaps we have met before, Mrs Fariday,' she said. 'Have you been to Cumbria much?'

'No, this is the first time. You're from Cumbria?'

He saw her struggle for an instant and realised she didn't like to lie outright. It was one thing to fool someone by omission or by allowing them to jump to conclusions, but quite something else to directly lie to their face.

'Born and bred,' George said, stepping in. 'Miss Winters has been with my family for years.'

'Oh.' Mrs Fariday shrugged and immediately lost interest, turning back to her husband, who held out his hand to her. Together they took a few steps along the terrace to marvel at the view.

Miss Winters's shoulders slumped as she got a respite from the curious eyes of Mrs Fariday. 'You know that woman?' George murmured.

'How would I know someone like that?' she said, but her tone was not convincing.

'You're from Sussex, then. Sussex is a long way away.'

'As is Italy,' she said, giving him a challenging look. He grunted. She was not wrong.

'I am happy to admit I fled England two years ago.

My first instinct was to get as far away as possible, but there is something special about Italy, something that made me pause.'

'I feel that way about here,' Miss Winters said quietly, and suddenly George felt bad for probing. He knew what it was to need a place of sanctuary, and he would not like it if his past tried to encroach on his new life.

'You know Mrs Fariday?'

'A little, in another life, another place.'

'I sense you do not wish to be recognised.'

'No.' She looked so panicked at the idea he felt a flicker of sympathy.

'I will make you a bargain,' he said quietly. 'You see to it Mr Sorrell is well looked after and I will finish showing the newlyweds around.'

'That is very kind, my lord. Are you sure?'

'Go.'

She smiled at him then, a genuine smile filled with warmth, and George felt as though he had been shot through the heart for an instant. Quickly he dismissed the sensation and moved over to the young couple, who were still entranced with the view. With any luck they would put in a good offer for the house and he would be able to conclude his business in England.

His eyes flicked to where Miss Winters was slipping back into the library, and for a moment he wondered if a delay of a few weeks would be a bad thing. He was intrigued by his housekeeper, intrigued and, if he was honest, a little beguiled.

'No distractions,' he murmured to himself, plastering a smile onto his lips and striding over to the Faridays. He needed to conclude his business here as soon as possible, and then he could leave England for good. Anything delaying that was unacceptable. When he had planned to return to Crosthwaite House, he had been worried he might be assailed by too many terrible memories, too many emotions. Thus far he had coped well and even had on occasion been pleasantly surprised by some of the good memories he'd encountered here, but he didn't want to risk the grief overcoming him again. After the death of his second wife, every room had reminded him of her, every piece of furniture, every walk around the estate. He didn't want to go back to that.

# Chapter Six

'It is Mary, isn't it?' Lord Henderson said.

Kate paused in the shadows to watch the interaction, her interest piqued. The earl liked to scowl and growl his way around the house, but Kate was beginning to suspect this was an act, something to make people keep their distance. He was too well liked in the village to be an ogre, and she had seen his kindness too.

Earlier when he had told her to leave showing the Faridays around the house to him, *that* had been kind. He had noticed she was genuinely upset by Mrs Fariday's presence and had swooped in to save her. As her employer, he hadn't needed to do it, but he had all the same.

'Yes sir,' Mary said, bobbing into a little curtsy.

'I think your sister used to work here.'

'Yes, my older sister, Lizzie.'

'Is she well?'

'Yes sir. She has three babies now and another on the way.'

'You must give her my congratulations, Mary.'

'I will, sir.'

Mary hurried off, beaming, and Kate marvelled at

what a difference it was to a maid to be acknowledged and treated like a person rather than just having orders barked at them.

'You're smiling at me, Miss Winters.'

She hadn't even realised Lord Henderson was aware of her presence.

'I'm smiling at the world, my lord.'

'Do you care to share the reason for your happiness?'

Kate stepped towards the earl, her eyes coming up to meet his. 'You were kind to Mary then, and you were kind to me earlier today.'

'So it *was* me you were smiling at.'

Kate felt her body sway forwards ever so slightly, as if there was an invisible force pulling her towards Lord Henderson. Already she was standing too close, but she couldn't seem to pull herself away.

Lord Henderson made no attempt to move either, his eyes holding hers for far longer than was appropriate or necessary.

'I wanted to say thank you,' she said quietly. 'For helping with the Faridays earlier.'

'There is a story there, and one day I hope you might tell it to me.'

'Perhaps one day.' She rallied and finally managed to take a step back. 'It is a beautiful evening. I wondered if you wanted me to prepare you a basket to take some tea out with you so you could have a break from all the paperwork you have been buried under.'

Mr Sorrell had left about an hour earlier after spending a good part of the afternoon closeted with Lord Henderson in his study, no doubt going over the paperwork needed for the selling of all the earl's properties. Kate had found an excuse to pop in a few times, bringing in trays of tea and cake and later coming back to clear the remnants. On each occasion, Lord Henderson had paused when she had entered, his eyes following her around the room. Mr Sorrell had seemed less distracted, continuing his animated discussion of prices and the practicalities of selling the estates in the south of England.

For a moment, she thought Lord Henderson might refuse and retreat back to his study, but then he nodded, stretching out his neck from side to side. 'I have been looking at the same set of papers for the last hour. A break would be good.'

'Wonderful,' Kate said, clapping her hands. 'I will put something together for you to take.'

'Make it for two.'

'Are you expecting a guest, my lord?'

'No. I want you to accompany me.'

Kate paused, not knowing how to react. Earlier she had heard him talking about the house to the Faridays when he had been showing them round. She'd listened as he had mentioned all the things he loved, from the dark wood of the staircase to the cosy nooks in the library. No matter what he said, there was still a lot of love in his heart for this house. *That* was what she wanted to nurture, to encourage to flourish. It would be easier to do that if she was there with him, pointing out all the advantages of the estate, but even so, Kate knew it was a bad idea.

'I'm your housekeeper,' she said softly.

'That is not the sum of who you are, Miss Winters.'

'It is who I am to you.'

'I am interested in hearing about how things have been whilst I've been away. I think you are best placed to inform me.'

Kate conceded with a quick nod. His reasoning made

sense. She was the only one who could update him on what had happened at Crosthwaite House over the last few months. Lord Henderson smiled in triumph, and Kate felt momentarily stunned. He didn't smile much, but when he did, it transformed his face.

'Shall we say half an hour?'

It was a glorious late afternoon when they set out from the house. The sky was heavy with dark clouds, but there were gaps where the sun would occasionally peek out, shining down and making everything look golden and warm.

'You do not trust the weather,' Lord Henderson said, motioning to the cloak she had draped over her shoulders, the hood currently down but ready to be whipped up at the first raindrop.

'I have been caught out far too many times. On days where there had been nothing but glorious sunshine, I have gone for a stroll and been caught in the most terrible storms, and when there has been a thick mist, I've postponed going out only to find an hour later it is warm and clear.'

'The weather here isn't like anywhere else in England.'

'Or Italy, I expect.'

'No.' Lord Henderson shook his head, and for an instant, Kate could see he was back in his villa, soaking up the sunshine. She cursed herself for leading his thoughts there when she was trying so hard to make him appreciate the beauty of this little slice of England.

'You are not bringing a coat?' she asked.

'Where is the fun in that? A stroll to the lake should come with some risk.'

'I'll remind you of that when you are running from tree to tree to find shelter on the walk back.'

'I have hardy northern blood in my veins,' he said. 'A little rain never hurt anyone.'

'Your family are from this area?'

'My mother is,' Lord Henderson said, picking out a path that led them round a small copse of trees before heading towards the lake. 'This was her family's home, where she spent much of her childhood.'

'And your father?'

'*Not* a northerner, although he fell in love with this place as soon as he set eyes on it. My father grew up in Hampshire, and I spent some of my childhood there, but it was up here I always longed to come.'

'I can see why.'

'When my mother died, my father clung to Crosthwaite House as a way to remember her, and I spent many of the holidays from school up here.'

'Were you young when your mother died?'

'Ten. Not so young I don't remember her.'

They lapsed into silence for a moment, following the path around the trees. This area was a little damp underfoot, and Kate was glad of her heavy-soled boots. They had served her well over the last few months and had been the best purchase she had made since leaving home.

'How about you, Miss Winters?' Lord Henderson asked. 'You are from Sussex, that much I now know.'

'Can you tell from my accent?'

'I would be hard placed to decide if you were from Sussex, Kent, or Hampshire, but you do have an unmistakably southeastern accent.'

'My family are from Eastbourne, on the south coast.'

'Could you get much further from home without leaving the country?'

When she'd fled her home and her family, she hadn't made a conscious decision to come as far away as possible, but she didn't deny that the distance from anything and everything she had once known was reassuring. This was why she had felt so shaken when Mrs Fariday, whom she had once known as Miss Edwina Connington, had appeared. In the six months she had been at Crosthwaite House, she had not encountered anyone she had ever met before, not until today.

'Sometimes it is nice to settle somewhere no one knows you or anything about you,' she said quietly, understanding this was giving too much of herself away. Most employers, if they found out the truth about her, would think seriously about dismissing her, citing the need to have their household free from people with a question hanging over their morals. She didn't think Lord Henderson would be like that—he was more concerned about the smooth running of the house in the few weeks or months it remained in his possession— but Kate had learned that people did not always act as you expected them to.

They were approaching the lake now, and Lord Henderson placed a hand on Kate's elbow ever so gently, guiding her to the left to a path that skirted the edge of the water.

'I know a perfect spot for a picnic.'

The ground was uneven and the walk further than Kate had anticipated, but as they approached the spot Lord Henderson indicated, Kate could see why he had chosen it. The view over Lake Bassenthwaite was uninterrupted, and with no houses or roads in sight, Kate could imagine this was what the lake had looked like hundreds of years ago.

After choosing a spot, Lord Henderson laid out the blanket he had with him and motioned for Kate to take a seat. She should have felt awkward and self-conscious—housekeepers did not normally enjoy picnics with their employers—but Lord Henderson was acting like this was the most natural thing in the world, and he had her believing it too.

'Please feel free to fulfil your daily engagement with the lake. I hear a paddle before a picnic is most invigorating.'

Kate bit her lip, but as the earl began busying himself setting out the food she had prepared, she decided to take up his offer and slip off her boots and stockings. As she stepped into the cold water, she gasped and stiffened.

She turned to find Lord Henderson's eyes on her. Although she was fully clothed, apart from the recent shedding of her boots and stockings, Kate felt as though she were naked under his gaze. She'd lifted her skirts to just below her knees, and there were only a few inches of leg on display, but suddenly she felt as though it were the most scandalous thing she had ever done.

Forcing herself to turn away, she tried to focus on the tingling sensation in her feet, on the vastness of the water in front of her, rather than the flare of heat from the man behind.

Only when she felt she had regained control of herself a little did she daintily step out of the lake and allow her skirts to fall back to her ankles.

'I would offer to take you swimming in there,' Lord Henderson murmured as she sat down beside her, 'but it is probably still too early in the year.'

'Perhaps in a few weeks, in the middle of summer.'

They both knew by the summer Lord Henderson hoped to have rid himself of Crosthwaite House and his other English properties and would be on his way back to a carefree life in Italy.

'Perhaps,' he said, holding out a glass of wine.

Kate blinked, hesitating before taking it. She hadn't packed wine, or the two glasses he had poured it into. Lord Henderson must have slipped the bottle and glasses into the basket when she was preoccupied with something else.

He had laid out the picnic on the blanket, and for a few minutes they ate, enjoying the cheese and bread and fruit Kate had packed. Once Kate's feet had dried, she had warmed considerably, but as the afternoon got later, there was a mild chill to the air.

'So tell me, Miss Winters, what do I need to know about Crosthwaite House? What notable things have happened since you took over as housekeeper?'

'Staff have come and gone. It has been hard to find a reliable man to help Mr Crosby in the gardens. He makes do with labourers in the spring and summer but struggles with maintenance in the winter.'

'He is getting on in years too,' Lord Henderson said.

'He is. There is also a new groundskeeper. Mr Williams. He lives in the gatehouse with his wife, but they are away visiting their daughter. Mrs Lemington was hopeful they would want to live in the house, but they were keen to have the privacy of the gatehouse.'

'Leaving you all alone.'

'It is unconventional, I know, but I enjoy the solitude, and the presence of Mr and Mrs Williams in the gatehouse keeps most of the gossip at bay about me living alone here.'

'Anything else of note?'

Kate shook her head. When Mrs Lemington had employed her, Kate had expected a longer transition period, but the old woman's health had been failing rapidly. As soon as Kate was able, Mrs Lemington had handed control of the house over. It hadn't been without its challenges, but the old housekeeper had left things well ordered and passed on her years of wisdom.

They fell silent, both enjoying the peace and view out over the lake.

'May is my favourite month,' Lord Henderson said as Kate pulled her cloak around her shoulders. 'There is that promise of warmth and sunshine yet to come.'

'I like July,' Kate said, momentarily losing herself in memories of July at the seaside in Eastbourne. As children, she and her sister would often give their nanny the slip and run giggling down to the beach to play on the sand. The days had seemed leisurely and endless, and it had been a time of innocence. 'Long, hot days to spend on the beach or in the sea.'

'You're thinking of your childhood?'

Kate nodded but didn't say any more.

'You are a very difficult woman to get any information from, Miss Winters. You would make a wonderful spy. If you were caught, the British government would not have to worry about you giving anything away.'

'Most employers are not interested in the lives of their housekeepers.'

'Perhaps I'm not like most employers.' He paused, waiting for her to look at him. 'Or perhaps it is because you are not like most housekeepers.'

Kate glanced up at him and saw the smile pulling at the corners of his lips. He seemed a little more relaxed today, as if the ghosts he had been expected to be plagued by hadn't materialised and he was finally allowing himself to breathe. 'I propose a game,' he said quietly. 'A challenge. Growing up by the sea, you must be able to skip stones?'

'A little,' Kate admitted. It wasn't the easiest thing to do with the waves lapping at the shore, but on a calm day she had spent hours skipping stones from the beach.

'Then we shall have a contest.'

'Why do I feel I am being set up?'

Lord Henderson chuckled softly. Kate liked this version of him.

'Did I tell you I was quite a lonely child?' he asked. 'No siblings, and a father with vast responsibilities that meant he had little time for entertaining a bereaved young lad.'

'Let me guess. You filled that time by become a world expert at skipping stones.'

'Perhaps not world expert, but I do admit I have skipped a few stones in my time.'

'What is the contest?'

'A simple exchange. We both select three stones and attempt to skip them across the water.'

Kate nodded. It seemed simple enough, and although she doubted she would win, she thought she could perform well enough to save herself any embarrassment.

'The number of skips we get equals the number of questions we can ask the other person.'

'Fine, I agree to your terms,' Kate said, feeling the pull of his enthusiasm. Her whole strategy here was to make Lord Henderson realise how much he loved Crosthwaite House and the grounds, how he could not give it up, even if he was not going to live here permanently. Light-hearted games whilst the sun began to set ahead of them sounded like a perfect way to do just that, even if it meant giving away a little of her history. 'But the questions can only lead to yes or no answers.'

'Cunning, Miss Winters. A good way to guard your privacy. I agree. Shall we hunt for our stones?'

Kate knew this was the most important part of the process and quickly stood, picking her way over the grass, looking for the perfect stone. She wanted something flat and smooth, preferably with rounded edges so it fit neatly against the curve of her fingers. Taking her time, she found three she was pleased with and returned to the water's edge.

'Ladies first,' Lord Henderson said, stepping to one side to give her enough room to manoeuvre.

Kate hadn't done this for years, and her first stone fell disappointingly into the water with a resounding plop without skipping even once.

With the second one, she bent her knees a little lower and released the stone with a flick, shouting in triumph as it skipped twice across the water.

'That is two questions you can claim. Do you wish to ask them now, or will you skip your last stone?'

'I'll skip,' she said, positioning herself again and letting the stone fly. It was no great success but bounced off the surface of the water once before sinking to the bottom.

'Three, not a bad show,' Lord Henderson said.

'Your turn.' Kate took a step back to allow him to the edge of the lake. As soon as he took up position, she knew the competition had been a bad idea. He skipped the first stone with ease, flicking his wrist as if he did this all day long.

'I counted six,' Lord Henderson said with a grin. 'Do you agree?'

'I think I've been tricked,' she mumbled, frowning.

Quickly he let the next two stones fly, one skipping five times and the other three.

'Fourteen questions,' he said, turning to her triumphantly. 'If I choose carefully, I should be able to find out a little about you, Miss Winters.' He took a step closer, and Kate felt a thrum of anticipation pass between them. 'Unless you want to abandon this and tell me all the interesting bits now?'

'A deal is a deal. Remember, the only answers I will give are yes and no.'

'But you must promise to answer with absolute honesty.'

'I promise.'

As Lord Henderson considered his questions, Kate returned to the picnic blanket, making herself comfortable and trying to hide the nervousness she felt building inside her. Her past was not a thrilling subject, but she had made some bad choices and had to live with that every day. Her family knew of her mistakes, of course, but no one else did. The anonymity was something she enjoyed.

'Before this job, have you worked as a housekeeper or servant before?' Lord Henderson said as he sat down beside her. He moved the basket out of the way so there were only a few inches of empty space separating them. It felt intimate, as if they were courting, even though Kate knew the situation was as far from that as it could be.

'No.'

'Do you come from a wealthy family?'

Kate screwed up her nose as she considered. 'Wealth is relative. What is wealthy to me might not be to you.'

'Fine, I'll ask a different question. Did you grow up in a household that employed servants?'

'Yes.'

'Have your family had financial troubles?'

Kate thought of her father sitting in his study when she had last laid eyes on him, surrounded by all the luxuries of a relatively wealthy man.

'No.'

This made Lord Henderson pause, and Kate realised he must have concocted a story in his mind about why she was here at Crosthwaite House, employed as his housekeeper. It would involve a family from the gentry, fallen on hard times and forced to send their daughter out to seek work. Something respectable but not quite their previous standard of living.

'Your family could still afford to support you?'

'Yes.' She was glad she had stipulated the questions could only elicit short answers. It meant she didn't have to try and find the words to explain the actions of her parents, the two people in the world who were meant to love her unconditionally.

Lord Henderson regarded her silently for a few moments, his expression intrigued.

'Was there some sort of scandal that prompted you to leave home?'

Kate considered. It wasn't a scandal as such, as no one except her family and the man she thought she would marry knew about it. She had been discreet even in her recklessness.

'Not a scandal,' she said quietly, 'but an unwise decision.'

'We all make unwise decisions,' Lord Henderson said with a nod of his head.

Kate stood abruptly, realising she didn't want to answer any more. She walked to the edge of the water, looking out into the distance and wondering how to get the lightness they had shared before back without delving into her past.

'I'm sorry,' Lord Henderson said, coming up behind her and placing a hand on her arm. 'I have always been curious about the lives of others. Sometimes I don't know when to stop prying.'

Kate turned and looked up at him, surprised by this genuine remorse for pushing her to reveal details of her private life. She didn't know many earls, but she would never have imagined one to express such sensitivity to her emotions.

# Chapter Seven

Miss Winters looked so sad standing there by the water that George had the urge to reach out and gather her in his arms. He wanted to console her, to show her she could seek comfort in him. It would be the fleeting kind, but satisfying all the same.

He'd seen the attraction flare in her eyes when their bodies had brushed against one another, seen the quickly suppressed desire fight to be allowed prominence. Perhaps it was purely physical, but he did wonder if there was a commonality between them, an acknowledgement they were two lost souls reaching out for someone who was equally as lost for solace.

Quickly he pushed away the notion, feeling a thrum of guilt. He was here to draw a line under his past, to enable him to move on from the terrible events that had happened here, but that did not mean he should have these sorts of thoughts about anyone else.

As he was about to speak, about to suggest they return to their picnic, he felt a fat raindrop fall on his head, followed by another and another. Miss Winters looked up to the sky, and he followed her gaze. The clouds that had been dark but patchy now covered the sky and looked as though they were about to burst.

'We should get back,' he said, knowing how quickly the weather could turn here.

Hastily they gathered together the remains of the picnic as the rain became heavier, and he cursed his decision to come out without a coat. Even walking briskly, it was fifteen minutes back to the house, and by that time he would be soaked to the skin.

'Are you glad you took the risk, my lord, to come out without your coat?' Miss Winters asked as she packed up the basket.

He stopped what he was doing and gave her a withering look.

'Are you finding it fun?' she asked. 'Getting caught in the rain.'

'I would be careful what your next words are, Miss Winters.'

'I'm feeling nice and warm and dry in my cloak,' she murmured, casting her eyes down.

He reached out and caught her wrist, a movement that surprised both of them. 'That cloak could very easily be taken from you.'

'I do not think it would fit you, my lord, although I am sure you would look fetching in it.'

She wriggled away from him and stood, ensuring her hood was pulled well over her hair. He regarded her for a few more seconds and then conceded. It was raining heavily now, and *he* was the one without a coat. It was only himself he was punishing here.

'Let's go,' he said, starting off in the direction of the house. He led the way, weaving around the edge of the lake before taking the most direct path to the house. Every few seconds he would check Miss Winters was keeping up. Her legs were having to go much faster than his due to the difference in their height, but she had no trouble moving quickly.

About half way back to the house, he heard her cry out and turn to see her slipping on the wet ground. She hadn't lost her balance, but her boots were streaked with mud, and he could see where she had slipped. He reached out and took her hand, offering to steady her. At first she hesitated, but after a moment she relented, seemingly deciding it was better to get back to the warmth and shelter of the house quickly than preserve her respectability but fall in the mud.

As they climbed the hill, there was a flash of lightning followed by a deep rumble of thunder. The thunder was like a harbinger of the storm, for the rain started pelting down, striking the ground so hard it was bouncing off.

'Follow me,' George said, gripping the housekeeper's hand tightly as they took a detour off the main path. Hidden in the trees was a small folly, nothing more than three enclosed sides and an open front framed with pillars, but it was deep enough it would give them some shelter from the rain. They could wait for just a couple of minutes for the worst to pass.

Miss Winters shivered as they stepped inside but gratefully lowered her hood, shaking the water droplets from the fabric.

'You're drenched,' she said, her other hand coming up to touch his sleeve, pausing in mid-air as she realised what she was about to do. Her eyes met his, and for a long moment it felt like the rest of the world faded away. There was just Miss Winters and her kissable lips in the enclosed space of the folly.

Even as he acknowledged all the reasons dallying

with his housekeeper was a bad idea, he felt his arm move, his hand reach out for her. It started with a light caress on her shoulder, nothing scandalous, but they both felt the tension surge between them. His fingers climbed up, onto the bare skin of her neck, feeling the velvety softness of the skin now wet from the raindrops. She gave a little shudder of anticipation as his fingers danced over her earlobe and then trailed onto her cheek. George saw her lips part and her body sway towards him and knew in that moment she wanted to be kissed just as much as he wanted to kiss her.

If he kissed her there would be no going back. Their relationship would be irrevocably changed. He wondered if it was worth the risk. His body, his desire screamed yes and urged him to kiss her, to claim her. The more sensible part of him reasoned that the house would be his for only a few more weeks, and finding another housekeeper for that amount of time if he scared Miss Winters away would be near on impossible.

Desire won out, and George took a step towards the young woman, one hand still on her cheek, the other coming to encircle her back. Her eyes were locked on his as he narrowed the space between them, and he could see the fire burning in them, fire that made him want her even more.

Before he could kiss her, there was a bright flash of light and a boom of thunder that sounded as if the sky was splitting in two right over their heads. Miss Winters jumped, pushing away from him, and quickly turned her face. Even though he could not see her expression, he could tell by her posture the moment had been lost, and already Miss Winters was heavily chastising herself for almost being so foolish as to dally with her employer.

He felt a roil of turmoil inside him and momentarily had to close his eyes, wondering if he would physically stumble. For two years he had eschewed any situation in which he would be expected to build a relationship with someone, not wanting to be embroiled in intimacy. The guilt he felt on a daily basis for surviving when his two late wives had not weighed on him heavily. He did not need the extra guilt of knowing he had moved on with his life. Neither Elizabeth nor Clara would get to kiss anyone ever again. It seemed an affront to their memory that he be allowed to move on.

Alongside the guilt, George felt a rush of disappointment and hated himself for it. This might be the first time he had felt desire in two years, but that did not mean he should act on it.

Turning away, he suppressed a sigh. Perhaps he should be grateful nature had intervened and saved him from himself.

Rallying, he turned back and felt a pang of remorse as he saw his housekeeper's slumped shoulders. For her it would probably have been a more serious entanglement, a more serious mistake. It always was for women. Despite her claim she was here because of a few poor decisions, he had an inkling Miss Winters's past contained some sort of scandal. Why else would a woman from a good family be so far from home and alone in the world? That didn't mean she could drop any facade of respectability.

'I think the rain is easing,' he said, forcing his voice to be light. It was probably best they just ignore what had almost happened between them. They could return to a more informal version of the normal master-housekeeper relationship, and everyone would be happy.

Miss Winters nodded, pulling her cloak up so it left

her face in shadow and it was almost impossible to read her expression.

'Take my hand,' George said, holding his out again. 'It will be slippery on the grass, and I don't want you to fall.'

She hesitated, but only for a second, before placing her hand in his. As her skin touched his, George felt the fizz of excitement but quickly pushed it away, instead bowing his head and leading Miss Winters out into the rain.

It had eased a little but was still torrential, and by the time they had made it back to the house and burst in through the front door, they were both soaked to the skin. Water sprinkled the floor as Miss Winters took off her cloak, grimacing at the mess they were making. As she hung the cloak on a hook, no doubt planning on retrieving it later, her gaze paused on him.

'You're drenched,' she said, a note of concern in her voice.

'As are you.'

They both looked at her dress, which was plastered to her skin and heavy with water in the skirts.

'I'll get a fire going,' she said, and he saw her shiver involuntarily. 'Would you like it in your bedroom?'

'The fire in the kitchen is still alight?'

The housekeeper nodded, and he motioned that they should go downstairs. The kitchen was tidy and quiet, and George assumed the two maids must have left for the day. The fire was smouldering, but it didn't take much to add a few extra logs and stoke it so the flames started to crackle again.

Out of the corner of his eye, he saw Miss Winters edge closer to the flame and let out a little sigh as the heat of the fire permeated through the thick cotton of her sopping wet dress.

'I don't mind lighting the fire in your bedroom so you can get changed, my lord,' she said after a minute.

'You need to get out of your wet clothes too,' he said, trying to colour that spread over her cheeks at his choice of words. Suddenly he had visions of him helping her shed her dress, unfastening the grey material and helping her slip out of it. In his imagination she did not have on all the silly layers that made up women's undergarments, and he glanced surreptitiously over at her to see if he could divine whether that might be true.

'I'm fine,' she said stoically, even though her skin was pale and she was desperately trying to stop her teeth from chattering.

'You need to change, Miss Winters. Either you take a few minutes to sort yourself out or I will come over there and do it for you.'

Her eyes came up to meet his, and he saw the hint of a challenge in them before she turned away and headed for her room.

'I will assist you with your shirt once I am changed, my lord,' she said.

The wound on his chest and shoulder was paining him, and he wondered if the water would affect the stitches or how the injury healed. Hopefully with a fresh bandage applied, it would not matter it had got soaked in the rain.

Whilst Miss Winters was changing, George pulled over a stool and set himself up by the fire. The flickering flames were already starting to dry his shirt, and at least he did not feel nearly as cold as he had.

Carefully he managed to kick off his boots, and by the time Miss Winters had returned, he had made himself comfortable by the fire.

'That feels better,' she said, summoning a smile as

she walked into the kitchen. She'd changed into another conservative grey dress, but this one didn't have such a high neckline. Her hair was loose about her shoulders, a shade darker than normal where it was damp. George felt something flare inside him, a feeling of possessiveness. Normally only a husband or lover got to see a woman with her hair loose and falling down her back. It made Miss Winters look softer, more vulnerable, and George had the unsettling urge to gather her in his arms and draw her to him whilst murmuring promises to protect her.

He coughed, quickly trying to dispel the image. Miss Winters did not need his protection, and she certainly had not asked for it. What was more, he was in no position to begin offering it. Soon he would leave England, never to return. That was not what a man with responsibilities could do.

'Let me see to your shoulder. Shall I go and fetch you a dry shirt?'

'I have warmed sufficiently. If you would be so kind as to help me off with my shirt, I can go and change in my bedroom.'

He stood as Miss Winters approached, trying to fix his mind on other, less alluring things than the pretty young woman in front of him. It was near impossible to think of anything else when she gripped his shirt and pulled it free from the waistband of his trousers as a lover might in the rush to undress him.

Her fingers were gentle on his skin, helping him hook his arm out before lifting the shirt up over his head. George was watching her closely, and although she was adept at keeping a neutral expression, he could tell she was as affected by their proximity as he was. There was the minute change in her breathing, a catch of her voice in her throat, as she asked him to move his arm, and her hand hesitated for a fraction of a second before making contact with his skin.

'Thank you,' he said gruffly when he was rid of his top. It would be easy enough to change his trousers and slip on a new shirt, and then it would be almost as if they had never got caught out in the storm. Almost.

'Your dressing is soaked through,' Miss Winters said, her fingers lingering on the skin below his collarbone. 'I should change it.'

He was pressed back into his chair whilst the housekeeper bustled round collecting her supplies. Only once the dressing had been removed and a clean dry one fashioned was she happy.

George stood again reluctantly. He enjoyed his life of solitude, of not having to answer to anyone. He revelled in being able to do what he wished when he wished it, but he hadn't realised quite how much he had missed having someone to care for him. Usually he could prepare a meal and see to his clothes perfectly well, but there was no substitute for human contact when you'd injured yourself or felt the weight of melancholy pressing down. He might growl and stomp around the house, but deep down he had to acknowledge it was pleasant having Miss Winters for company, despite their different positions in the household.

'You're going soft,' he muttered to himself as he grabbed his shirt and left the kitchen, forcing himself not to look back at Miss Winters busying herself tidying after him. He would dream of her tonight no doubt, with her hair loose around her shoulders, although he expected she would be wearing a lot less than the sensible grey dress in his dreams.

# Chapter Eight

Kate bustled over to the sink with a determined expression on her face. Today she would not be distracted by anything or anyone.

'What has that pot ever done to you?' Marigold said, her eyes wide as she regarded the normally serene housekeeper.

She looked down and realised she had been scrubbing with more force than normal and was in danger of scratching the pot beyond repair. Slowly she put it on the side, ready to be dried and put away.

Kate saw Marigold backing away and turned to the maid with a smile.

'I was in a world of my own. How are you today, Marigold?'

Marigold launched into a comical tirade at how long it had taken her to get out of her house, weighed down by all the demands of her younger siblings. Kate listened, but only with half an ear. Already her thoughts were wandering to Lord Henderson and the kiss they had almost shared the day before.

She blamed herself. All afternoon the tension had been mounting between them, and the picnic by the lake had begun to feel like a courtship not a pleasant interlude between servant and employer. She thought of how his fingers had set her skin on fire. Just a gentle caress of her neck and cheek and she was almost on her knees begging him for more.

She was starved of affection. That was all it was. For the past year, the only human touch she'd experienced was if her hand accidentally brushed against Marigold's or Mary's when they were making a bed or dusting one of the heavy picture frames.

Shaking herself, Kate resolved to keep her distance. At times Lord Henderson could be much more amiable than she had originally judged, but that didn't mean she needed to be anything but professionally courteous. A dalliance with Lord Henderson could ruin the life she had built here, away from any whispers of scandal. She closed her eyes and braced herself against the sink for a moment, forcing herself to breathe deeply. When she had first left home, she hadn't had enough energy to do more than survive each day. Once she had settled here at Thornthwaite, she knew some of her emotional wounds had begun to heal, and in the last few months, she had begun to consider what she might want from her future. She knew she didn't want to return home, to be subjected to the rules and strict scrutiny from her father, but she struggled to know what she did want. Initially she had thought earning her own money, being independent, would be enough, but slowly she was coming to realise she wanted more than that. One day she thought she might want a husband, a family, a chance at the future she felt had been ripped away, but she was determined it would be on her own terms. No one would tell her whom to marry or what to do. The thing she prized most now was her freedom to make her own decisions.

'Good morning, Miss Winters. Good morning, Marigold,' Lord Henderson said as he clattered down the stairs into the kitchen. Although this was her first position as housekeeper Kate knew most masters rarely visited the kitchen, let alone burst into it with such regularity. She cursed Lord Henderson's lax interpretation of etiquette.

'Good morning sir,' Marigold chirped, grinning broadly. 'It's a lovely day today.'

'Indeed it is, Marigold. I think all the rain for the entire month fell in the space of an hour yesterday evening.' As he spoke, Kate felt his eyes flick to her, but she resolutely continued to look at the water in the sink.

'Are you continuing to organise the papers in the study today, my lord?' Kate said, still focussing on the washing up. It had only been a couple of days, but the property deed was still in her possession and making her feel increasingly guilty every time she looked at it. Soon she knew she would have to return it, to allow Lord Henderson to move on, but she wanted just a couple more days to persuade him not to sell.

'No. I am planning a trip out today, and I hope you will join me, Miss Winters.'

This made Kate stir, and she quickly wiped her hands on her apron, turning to face Lord Henderson.

'I plan to go over to see Mrs Lemington in Keswick,' he said. 'I am sure she would be eager to see you, and I thought you might like to accompany me.'

Kate hesitated. She was sorely tempted. Mrs Lemington had been kind to her when Kate had most needed it, taking her in and teaching her everything she knew about running a house. Since the older woman had gone to live with her daughter, Kate had visited three times, hitching a ride on the back of a farmer's cart. The last occasion had been about a month earlier, and then the old housekeeper had seemed increasingly frail. They had laughed and talked, Kate telling Mrs Lemington about Mary's and Marigold's antics. When she had left, Mrs Lemington's daughter had caught her in the hallway, thanked Kate for coming, and urged her to visit again if she could.

It would be wonderful to see Mrs Lemington, but a whole morning spent with Lord Henderson was not wise given her reaction to him the evening before.

'There is a lot to do here…' she began.

'I'm sure Marigold is perfectly capable of taking charge for one day.'

Marigold nodded furiously, her eyes gleaming at the prospect. No doubt she would spend the day ordering Mary about and reminding her friend she was the one chosen to stand in for Kate whilst she was away.

'Go on, Miss Winters,' Marigold said. 'You know Mrs Lemington loves it when you visit.'

'Perhaps she would like to see you on your own,' Kate suggested to Lord Henderson. 'It has been a long time.'

'I am sure she will be happy to see you,' he said abruptly, 'but it is your choice. If you decide to come, meet me outside in fifteen minutes.'

Kate couldn't think of a convincing argument as to why she couldn't go, so found herself nodding.

Kate was out the front of the house first, waiting for Lord Henderson, when she heard the steady clop of hooves and frowned. For some reason she had thought they would walk, although now that she considered the matter, she realised it would probably take too much time out of the earl's day to cover the four miles by foot there and back.

'You only have one horse,' Kate said as Lord Henderson appeared around the corner of the house leading Odysseus. He was a fine-looking horse, sleek and well groomed. Kate wondered if she would be expected to walk alongside.

'Odysseus is strong. He is certainly capable of carrying us both for the short trip to Keswick and back.'

'You want me to sit on the horse with you?'

'Unless you prefer to run behind.'

Kate hesitated. It might be preferable to an hour with her body pressed close to Lord Henderson's.

'I'm wearing the wrong sort of dress,' she said, wondering if it was too late to back out of the trip completely.

'Thousands of women around the world manage to ride without a side saddle and riding habit, Miss Winters. I am confident you will cope.' He held out a hand, motioning for her to step closer. 'Come, I will get you settled before I mount.'

Knowing she would regret not walking away, Kate stepped forwards and placed a hand on Odysseus's neck. She had ridden a lot growing up. Her family owned two horses, and she would often spend time racing round the Sussex countryside on horseback, being chased by her older sister. It would not be the first time she shared a horse, either, but riding sedately with her father or sister to the next village was a little different to being seated with an attractive earl.

Carefully she placed her boot in Lord Henderson's hand and allowed him to boost her up so she could swing her leg over the horse's back. Predictably her skirts got a little caught up in the manoeuvring, and

Kate had to tug them down to avoid flashing too much of her legs, but after a few moments she was comfortable.

Lord Henderson mounted his horse, and she saw him grimace as the wound on his chest and shoulder must have pulled, but after a moment he was sitting in the saddle and taking hold of the reins around her waist. He wrapped one strong arm around her, pulling her closer to him, and as he nudged Odysseus forwards, Kate realised he wasn't planning on letting go. She felt safe, stable, being held like that, but it was how a married couple might ride, not two strangers who barely knew one another.

'Are you comfortable?' Lord Henderson enquired as they rode out through the gates of Crosthwaite House.

'Quite comfortable.'

'Let me know if there is anything you need.'

His breath was warm on her neck, and Kate had the urge to lean her head back and rest it on his chest. Instead she straightened her back further, tensing her muscles to remain completely upright.

They rode in silence for a few minutes, travelling down the windy lane that led from Crosthwaite House. It was about two miles to the village, and from there they would join the bigger road that led to Keswick.

'It is a pleasant day,' Lord Henderson said, seeming to be oblivious to her discomfort. He growled out the words as if he was forcing himself to be genial but struggling with the execution. Kate wondered if he felt anything in their closeness. Yesterday she was certain he had been ready to kiss her and perhaps more as they sheltered from the rain, yet here he was commenting on the weather as if he was taking his aged aunt to church.

'Very pleasant,' Kate murmured, feeling a twinge of tension in her back from her rigid posture.

'You can relax, Miss Winters. The ride is likely to take well over an hour. I suggest you do not sit like that the whole time.'

'I am perfectly alright.'

'I highly doubt that,' Lord Henderson said, adjusting his arm so it snaked around her waist a little more. 'I can pull you into my lap if you would prefer.'

Kate wriggled in alarm, making Lord Henderson hold on to her more tightly.

'Settle down,' he commanded. 'You'll spook Odysseus.'

Not wanting to be the reason the animal bolted, Kate did her best to stay still, acutely aware of Lord Henderson's body close to hers. He seemed quite comfortable, as if he rode with strange women in front of him all the time. Kate wondered if this was true.

From what the locals had told her, and listening to the gossip from Mary and Marigold, he had withdrawn into himself after the death of his second wife, but before his marriage, he had been a handsome and eligible young earl who was never short of company. Perhaps after he had mourned his wife, the same had been true these past couple of years in Italy, although somehow she didn't think so.

Kate gave a minute shake of her head. It wasn't any of her business or concern what Lord Henderson had been getting up to with or without company. It was his choice if he lived the chaste life of a monk or invited three different women every week to share his bed.

'You're deep in thought,' Lord Henderson said, his

voice cutting through her daydream and making her jump. 'What has you so preoccupied?'

Kate coughed, trying to buy herself time to think of a lie. There was no way she could tell the earl she was thinking about the women he shared his bed with.

'I was thinking of Mrs Lemington,' Kate said softly. 'She was very frail the last time I visited. Her daughter implied she didn't think she had long left in this world.'

'That is sad,' Lord Henderson said, his voice low and sombre. 'The Lemingtons have been at Crosthwaite House since I was a boy.'

Kate twisted round in her seat to look at him. 'I'm sorry. It must be hard coming home to find so many things have changed.'

'The world changes, life moves on,' Lord Henderson said quietly, 'but it is hard for those of us who get left behind.'

'You feel like you have been left behind?' She frowned. He was a wealthy man with all the freedom he could desire. She didn't see how he could feel abandoned by the world.

For a long moment, Kate thought he wasn't going to answer her. The silence stretched out, and then finally he spoke. 'I am sure you are aware of my past, my history. I have been married twice and widowed twice.'

Kate nodded. She got the feeling he didn't like the fact everyone discussed his personal life and the tragedies that dominated it.

'My first wife, Elizabeth…' He paused as his voice caught in his throat. 'We were not married long. She died three months after our wedding. It was a match arranged by my father before he passed away.'

Kate understood what he was telling her without putting it into words. They had not loved each other, at least not at first. They had probably barely known each other on their wedding day.

'Her death was unexpected. Despite our short marriage, I had come to care for her, and suddenly she was ripped away from me. I mourned Elizabeth, and I also mourned the loss of the life I thought we would share together with our child.'

She glanced around again and saw the darkness in his eyes. He'd lost a lot of people he was close to. First his mother, then his father, then his two wives. It would make you reassess your priorities.

'Life moves on, but you are left confused and adrift, uncertain of your place in the world without the person you thought you would spend it with by your side.'

'You mourned your first wife for a long time?'

'Officially I observed the correct period of mourning, but I was in no rush to remarry. I doubt I would have at all if I hadn't met Clara.'

'Clara was your second wife?'

'Yes.' There was a tightness in his voice, and Kate could tell he was trying to suppress the emotions that must be raging within him. 'She was the sister of a good friend, but I had not seen her for years, not since we were children. The day we met again, she told me she was going to marry me.'

'Determined woman,' Kate murmured.

'She was. That's what made it so hard…' He trailed off, shaking his head. 'When someone is young and full of life, you can't imagine them not being around. Clara filled Crosthwaite House with her energy and her happiness, and then suddenly she was gone.'

'I can't begin to understand what it must have been like for you.' She knew he had lost his unborn child at the same time, a double tragedy to cope with, to push him to the limit of emotional endurance.

'Everyone was sad. Everyone mourned for her, but then little by little they got on with their lives.'

'But you were unable to.'

He shrugged, the movement unbalancing her a little so she had to lean back into him.

She wondered if he saw leaving England, fleeing from everything he had once known, as a way of moving on. She could understand the desire to start afresh, but knew dealing with grief wasn't as simple as moving away from where a tragedy had occurred.

'After a year, people think you should be ready to start again. If you are not...' He trailed off, and Kate could feel he was shaking his head.

'I am sorry for everything you have lost,' she said quietly. Although this past year she had suffered a sort of bereavement in the loss of the life she had once expected, she had been fortunate that no one close to her had died young. She had lost her grandmother a few years earlier, but she had been well into her seventh decade and had been ailing for a while. Then there was a childhood friend who had succumbed to a winter fever and had been heavily mourned by everyone in the village, but Kate had never lost a beloved family member in the prime of their life. It wasn't her place to ask why he hadn't moved on, why he wasn't willing to try again for the life he had once desired.

They lapsed into silence, and Kate could feel the tension coming off Lord Henderson as he no doubt remembered his two late wives.

Kate had a sinking feeling in her stomach. Listening to his revelation, she knew that she was never going to inspire a love for Crosthwaite House or Bassenthwaite again. It had been a naive idea, one she felt a little ashamed of now. She could feel the tension in his body as her back pressed against his torso and realised he wasn't going to change his mind because of some subtle reminders of the good memories he associated with the house.

It meant she was going to have to accept moving on. It wouldn't be immediate, but at some point in a few months, Crosthwaite House would be handed over to the new owners, who would probably have a housekeeper of their own alongside a full complement of staff.

When she had arrived in Thornthwaite all those months ago, she hadn't expected to stay as long as she had. It had become her sanctuary, but perhaps she would find somewhere equally as peaceful and healing.

Kate knew she needed to start thinking about a longer-term plan. Going home wasn't an option. She had saved a little money from her salary, but she would need to start looking for another job soon. She liked the work of a housekeeper, enjoyed keeping busy, but she wasn't sure what she wanted in the months and years going forwards. Much like Lord Henderson, she had expected her life to follow a certain path, and when that had been pulled away from her, it was hard to decide what to do next.

'Is something amiss, Miss Winters?' Lord Henderson said as they slowed to let a carriage pass by.

'No,' Kate said, trying to inject a cheery note into her voice but failing miserably. 'I'm just thinking about the future.'

'Ah, the future,' Lord Henderson said, then fell silent again.

# Chapter Nine

The centre of Keswick was bustling and busy with people strolling past the shops and gathered in little groups to catch up on the local gossip. It was a pretty little place, close to the water and with an air of gentility. George always enjoyed a trip here.

Mrs Lemington's daughter lived on the outskirts in a smart cottage that had a beautifully tended front garden with roses that were almost ready to burst into flower where they were weaved around a trestle over the front door. It would be a colourful display and set the cottage apart from its neighbours.

'It is this one here, on the end,' Kate said, indicating where to stop. George hadn't visited before even though he had known vaguely which direction to take from the centre of Keswick.

He would be glad to dismount and didn't doubt Miss Winters felt the same. At least he had been in his saddle. She would have felt every bump and jolt through Odysseus's back, and although she had not uttered one word of a grumble, he did not imagine it had been the most comfortable hour and a half of her life.

'Let me dismount, and then I will help you down,'

he said as she began to wriggle. Quickly he slid out of the saddle and found his footing, turning back to Miss Winters before she could leap from Odysseus's back. He gripped her tightly by the waist as he steadied her down, trying to ignore the flare of attraction he felt holding her so close. The wound on his shoulder burned as the skin pulled on the stitches, but he was so distracted by Miss Winters being so close that he barely noticed.

Forcing himself to turn away, George tied Odysseus to a fence post where he couldn't eat too many of the flowers in the garden and then started along the path to the front door of the little cottage.

He knocked on the door, at the same time wondering if he should have sent word that they were coming first.

The door was opened almost immediately by Ann Smith. He'd known her in childhood. She was about ten years older than him but had lived with her parents in a little cottage on the estate when he was young before she had married and moved to Keswick to start a family of her own.

'Lord Henderson.' She smiled, all genuine warmth and hospitality. 'This is a most wonderful surprise.'

'It is lovely to see you Mrs Smith. You're looking well.'

'Please come in.' Mrs Smith beamed at him and then saw Kate standing behind him. 'Miss Winters, it's wonderful to see you again. My mother is always invigorated by your visits.'

They followed the old housekeeper's daughter into the neat cottage, making their way into the sitting room that looked out over the front garden.

'My condolences on the loss of your father,' George said. 'He was a brilliant man, and the world is a little poorer without his presence.'

'Thank you. It was his time, I know, but I miss him every day.'

'How is Mrs Lemington?' Miss Winters said, concern on her face.

Mrs Smith lowered her voice and glanced up at the ceiling. 'She weakens every day. The doctor says it is her heart and implies she does not have long, but she is strong willed and, I am happy to say, comfortable.'

'Do you think she would be up to a quick visit?' George asked. 'I do not want to strain her.'

'Nonsense, my lord. She would be livid if she found out you were here and I had kept you from her. You know she dotes on you like a son. Let me go upstairs and ensure she is presentable, and then I will fetch you.'

Mrs Smith disappeared upstairs, and in the silence that followed, they could hear the creaking of floorboards as she moved about above them. George watched Miss Winters as she perched on the edge of a chair, looking out of the window, deep in thought.

He hadn't meant to reveal so much about himself to the young woman, but he couldn't deny it had been cathartic. Miss Winters made him want to tell her things, to share his darkest secrets. Perhaps it was the empathy in those sparkling green eyes, or perhaps it was the gentle way she listened without interrupting, never trying to impose her opinion or her own experience on his. So may people did that when they heard of his tragedies; they tried to compare it with the loved one they had lost, reducing it to a judgement of value, a decision on whose trauma was greater. Miss Winters was unique in that she simply listened and allowed him to talk, to unburden himself. It was refreshing even if a little disconcerting.

'My mother is ready to see you,' Mrs Smith said.

'She could not believe it when I said you were home, my lord.'

They stood and made their way to the stairs, Miss Winters allowing him to ascend first.

'The room is small, so I will wait outside,' Mrs Smith said as they reached the miniscule landing, no more than a square with a door leading off either side. 'I do not doubt she will tire quickly. Please call for me if anything is needed.'

'We will make sure we do not exhaust her,' George said, stepping into the room.

He was pleased to find it was not like many rooms of the sick or infirm he had been into. The curtains were flung open, as was the window, letting a cool breeze into the room. The sun shone brightly, making it look cheery and not a place where an elderly woman was growing weaker by the day. On the walls were framed dried flowers, and the bedcover was brightly coloured patchwork, no doubt lovingly made by Mrs Smith.

'I can't believe it,' Mrs Lemington said, pushing herself a little further up in bed. She was propped against the pillows with the covers pulled up to just below her chin. 'I thought I would die before I got chance to set eyes on you again.'

She reached out a bony hand and grasped George's, and he felt a well of emotion. After his mother's death, Mrs Lemington had done many of the things a mother would normally do for her son. She had patched up his wounds if he fell from a tree or scraped his knee playing with the local boys, and she had listened to his tales of school in the holidays whilst he sat in the warm kitchen eating freshly baked biscuits by the fire.

'I'm sorry I was away for so long,' he said quietly.

'Hush now, I understand why you had to spend some

time away. A man cannot suffer like you did and not withdraw to heal his wounds.' She smiled, her eyes full of love and warmth. 'I'm just glad you're back now. Back at Crosthwaite House where you belong.'

George swallowed, flicking a glance at Miss Winters. Almost imperceptibly she shook her head, and he felt relief wash over him as silently they agreed not to tell Mrs Lemington of his plans to sell Crosthwaite House to strangers and flee the country with no plans ever to return.

'How are you, Miss Winters?' the old housekeeper said, turning to her younger replacement.

Miss Winters stepped up to the bedside and perched on the edge of the bed, seemingly comfortable in the older woman's company.

'I am well, thank you, although everyone misses you at the house. Mary and Marigold send their love.'

'They're good girls.' Mrs Lemington dropped her voice. 'How are you finding it now Lord Henderson is home?' She flicked a mischievous grin at him and continued. 'He can be demanding.'

'These things are put in our lives to challenge us,' Miss Winters said.

'I am no bother at all,' George said.

'He *thinks* he's no bother, but I bet he has got himself into any number of scrapes since his return. Scrapes you have had to pick up the pieces with.'

'Some you would not believe,' Miss Winters said, dropping her voice to a confiding hush. 'The first night he arrived, he entered through the kitchen window. I thwacked him over the head with a saucepan because I was so convinced he was a burglar.'

'I don't doubt, if he came in through the window. What civilised person does that?'

'Then the second night he was here, he got gored by a stag.'

Mrs Lemington's eyes went wide for a second, and then she started to chortle. 'Would it surprise you to hear it isn't the first time?'

It was Miss Winters's turn to look astonished.

'Enough,' George interrupted quickly. 'No one needs to hear stories of my selfless charity, tending to these poor, wounded creatures.'

'Charity is noble, but most people manage to do it without getting dreadfully injured,' Mrs Lemington said with a smile.

'A mere scratch, both times.'

'I cannot believe it is not the first time you have been injured by a stag,' Miss Winters said, her eyes searching his.

'I am sure Lord Henderson will tell you the story.' Mrs Lemington struggled again to get a little more upright against her pillows, and immediately Miss Winters came to her aid, fluffing up the pillows behind her and helping the older woman sit up. 'I wonder if you would be a dear and ask my daughter for a cup of tea for me?'

'Of course.' Miss Winters stood and left the room, and after a moment there was the hum of distant voices.

'Isn't she a lovely girl,' Mrs Lemington said, her eyes bright and determined as she turned to George.

'Very capable,' he murmured.

'More than capable. I expect you have realised she is more than she likes to let on.'

George nodded, thinking of the game they had played by the lake and the details she had let slip. There was something painful in her past, something that had caused an irreparable split with her family and made her flee Sussex for the opposite end of the country.

'She was badly wounded when she came to me.' Mrs Lemington saw his expression and quickly went on. 'Not physically, but emotionally. Poor child, but I knew the peace and serenity of Crosthwaite House would work its magic. She is like a new woman.' Mrs Lemington looked at him out of the corner of her eye. 'Unless that is your influence?'

'No, I have been home only a couple of days.'

'I always said that house was something special. Not many people are aware of the restorative power natural beauty has on the soul.' Mrs Lemington looked at him with the wisdom of a woman who had lived a good and long life. 'You are something special too, George.'

'You are biased.'

'Now is not the time to hide behind humour. I am well aware this is probably the last time I will ever see you, so listen to me carefully.'

George felt a lump in his throat at the thought of losing the kindly housekeeper. She had been part of his life for so long he couldn't imagine a world where she no longer existed.

'No one could deny you have had a tough few years, and I doubt you will ever truly get over what happened, but don't push yourself into a cycle of perpetual mourning. You deserve happiness. It isn't an insult to the memories of your wives to go out and look for it. Those two women were vibrant and generous. They would want you to be happy, to find someone to love, to have a family.' She looked at him, and he could see how it had exhausted her to make her speech, but she was desperate to continue. 'Your life is not cursed. You do not believe in those ridiculous superstitions. You were unlucky, that is all. If you allowed yourself to fall in love again, to marry again, then there is no reason you cannot have everything you have ever wanted.'

He nodded, not about to argue with a woman whose heart was failing. Much of what she said was true, and he knew it came from a place of pure love. She didn't want to think of him spending the next thirty or forty years alone, never risking his heart for the fear one day it would get broken again.

George didn't want that for himself either, but he didn't think it was a conscious choice. He couldn't help feeling the grief he did or the reluctance to form any lasting relationship in case that person was ripped away.

'Miss Winters is very pretty,' Mrs Lemington said, closing her eyes and resting her head back on the pillow. 'And she has a backbone. I can imagine her standing her ground and not giving in.'

'She is my housekeeper, Mrs Lemington.'

'For now.' She opened one eye a crack and looked at him slyly. 'You agree she is pretty.'

'I can hardly argue with that. Of course I agree she is pretty.'

'Good. That is settled then.'

He blinked, feeling he was being expertly manoeuvred.

'What is settled?'

'You agree to at least consider a relationship.'

'With Miss Winters?'

'If that is what you desire.'

He did desire her, more than Mrs Lemington could know, but he wasn't about to admit it.

'I promise to think on everything you have said,' he murmured. '*Except* the ridiculous idea that I should look for romance with Miss Winters.'

'Then you are a fool, George Henderson.'

Suitably chastised, he fell silent. It was just in time, for Miss Winters returned with a steaming cup of tea for the older woman. As she sipped the tea, George told her of his villa in Italy and what he had been doing the last two years. Miss Winters talked of Mary and Marigold and the other people who visited Crosthwaite House that Mrs Lemington remembered fondly.

After about fifteen minutes, the housekeeper started to look increasingly pale and drawn, and Miss Winters moved to take the teacup from her hand. She glanced at him and he nodded, agreeing it was time for them to go.

'Thank you,' George said quietly as he leaned in to hug the frail old woman. 'For everything.'

'It has been my pleasure. Watching you grow up has been a gift. Will you grant a dying woman one promise? Let go of the guilt and allow yourself to be happy.'

He nodded, his voice catching in his throat. 'I will.'

# Chapter Ten

Kate found it hard to hold back the tears as they bid farewell to Mrs Lemington's daughter and stepped outside. Lord Henderson was equally pensive, walking onto the road without uttering a word and bowing his head as he untied Odysseus.

He didn't suggest they mount at first, instead leading Odysseus by the reins and offering Kate his arm. Tentatively she took it, falling into step beside him.

'Do you think there is anything she needs?' Lord Henderson asked eventually.

Kate shook her head, pleased he would seek her opinion. 'No, her daughter is so kind and accommodating. I don't think Mrs Lemington wants for anything.'

'I feel like I want to do something for her, but I don't think there is much she needs now.'

Kate considered a moment. 'Do you truly want to? It isn't just a feeling of obligation?'

He shook his head. 'Mrs Lemington loved me like a son. She was always there in the background, picking me up whenever I fell.'

'Then do something for her daughter. Mrs Lemington cares more about people than material things. Provide for her daughter in some way, and you will make Mrs Lemington very happy.'

Kate could see Lord Henderson was seriously considering her suggestion, and after a moment he nodded. 'I have an idea. Let me think on it.'

It was a pleasant early afternoon, and for a while they strolled along quietly, both contemplating what Mrs Lemington had said without feeling the need to fill the silence with idle chatter.

'We should stop for lunch,' Lord Henderson said after a while, and Kate realised how hungry she felt. Often she would skip lunch, making sure she had a hearty breakfast and a filling dinner. She didn't always need a meal in the middle of the day. Sometimes she might take an apple out into the garden and pick a spot to enjoy a few moments before she returned to her work, but she didn't often stop for a full meal. Today, however, she felt ravenous. 'I know a place,' he said.

They were well out of Keswick now, and Kate hadn't seen anywhere along the way that seemed a likely option.

'Let me help you onto Odysseus.'

It was harder here out in the open with no box to help her pull herself up onto the horse's back. Odysseus was huge, and Kate had no chance of getting up there unaided.

'Here,' Lord Henderson said, placing his hand on her waist to position her better. Kate felt her body tense at the contact and cursed herself for being so easy to read. 'Put your foot in my hand and I will lift you.'

He boosted her up as if she weighed no more than a feather and then, with apparent ease, vaulted into the saddle behind her. Only the almost-hidden wince showed her how his shoulder must pain him. This time

Kate forced herself to relax more, knowing the only person she was harming from sitting completely upright with as little contact as possible with Lord Henderson was herself. Instead she let her body sink into his, her back resting against his chest. It felt intimate, as if they were more than just master and servant, but she was much more comfortable.

They rode for half an hour before turning off the main road down a series of narrow and winding lanes until they stopped outside a picturesque tavern, hidden in amongst the hedgerows and rolling hills. It was the sort of place you would only know about if you were local, although it looked popular and bustling with customers.

'This place has been here years,' Lord Henderson said as he dismounted and helped Kate down. A stable boy ran out and took hold of Odysseus's reins, nodding at the instructions to rub the horse down and give him some hay. 'My father used to bring me here after my mother died when I was a boy, home from school in the holidays.'

'Lord Henderson, as I live and breathe,' a portly man said, coming out of the front doors wiping his hands on a cloth.

'Mr Firth, you don't look a day older.'

'You always were a good liar, Lord Henderson. I cannot believe it is you. It has been years since we last saw you,' the landlord said, ushering them inside. 'I have the perfect table for you, out in our garden. Do you want food, or is it just a refreshing drink you would like today?'

Before Kate knew what was happening, they were swept up in a whirlwind of enthusiasm from the landlord and whisked through the tavern into a beautiful garden at the back.

'This is my hidden gem,' Mr Firth said, winking at Kate as he saw her expression.

The garden was indeed a gem, stretching back a long way and planted as if it were the garden of a wealthy country squire. Tables were dotted about, none of them too close together, to give the patrons some privacy in their discussions.

'Some food would be good.'

'I expect you have been to visit poor Mrs Lemington,' the landlord said, shaking his head.

'We have. She was in good spirits.'

'That warms my heart to hear. I'm fond of her and knew her husband well.' The landlord rallied, and the smile returned to his face. 'I'll bring you the daily special and some drinks.'

Before Kate could open her mouth to order anything, the landlord had hurried off, disappearing back inside the tavern and leaving them by a table with views over the countryside beyond.

'How does he know what we want? Or that we've been to see Mrs Lemington?' Kate said, taking the seat Lord Henderson motioned to.

Lord Henderson smiled and shrugged. 'He has this knack of guessing. And sometimes he seems to know better than you know yourself.' He took his seat and leaned back in his chair, looking more relaxed than she had seen him before. 'I suggest you allow Mr Firth to work his magic.'

Kate looked out at the view, and slowly felt herself relax. It had been a strange couple of days, and her mind hadn't quite caught up with everything that had happened and the consequences of it yet. Slowly she was starting to accept her time at Crosthwaite House was coming to an end, and she would have to find a different position or occupation, but as she gazed at the view, taking in the rolling hills and the sparkle of the lake in the distance, she realised she wanted to stay up here in the Lake District. There were many beautiful places in the country, but it was here in Thornthwaite that she had finally found some peace.

After a few minutes, Mr Firth reappeared with two tall glasses of amber liquid and placed them on the table.

'Best cider in the county,' he announced, beaming at them before disappearing.

Kate looked at her glass dubiously. She had only drunk alcohol on a couple of occasions before, and then it was a few sips of wine at a dinner party. Never had she set foot in an inn or tavern apart from to sleep in on her journey north, and then she had avoided the tap room.

'The man is not lying,' Lord Henderson murmured as he took a long gulp of cider.

Slowly she raised the glass to her lips, taking a small sip, pleasantly surprised by the refreshing coolness of the sweet drink. She took another and another sip and then relaxed back in her chair. If this was how Lord Henderson wanted to spend his afternoon, she would just enjoy it. There was nothing she had to do at the house that was pressing for today, and Mary and Marigold were perfectly capable of doing all the vital jobs whilst she was away.

The food appeared in no time at all, and there seemed to be far too much for two people, but Mr Firth kept bringing out more and more plates. There was a basket of freshly baked bread and a little bowl of butter, a rich chicken stew, some sort of fresh fish, and three bowls of different vegetables.

'Enjoy,' Mr Firth said as he placed the last dish on the table.

They ate in silence at first, both enjoying the food and taking a moment to appreciate their surroundings whilst they had their meal. Kate sipped at her cider as she ate, and before she knew it, another appeared in its place, set gently on the table by the accommodating landlord.

'Mr Firth seems to know you well,' she said.

Lord Henderson nodded, looking over his shoulder at the old tavern.

'My family owned the land and the tavern a few generations ago. Mr Firth ran it from when he was young, and my father sold it to him for a good price. He's always treated us like family ever since.'

'You have a lot of ties here,' Kate said quietly. She had given up on her idea of persuading Lord Henderson to stay, to keep Crosthwaite House, for her own benefit, but that didn't mean selling it was necessarily the right decision for him. There might be bad memories associated with the place, but by selling and never coming back, he would lose all these close associates, people admittedly of a different social class but who seemed to hold the earl in their affections all the same.

'I do. More than anywhere else in the world.'

'People who care about you.' She smiled, feeling an unusual warmth flood through her. 'I know now why you are so insistent you want to sell Crosthwaite House. These good people of Bassenthwaite know all your secrets, don't they?'

He looked at her for a long time, not answering, and Kate wondered if she had adopted the wrong tone. He had been quiet on the journey here from Keswick, lost in thought. Then he gave a little half smile and replied.

'All my youthful indiscretions?'

'Were there many?' Kate knew it was not the sort of question a housekeeper should ask her employer, but she felt light and carefree as if recklessness was running through her veins.

Lord Henderson looked around as if assessing for people trying to listen in on their conversation. Then leaned in closer, dropping his voice. 'Dozens.'

'None of them can be that terrible,' Kate said, taking another sip of cider and finding with surprise that the glass was almost empty again. As if by magic, Mr Firth appeared out of the back door of the tavern, bringing two new glasses filled to the brim with cider. Kate waited until he placed the drinks on their table and left before she spoke.

'Everyone still loves you. *And* they respect you.'

'Perhaps they never knew the worst of the lot.'

Kate saw the twinkle in his eye and wondered if this was what he had been like all the time before the death of his wives. There were flashes of it now, but it was interspersed with spells of melancholy and withdrawal. He was a charismatic man, and she could only imagine the stir he had caused in London as an eligible young bachelor, blessed with charm and good looks alongside his wealth.

'What was the worst?'

'You want me to tell you my darkest secrets?'

Kate held Lord Henderson's eye. 'I bet you were a good boy.'

Lord Henderson stood, picked up his chair, and moved it round the table so he was sitting next to her. It was an intimate position, side by side, as lovers or a husband and wife might sit to discuss their secrets in private.

'No one knows about the time I broke a priceless stained glass window in the church,' he murmured, his lips almost on her ear. 'Or the time one of the local girls tried to sneak me into her family home. Her parents were meant to be away, but they came back early, and I spent a very uncomfortable hour hiding under the dining table before I could make my escape.'

'They didn't see you?'

'I was as quiet as a mouse.'

'What happened with the church?'

'I liked sneaking into places I wasn't meant to be. One night I crept into the church, but I got locked in and panicked. When I was trying to make my escape, I slipped, and my foot went through the stained glass window.'

'No one ever knew it was you?'

He grimaced. 'I was never identified, although my father was quick to offer to pay to replace the window, so I think he suspected.'

'You sound like you were trouble when you were young.'

'Thankfully I have grown into a model citizen.'

Kate scoffed, remembering how he had decided to enter his own house the night he had arrived in Bassenthwaite.

'What about you, Miss Winters? Any youthful misdemeanours?'

'I was a good girl,' she said with a smile.

'Not a single broken vase, pinning the blame on the family dog, or creeping out to sneak into the assembly rooms?'

'Brutus was a very handy scapegoat,' she mused, remembering the loving Labrador that had got the blame for anything that broke in their house.

'Your dog was called Brutus?'

She nodded. 'I think my father thought it would make him more menacing, more of a guard dog, but he was just a sweetie.'

Kate felt her head begin to spin a little, taking another long sip of cider to try and calm it. She was feeling unseasonably warm, and a wonderful contentment was spreading through her.

'Perhaps we had better get you home,' Lord Henderson said, eyeing the glass in her hand.

'Five more minutes,' she said, closing her eyes and turning her face up towards the sun.

'Five more minutes,' he agreed as Mr Firth came out with another couple of drinks.

## Chapter Eleven

In the end they stayed another two hours, joined by various locals who were happy to see George home where they thought he belonged. He had seen the odd looks some of the locals had given Kate, as if she were taking liberties with a too indulgent master, but no one had said anything.

Now he was faced with the prospect of getting Miss Winters back to Crosthwaite House when he was not certain she was sober enough to remember to stay upright on Odysseus's back, let alone hold onto the reins. They could walk, but she was veering a little, and he suspected it might take a couple of hours to make the two-mile journey home.

'Wait there,' he said as he swung himself onto Odysseus's back, settling into the saddle. He would lift her up in front of him. At least that way he was there to hold her so she wouldn't slip off whilst he mounted. 'Can you put your foot in the stirrup and push yourself up? I'll help from up here.'

After a few attempts, they were successful in getting her seated in front of him. Almost immediately she tried to turn round, then collapsed back onto his chest.

'Isn't this nice,' she gushed, her eyes wide as she took in the view. 'I never knew riding a horse could be so cosy.'

He felt a little guilty. The stop at the tavern was only meant to be a quick diversion to get something to eat. In the end they had been there nearly three hours, and in that time George had lost count of how many glasses of cider Kate had finished. By the way she was behaving now, he would wager she was not a habitual drinker, and no doubt her head would be pounding tomorrow morning.

'I much prefer riding with you,' she said in a loud whisper that no doubt she thought was discreet.

George suppressed a smile and urged Odysseus on, allowing the horse to pick his own speed as Miss Winters fiddled with the reins.

'Isn't it funny how life works out,' Miss Winters said, her head resting back on his shoulder. In this position, he could look down at her and see the expressions on her face only a few inches away from his own.

'What do you mean?'

'If you had told me two years ago I would be riding around the edge of a lake on horseback with a very handsome earl, I would never have believed you.'

'What did you think your life would hold?'

Kate waved a dismissive hand. 'Oh, you know, all the usual things. A husband, a family, little shopping trips with my friends, and nights out at the theatre.' She ridiculed and moved her head so she could look up at him. 'All those ridiculous dreams young girls have.'

'It doesn't sound ridiculous.'

'No, I suppose not,' Kate said quietly. 'But it seems so far from my life now that I can hardly imagine even dreaming about it.'

'Is that what you would choose for yourself, if you could?'

'Not with Arthur, no thank you. I have learnt my lesson there.'

George paused before saying anything more, realising this was the first time she had spoken of a man who broke her heart.

'I don't think I would want the life my sister has. Trips to the modiste and organising dinner parties and welcoming her husband home with a smile but all the time knowing what a scoundrel he is.'

He felt as though he had missed half of the conversation. She was talking as if he should be aware of the intertwined relationships she was thinking about, and he felt lost, but allowed her to ramble on without interrupting.

'Perhaps he isn't a scoundrel. Perhaps it was just me.'

'You are not a scoundrel, Miss Winters.'

'But I am a fallen woman,' she said, her eyes widening at the revelation that slipped from her lips. 'And society thinks that's even worse than being a scoundrel.'

'This Arthur took advantage of you?'

She nodded, and he felt a surge of anger. She was still only young, innocent to many of the ways of the world, yet something had happened in her past to upend her entire life.

'And now he's my brother-in-law. My sister insists I should call him *brother*.' She mimed being sick in a show of theatrics, and George couldn't help but grin. The alcohol had loosened her inhibitions as well as her tongue.

'Not that I have ever visited the happy couple.'

'Your sister and this Arthur?'

She nodded, and he began to see why things might

have been so frosty at home. If she had been caught in a dalliance with the man her sister was meant to marry, there would have been a scandal. Perhaps they had managed to contain it within the family, but these things always had a way of eventually seeping out.

'He was ever so handsome,' she said, leaning her head on his shoulder again. 'And charming. Rather like you.'

'You think I'm handsome.'

Miss Winters shrugged her shoulders. 'There's no thinking about it. You are so attractive women swoon as you walk past.'

'Now I know you are mocking me, Miss Winters.'

'Only a little.' She turned, almost falling off Odysseus's back in the process but allowing him to slip a supportive arm under her back. 'I find you attractive,' she said, and if she hadn't been tipsy he would have kissed her then. She looked so earnest, so open, that he wanted to gather her in his arms and kiss her until they both forgot the pain they were carrying. 'I'll swoon next time you walk past me.'

'I'll hold you to that,' he murmured as she turned around, seemingly unaware of the effect she had on him.

'You're not really like Arthur, though,' she said, returning to her previous line of thought. 'You're nice, underneath that facade of grumpiness. You might try to hide it, but when you let your true self shine through, you are undeniably nice.'

'A ringing endorsement.'

'There is absolutely nothing wrong with being nice. It is better than being a cad. Or a lying toerag. Or a snivelling little wormbucket.'

'I take it Arthur is all three.'

'He is.'

'Do you want to tell me what happened?'

He was curious, and she seemed to want to talk, but he was aware she might regret it once the effects of the alcohol wore off.

'You don't have to,' he added quickly.

'He was engaged to my sister,' Miss Winters said, shuffling her bottom so it was pressed up right against him. She had done it to make herself comfortable, but now he was aware of every little movement of her body, and it would make the rest of the ride home almost unbearable. 'They hadn't seen each other for years. It was arranged by my father before Caroline was even old enough to understand what marriage was. Then Arthur was away seeing to his family's business in the Caribbean. When he returned, Caroline was on a trip to Europe with a rich old aunt who favoured her.'

'It does not sound as if they were destined to be together.'

'That is what Arthur said to me.'

George could imagine what had happened. Fresh from his trip to the Caribbean, Arthur had laid eyes on the innocent and pretty Miss Winters and decided he didn't want to wait for the older sister to return.

'I was such a fool,' Miss Winters whispered. 'I believed every dastardly lie that came out of his mouth.'

'He made you promises?'

'He said we would be together. He would break off the engagement to Caroline and we would marry.'

Even though she had an air of authority, now he suspected she had gained that through being thrown out into the world this past year. The Miss Winters of a year ago would have been innocent to the smooth words some men used to trick women into thinking there was more to a relationship than there really was.

'He lied.'

'Again and again.' She sounded morose. 'I was stupid for believing him, but I'd lived a sheltered life where everyone was kind and caring and no one taught me how to recognise the scoundrels of this world.' She paused for a long moment, her eyes closed as she rested her head back on him, staying still for so long George was beginning to wonder if she had fallen asleep.

'What I don't understand,' George said as she stirred and looked up at him, 'is what happened with your family. Surely they could see none of this was your fault.'

'My family are not part of the aristocracy,' Miss Winters said slowly. 'I didn't have to be presented to the queen before I could begin my first season, but even so, there are rules. My father is wealthy. He owns a vast estate, and there is more land in Kent. I was expected to make a good match. The *only* purpose a daughter of such a man can have is to marry well. Either to marry a man with a fortune or to take my sizeable dowry and exchange it for a title.'

'Your father was displeased with the scandal?'

'There wasn't a scandal. He was displeased with the *possibility* of one. No one except my mother, father, and Mr Arthur Evans knows that I threw away my virtue, but still my father was livid I could have put all his hard work to climb up the social ladder in jeopardy.'

'Why didn't he just change the agreement he had made and marry you off to Mr Evans instead?'

'My father would never condone rewarding my immoral behaviour. He was clear I was to be punished, and in his eyes that did not include being rewarded with marriage and a family with a man I had chosen to have a liaison with.' She pressed her lips together, and he could see the tears in her eyes.'

'They didn't care about your happiness?'

Miss Winters scoffed. 'It was never about happiness. It was about behaving properly and what looked best. Now Caroline is married to the man she is supposed to be married to, and I am off looking after a poorly great-aunt I am devoted to in Cornwall.'

'That is the story they have used to explain your absence?'

Miss Winters nodded, a frown darkening her face. 'Do you know how it feels to never be the most important person to anyone? My parents chose their own reputations over my happiness. Arthur chose my sister and an easy life.' She shook her head in disgust. 'Life is not like how you dream it will be when you are fourteen.'

'It most certainly is not,' George murmured, hardly able to remember his hopes as dreams as a fourteen-year-old lad. They had probably been impossible notions of discovering a new land whilst in command of his own boat or fighting pirates off the coast in the Caribbean. He'd been a fanciful boy.

'You've had that kind of love,' Miss Winters said, trying to turn in her seat again as if she forgot she were on horseback. 'Is it as wonderful as everyone says?'

'Yes.'

They both fell silent, and then Miss Winters looked round with a mischievous grin, seemingly forgetting the gravity of their conversation a few minutes earlier.

'I don't know what Mr Firth put in that cider, but I feel like I can fly,' she said, stretching her arms wide and surging forwards. George lurched to catch her, his injury momentarily slipping her mind and the weakness it foisted upon his left arm. To his horror, the petite housekeeper slipped from his grip and tumbled off Odysseus's back.

She landed in a heap on the ground and then looked up at him and giggled.

'You look so serious.'

Quickly George dismounted, trusting Odysseus not to wander too far, and crouched down beside Miss Winters.

'Are you hurt? Can you move your legs?'

She gave a wonderful display of how all four limbs worked, wiggling them up and down, hardly noticing how her skirts fell to her knees, exposing her legs to the world. When she didn't pull them down, George reached over and tugged at the hem, covering her up.

'Does the sight of my legs upset you, my lord?'

'No.'

'Does it unsettle you, then?'

'You have very pretty ankles, Miss Winters, but alas, the mere sight of them is not going to make me lose my composure. Come, let's get you on your feet.'

They were in the middle of the road, but it was quiet. The narrow lane only led up to Crosthwaite House, so although it wasn't part of the estate, no one used it except to visit the property. He straightened and then took her hand and pulled her up, steadying her as she tottered and sidestepped.

'You have had far too much to drink, Miss Winters,' he murmured.

'I only had two glasses of cider.'

'You had at least six, maybe seven.'

Her eyes widened, and she shook her head. 'No, that was you draining all the glasses. I only had little sips.'

'Lots of little sips add up.'

She looked like she might protest again but then shrugged.

'I've never really drunk before, but it seems I can handle my alcohol well,' she said, veering off to the left so much she almost fell off the path.

'Impeccably, although might I suggest we lean on one another for mutual support?'

He thought she might refuse, but after a moment she nodded and half skipped, half stumbled her way back over to him. Taking Odysseus's reins in one hand, he waited for Miss Winters to slip her delicate hand into the crook of his arm before they set off.

'It's very quiet out here,' the housekeeper said after they had made a little progress. Her speed was painfully slow as she kept stopping to admire mundane objects. They paused to look at a particularly interesting stick, an exceedingly green weed, and a trail of ants carrying a leaf back to their nest. 'It really is the perfect place to steal a kiss.'

Now it was George's turn to pause. 'A kiss?'

'Yes. If two people wanted to kiss, there would be no need to creep into the bushes. They could do it right here in the middle of the road and only have squirrels for witnesses.'

'And squirrels are notoriously tight-lipped,' he murmured.

She spun, looking up at him, and he knew she was thinking about kissing him. Never would he take advantage of a woman in an inebriated state, but the hungry way she was looking at him made him wish she wasn't quite so tipsy.

'Kissing is nice,' she said, her eyes closing and a wide smile blooming on her face.

'If you think kissing is merely nice, your companion hasn't been doing it right.'

'Oh.' Her eyes shot open, and she stumbled into him. George gripped her hand to steady her, and for a long moment a wave of desire pulsed between them.

George coughed. He needed to get her home before he did something they both regretted. Miss Winters might not be an innocent—dastardly Arthur Evans had seen to that—but she was hardly a woman of the world, and he did not want her to wake up with regret in the morning.

As he continued to guide her along the road, he wondered if *he* would regret dallying with his housekeeper. It was invigorating to feel desire again, after all this time to be drawn to someone. Part of him wanted to give in, to revel in the pleasure he knew they could give one another. Quietly he shook his head, knowing it wasn't as simple as all that. He couldn't just shrug off the guilt he felt about moving forwards with his life when Clara and Elizabeth would never be able to move forwards with theirs. Any dalliance would not be the straightforward giving and receiving of pleasure. He would always have the spectre of his guilt hanging over him. He couldn't deny a liaison with Miss Winters was tempting, but he would be foolish to think they both wouldn't pay an emotional price.

Still, he couldn't ignore the pull of desire, the overwhelming attraction he felt for her.

Thankfully the facade of Crosthwaite House came into view before either of them did or said something they would regret, and after a little persuasion, Miss Winters allowed him to stable Odysseus whilst she went inside.

## Chapter Twelve

'She's like a bear with a sore head,' Mary grumbled in the next room, unaware Kate was able to hear her. It wasn't an inaccurate description, although *sore* seemed a bit of an understatement.

Her head throbbed. The light made her want to poke her eyes out, and somehow every muscle in her body ached even though she had not done more than gentle physical activity. Loud noises cut through her like a sword through a soft cake, and she wanted nothing more than to crawl back under the covers and spend a day feeling sorry for herself.

'Good morning, Miss Winters,' Lord Henderson boomed as he rounded the corner into the pantry. She'd been hiding out in the cool darkness of the storeroom, enjoying a little peace. She must have visibly winced, for he lowered his voice to a theatrical whisper before continuing, 'How is your head?'

'Perfectly fine, thank you,' she lied, having to grit her teeth to enable her to answer.

'Liar.'

'How come you are so cheerful this morning? You drank as much as me.'

He looked down at himself and then pointedly at her. 'There's twice as much of me. Besides, it's not my first time. You ran off so quickly yesterday afternoon, I couldn't tell you to drink lots of water and have something to eat before bed.'

She had disappeared. At the time a mild wave of nausea had overtaken her, and she had been worried she might be sick. Thankfully Marigold had still been in the house and had cheerfully agreed to stay a little later to see to anything Lord Henderson might need whilst Kate had crawled into bed.

'Why do people drink?'

He grinned. 'You were good fun on the journey home. Trouble, but good fun.'

Desperately Kate tried to piece together what had occurred on the journey. She could remember snippets, little bits of conversation, but certainly not everything.

'Did I…' She trailed off, not wanting to give away how little memory she had of the previous afternoon. She cleared her throat and pushed on. 'Did I do anything regrettable?'

Kate thought she saw a twinkle of mischief in Lord Henderson's eyes, but he shook his head.

'Good.'

'I came to tell you a messenger arrived saying there is a man coming to view the house today. He should be here this afternoon.'

'Everything is in order.' Everything except her. She expected she looked terrible. A quick glance in the small mirror above her washbasin was all she could manage this morning, and the dark rings round her eyes and pale complexion hadn't signified a housekeeper who was a picture of health.

'Good. I think it would be helpful if you accompanied us in case there are any practical questions about the running of the house I cannot answer.'

She nodded, regretting the movement immediately as her head started throbbing even more.

'Might I suggest you take an hour or two to lie down first? Mary and Marigold are busy about their work, and it might make you feel a little more functional if you slept for a short time.' He regarded her with a hint of concern, frowning. He seemed to have lost some of the heaviness that had weighed on him since returning to Crosthwaite House and even managed a smile. 'And I happen to know you have a very understanding employer.' Lord Henderson turned to leave, stepping out of the darkness of the pantry.

'He should be understanding. He got me drunk,' Kate muttered. She knew Lord Henderson heard her by the way his shoulders shook with laughter as he walked away.

Deciding she would take his advice, Kate ensured Mary and Marigold were occupied and happy before retreating to her room. It was only mid-morning even though it felt as though she had been up hours and hours, so she had plenty of time to lie down and rest her eyes before getting up to be prepared for the potential buyer's visit after lunch.

As she sank into her bed, she felt the throbbing in her head subside a little, and within a few minutes she was asleep.

'Do you feel any better?' Lord Henderson said as they watched the carriage roll to a stop and the driver jump down to open the door for the occupant.

'Much better, thank you,' she said. It was true. After sleeping for a couple of hours, Kate had woken rejuvenated and refreshed, hardly able to believe how terrible she had felt just a few hours earlier. 'Who is this?'

'Lord Willcox. He owns a lot of land around Lake Windermere and always has his eye on opportunities to acquire more.'

Lord Willcox descended from the carriage, taking a moment to look at the impressive facade of Crosthwaite House. The sun was shining and the flowers were coming into bloom on either side of the front door, and it made for a pretty aesthetic.

'Henderson, good to see you. I didn't know you were back in the country.'

'A short trip only. How are you?'

'Excited to hear your property might be coming up for sale. My father tried to buy it from your father on a number of occasions, but the old man was always turned down. It has a prime position here. Glorious views, I would imagine.'

Lord Willcox was a large man who seemed to be in his forties. He was tall and well built, although not fat. He looked like a man who spent most of his time outside and had a ruddy complexion and windswept hair.

'I'm happy to show you around.'

'Are you definitely selling?'

'Yes,' Lord Henderson said without hesitation.

'Money problems? Creditors banging on your door?' It was a highly personal question, but Lord Willcox didn't flinch as he asked it.

'I plan to make my home in Italy. I have no need for a property here.'

'Well, that's good for me.' Lord Willcox's eyes settled on Kate, and she felt herself shift uncomfortably. She could withstand a scrutinising gaze, but this felt predatory. 'Who is this?'

'Miss Winters, my housekeeper.'

'Lucky chap. Does she come with the house?'

Kate felt her skin crawl as he regarded her with a sort of hunger.

'No. Shall we start?' Lord Henderson said abruptly.

'Lead the way.'

Kate fell into step behind the two men, careful to keep out of arm's reach. She didn't trust Lord Willcox not to try and grope her when Lord Henderson's back was turned. With a sinking heart, Kate realised this was what her life could be like once she left Crosthwaite House. Many servants lived with decent employers who cared about their well-being, but many did not. She had heard horror stories of young female servants being harassed again and again, their lower status in the house making them fair game for their masters' attentions. The idea made her feel sick again.

She needed to work. She needed the money. For a moment, she wondered about returning home to ask for some support from her parents but knew she could never do it. The look of disgust and disappointment in her father's eyes had driven her away, that and the heartbreak of finding the man she loved had so easily given up on her and married her sister instead. She would not return home and become prisoner to their terms, being hidden away in exchange for a few measly pounds a year.

Glancing at Lord Henderson, she allowed herself a moment to examine the feelings she knew were developing for him. With Arthur she had been infatuated, tricked by his flattery into thinking there was more between them than a mere attraction. Looking back, she could see now she hadn't ever loved him, not really. She had been swept up in his compliments and pretended affection. At home with a cold father and cowed mother, she didn't receive much warmth, much love, and she had grabbed on to the first thing that looked a little bit like the romance she had dreamed of as a young girl. Now she could see none of it was real, even the feelings she had told herself she had for Arthur.

Lord Henderson spoke of love differently, of wanting to put someone else's feelings above yours at all times, of caring for someone more than anything else in the world. If she was completely honest with herself, *that* was what she wanted, what she craved.

Shaking herself, she hurried to catch up, quickly suppressing the rebellious thought that she would like to experience that affection with Lord Henderson. It hadn't been offered, and with him leaving very soon, it wouldn't be, either.

Lord Henderson gave a good tour, showing all the main rooms downstairs before taking Lord Willcox up to see the bedrooms.

'We have ten bedrooms, including a grand master bedroom, which links to a second bedroom via a small dressing room.'

'Are you selling the furniture with the house?'

'Yes. Everything except a few sentimental pieces.'

They entered the master bedroom. 'Looks a comfortable bed, eh?' Lord Willcox said, turning to Kate. Until now he had largely ignored her after his first remark, but Kate felt his eyes roaming over her body as he watched her.

'All the beds are finest quality,' Lord Henderson said, frowning at the other man. 'Please have a look through to the adjoining bedroom.' He waited for the large man to step into the dressing room and pushed the door to behind him. 'I'm sorry,' Lord Henderson said to Kate.

'I barely know the man. I was not aware he was such a pig.'

'I suppose I have to get used to it.'

'You wouldn't work here under him?'

Kate shrugged. 'I have to work somewhere.' She saw his aghast expression. 'Although I would not stay and subject myself to that willingly.'

'Good, I...' Lord Henderson began, but was cut off by Lord Willcox reappearing in the doorway.

'Very nice,' he said. 'Great views. Bassenthwaite is so rugged and beautiful. I think I would enjoy a property up here on its shores.'

They trailed through each of the bedrooms and then headed back to the main staircase.

'Miss Winters will show you the kitchens and downstairs quarters,' Lord Henderson said, allowing Kate to lead the way but ensuring he stuck close behind. She was grateful for that, although she was aware she would soon likely have to learn how to manage men like Lord Willcox on her own.

As they entered the kitchen, Kate began giving a little information about the size of the servants' quarters, leading Lord Willcox through the maze of rooms.

'Sorry to interrupt, sir, but there is a messenger just arrived. He brought this,' Marigold said as she appeared in the corridor. 'He's waiting in case you want to send a reply.'

'Thank you.'

Lord Henderson looked at the note, his expression serious. 'Excuse me,' he murmured, his eyes still racing across the words. 'I'll be back in a minute.'

Marigold disappeared too, returning to whatever task she was seeing to upstairs, and Kate felt a moment of unease at being left alone with Lord Willcox. Quickly she rallied. He might be a suggestive scoundrel, but he was hardly going to try anything with another man's housekeeper whilst left alone for a mere few minutes.

'What's along there?' Lord Willcox asked, pointing to the far end of the downstairs corridor.

'More storerooms, an old laundry, and at the very end are steps leading out to the side of the house. The door has been locked for years, but there's nothing wrong with it, and it could be used as an alternative entrance if you had a large household with lots of servants coming and going.'

'Shall we take a look?'

It was dark along the corridor with no natural light, and Lord Willcox had already set off, striding ahead so she had no time to find a candle and light it. She followed, hoping he would take a quick peek at the disused rooms and then turn back.

'Lots of dark nooks and crannies in here,' he said, turning to leer at her.

'There isn't much natural light,' Kate said, keeping her voice neutral. He didn't need to see how much he unsettled her.

They had entered the room at the very end of the corridor that was set up as a laundry with big sinks along each wall. As Lord Willcox turned around, he barrelled into Kate, and she wasn't sure if it was entirely by accident. Certainly the hand that roamed over her back and buttocks as he steadied himself was intentional, as was the horrific way he leaned in closer and sniffed her hair, letting out a little murmur of appreciation.

Thankfully Kate was closest to the door, and she was able to slip out of his grasp and escape into the corridor. Out in the open, she thought that would be the end of his unwanted attention, but he strode out and caught her wrist.

'Not so fast, Miss Housekeeper. How about a smile as you give me the tour? I bet you're even prettier when you smile.'

Kate couldn't have made her lips obey even if she had wanted to. She stood there stony faced, her wrist still encircled by his hand, knowing that if he chose to, he could overpower her in a second.

'Go on, give me a smile. That's all I want. One little smile from that delicious little mouth of yours.'

Still she did not smile, hoping that if she stayed still and silent for long enough, he would realise what he was doing, find some sliver of conscience and let her go.

'Unless you want to put your mouth to better use. We probably have time before your master comes back, and I'd pay well for the service.'

Kate felt a wave of nausea and fear take over her body. She wanted to scream, to pull away and run, but she knew there was a likelihood no one would hear her. Lord Henderson would be returning soon, but that could be in thirty seconds or ten minutes, and a lot could happen in ten minutes.

She tried to force herself to remain calm. It was highly unlikely Lord Willcox was going to do anything to her whilst he was here as a guest of her employer. Probably he viewed this as good-natured teasing, words only, and she was panicking for nothing.

He exerted a light pressure on her wrist, pulling her towards him. Kate resisted, trying to keep her feet from moving, knowing whatever his intentions she did not want to be any nearer to this man.

'Shall I help you?' he said, using his free hand to pull at the corners of her mouth.

Kate recoiled at his touch, jerking her head away so hard and fast it whacked into the wall.

'What's happening here?'

Kate had never been so pleased to hear someone's voice in all her life.

Lord Henderson strode down the darkened corridor, a ball of pent-up energy and anger. As he drew level with Kate and Lord Willcox, he none too gently ripped the older man's hand from Kate's wrist.

Lord Willcox stepped back, raising his hands in a gesture that seemed to signify he meant no threat.

Ignoring the other man for a moment, Lord Henderson turned to her, concern etched on his face.

'Did he hurt you?'

'Course I didn't hurt the girl. It was just a bit of playful teasing, nothing more,' Lord Willcox blustered.

Lord Henderson acted as if the viscount hadn't spoken and focussed completely on Kate.

'Did he hurt you?'

She shook her head.

'Good.' Turning finally to face the older man, Lord Henderson shook his head in disgust. 'Get out of my house.'

'Come on, Henderson. It was innocent joshing. The girl didn't mind, did you?'

'Get out of my house,' Lord Henderson repeated, his voice low and dangerous.

Lord Willcox bristled this time and then scoffed.

'Keeping her for yourself. I know your game, Henderson. *That* I can respect.'

In a flash Lord Henderson spun around and his fist flew through the air, connecting with the older man's lower jaw. Kate saw the wince of pain as the punch must have pulled on his wound, even though it was on the other side of his chest. Lord Willcox staggered back, holding his jaw and looking shocked at what had just happened.

'Don't make me throw you out,' Lord Henderson said quietly.

The viscount moved quickly, muttering under his breath as he scurried away. Both Kate and Lord Henderson watched him go, neither moving until he was out of sight and they heard the slam of the front door behind him.

'Are you hurt?' Kate raised her hands to his chest before she could stop herself, probing for the edge of the bandaged wound.

Lord Henderson caught her wrists in his fingers, holding her lightly.

'I'm sorry I left you alone with him. I knew he had a reputation for being a blaggard, but I never thought he would try anything in someone else's home.'

'I can't believe you hit him for me.' She really was astonished. Not that Lord Henderson would stand up to a man like Lord Willcox. He was good and kind and cared about other people. She was more astonished that he had hit him to defend the honour of his housekeeper.

'Probably was a terrible idea. Now he'll put it about I'm cloistered away here with my pretty housekeeper doing all number of unspeakable things.'

She felt shaken, as if her insides were in turmoil, which stopped only when Lord Henderson reached out and took her hand. It felt as though he was anchoring her to the ground, the only thing stopping her from spiralling out of control.

'Breathe,' he murmured, his voice low and calm, a balm to the feeling of panic in her chest. 'You're safe. No one can hurt you.'

For a minute Kate did just that. She focussed on sucking air into her lungs and blowing it out again. The rhythmic movement of her chest acted to calm her. She hated that a man like Lord Willcox could make her respond this way. After everything with Arthur, she had told herself she would never let a man dictate how she felt ever again. She'd been determined to be independent and self-sufficient in every sense of the word.

'Can you move?' Lord Henderson said softly.

She nodded, allowing him to lead her upstairs and out onto the terrace with views over the lake. He guided her to a bench and made sure she was comfortable, bringing a chair over so he could sit close but not immediately beside her.

The fresh air was exactly what Kate needed. As she felt the gentle wind whip about her cheeks, it seemed to clear some of the panic she still felt until her heart settled into a normal rhythm.

'Thank you,' she murmured, looking over at Lord Henderson.

'You have nothing to thank me for.'

For a few minutes they sat in silence, Kate wondering if she could have handled things differently. With a shake of her head, she dismissed the thoughts. It was not she who was the problem. She had done nothing wrong, and she wouldn't let herself get sucked into a cycle of self-recrimination and loathing. With Arthur she had fallen into that trap, and it was only time and distance that had allowed her to accept that primarily she had been a victim. She was not innocent—she would never claim that—but Arthur had spun a web of lies and showered her with false promises and compliments, and she had been naive enough to believe them. Now she wouldn't waste any more time blaming herself.

# Chapter Thirteen

Sitting on her bed, Kate stared down at the piece of paper in her hands. It was the property deed Lord Henderson had returned to Crosthwaite House to find, the one thing that was keeping him here.

She knew in her heart it was time to return it. It had been a mistake to take it, something she regretted. It was not her place to influence him as to what he should do with the house. These last few days, she had seen a change in him, as if being here had allowed him to confront the assumption he had made that only bad memories assailed him. There were still moments of darkness, times when he seemed to stomp around with a frown on his face, but they were less frequent than when he arrived, and there were more and more flashes of the man she knew he was underneath all of that. The change had seemed to come after their trip to see Mrs Lemington. She didn't know if it was being out in the local area, seeing the people he had grown up around, realising he did still belong, or if it was something else, but she was grateful for the change, whatever had driven it.

Now, however, she knew she had to right the wrong she had committed when taking the deed. It would be up to him then whether he stayed or whether he left immediately as he had originally planned. She hoped he might decide to wait a little longer, perhaps finish the job of sorting the pile of papers in his study and oversee the selling of the house. Perhaps even he might decide it wasn't the time to sell, not now he had confronted some of his demons returning here and survived.

Whatever he decided, she could not influence him any more. Kate knew she needed to focus on her own future. First she would begin her search for another position, something that allowed her to maintain her independence, and then she would slowly ask herself what exactly it was that she wanted. It wasn't a question she had allowed herself to think about much this last year, having to instead focus on rebuilding her shattered confidence and trust, but perhaps in a few months, when she was settled somewhere else, she could finally work out what she wanted from life.

Standing, Kate took the piece of paper and tucked it into the pocket of her apron. There was no point delaying any longer. She headed upstairs, knowing the study would be empty. Ten minutes earlier, Lord Henderson had headed out for a ride, and she knew he would be gone at least an hour. It was the perfect time to slip the deed near the top of the pile of papers he was sorting through so he would find it next time he sat down to work.

Kate had wondered if she should confess her bad action to Lord Henderson, but after a conflicted night, she had decided there was nothing to be gained from it and instead would return it without him ever knowing she had taken it.

Briskly she knocked on the door of the study just in case he had returned without her knowledge, but there was no answer, so she slipped inside. Carefully she assessed the piles of paperwork, much more ordered than they had been a few days earlier, and chose one to slip the deed into. She was just lifting up the pile when she heard a noise behind her and the door opened.

Kate froze. Desperately her mind was telling her body to move, but instead she stood unmoving with the papers in one hand and the deed in another.

'Miss Winters,' Lord Henderson said, 'what are you doing?'

Kate could have said anything and she doubted he would have questioned her, but she knew she couldn't lie. It was one thing planning to slip the deed back without confessing she had taken it, but quite another to lie to his face when caught red-handed.

'What are you doing?' he repeated, and she heard the note of danger in his voice.

She took a deep breath and held up the deed. 'Returning this,' she said, holding his gaze for as long as she was able.

'What is it?' He strode over and took the paper from her, frowning as he saw the importance of the document. 'Why do you have that?' His tone was sharp, disbelieving.

'I found it the first morning you returned when I helped search your papers,' Kate said, hating how he was looking at her. 'I slipped it into my apron pocket. I'm sorry. It was a mistake.'

'A mistake? You can hardly have done it by accident. Why did you take it?'

'I had this notion I could persuade you to not sell the house if only you would stay for a little longer,' she said quietly.

He looked at her for well over a minute, not saying a

word. Kate wished he would rant, shout at her, anything but the look of hurt and disdain in his eyes.

'What makes you think you have any right to influence me over what I do with *my* property?'

'I am sorry. It was a mistake. I regretted from the moment I took it.'

'Yet it has taken you until now to return it.' He shook his head, turning away as if unable to look at her. 'Is that why…' He trailed off, not finishing the sentence. Instead he spun on his heel and walked from the room.

Kate sank down to the floor, her legs shaking too much to hold her up. She felt wretched. He was right, of course—her actions were unforgiveable—but she hated for him to think of her this way. These past few days, she had felt a growing respect between them, alongside the undeniable attraction, and now she knew that had been shattered completely.

Tears streamed onto her cheeks, and she let them flow freely, wondering if that was the last she would see of Lord Henderson. The departure was abrupt but it wouldn't surprise her if he left now and never returned.

The idea of never seeing him again made her heart ache, and for a moment Kate allowed herself to wonder what that meant. He was a complicated man, but there was kindness at his centre, and she knew she was beginning to care for him more than she had any right to. With her fingertips she brushed away the tears, wondering how these feelings had crept up on her. After everything that had happened this past year, she hadn't sworn off love. She knew that was foolish. One day she would like a husband, a family, but she had promised herself she wouldn't allow her feelings to run away from her, to risk her heart without very careful consideration.

Which was exactly what she had done.

Forcing herself to stand, Kate hurried downstairs, hoping she didn't encounter Mary or Marigold on the way. All she wanted to do was shut herself away in her room and bury her head under the pillow.

George was fuming. He could not believe Miss Winters had taken the deed, that she'd kept it hidden these past few days. He'd trusted her, opened up to her, even let her see some of his pain and vulnerability.

He was riding hard, bent low over Odysseus's back, relishing the harsh whip of wind against his face. Only when he sensed his horse was tiring did he slow, his blood pounding in his temples and his breath coming hard and fast.

With a loud, primal shout, he let some of the anger escape through his lips. Her actions weren't even logical. A delay of a few days was hardly going to make him change his mind on whether he would sell or not.

Slumping forwards, George loosened his grip on the reins, allowing Odysseus to start walking again, choosing his own pace.

The worst part was that he was beginning to trust Miss Winters, to give in to the desire to spend more time with her. He pictured her smiling face and wondered what else had been a ruse. Running a hand through his hair, he knew he was being uncharitable, unreasonable even, but he felt so angry.

It took Odysseus about thirty minutes to pick a path back to the house, and George had lost some of the initial anger by the time he had rubbed the horse down and ensured he was comfortable in his stable. Still he knew he had to confront Miss Winters, to show her how harmful her actions had been.

'Where is Miss Winters?' George said as he stomped down to the kitchen.

Marigold eyed him nervously and bobbed into a little curtsy.

'I think she went to her room, sir.'

Without another word, he stalked along the corridor to the housekeeper's room and rapped sharply on the door.

Some of the fire in him flickered and died as he saw Miss Winters's tear-stained face. She looked devastated. He felt a pulse of sympathy and then quickly pushed it down. It was her own fault.

He walked past her into the room, pulling the door closed behind him, and then spun to face her.

'I'm sorry,' she said. He was surprised to see she held his eye and spoke with less panic than earlier. Taking the deed was easily a sackable offence, and she must realise her job was on the line. His eyes swept the room and he saw the fabric bag on the bed, already half-stuffed.

'You're leaving?'

'I thought you would want me to.'

He closed his eyes. It would be easy to agree with her. To send her on her way, grab the deed, and leave Crosthwaite House forever himself. That way he wouldn't have to confront the emotions swirling inside. He could run back to Italy and try to forget the way his heart clenched when Miss Winters smiled or how he found any little excuse to spend time with her. Perhaps he could lessen the guilt he felt rather than adding to it.

'What were you thinking?' he asked, to give himself more time to make his decision.

'You don't want to know.'

'I asked the question. It is only fair you give me an answer.'

Miss Winters sighed and was silent for a long moment before speaking. He could almost see the thoughts running through her head. Then she perched on the edge of her narrow single bed and looked down at her hands.

'This wasn't the first place I went after I left my family,' Kate said quietly. 'I drifted from here to there, finding a little work, rapidly spending my dwindling savings. Then I saw the advertisement for a housekeeper at Crosthwaite House, and it was as if something was calling to me.' She glanced up, but just for a second. 'When I arrived here, I was broken and low in confidence. I didn't trust my own judgement, and I still blamed myself for what had happened with Arthur. Despite that, Mrs Lemington took me in and showed me the job, and in that time we spent together, she restored some of my self-belief.'

George could well imagine it. Mrs Lemington had always had a soft spot for lost souls and had a firm but kind way of making you realise it did no good to mope.

'In the months I have been here, I have healed. I began to believe in myself again. I found satisfaction in doing my job well, in making a success of myself. I even enjoyed the physicality of the work, and slowly I realised that all those things I had allowed other people to tell me about myself were not true.' She spoke softly, so he had to lean in a little closer to hear. Her words melted some of the frostiness in him, and he had to resist the urge to reach out and take her hand.

'I do not know what I want from my future. I think one day I would like a husband and a family, but right now I need a little more time just learning to like myself again. Time to work out what *I* enjoy and what I don't. Time away from living under the iron rule of my father, where I could make no decisions for myself. The only rule I have is that I say yes to things that make me happy.'

'That is why you took the deed?'

'Yes. I am happy here, and I wanted more time. It was selfish and wrong, and I regretted it immediately, but I did it, and I am sorry. When you turned up with no warning and told me it was the end of my time here, I felt as though you had ripped out the rug from under my feet. I panicked and made a bad decision.'

When she said it like that, it was hard to be angry with her. She looked so forlorn sitting there, bag half-packed on the bed.

George looked down at the floor, trying desperately to work out what to do for the best. He *should* stick to his plan—to make haste for his solicitor, deposit the deed with him, and then arrange for a passage to Italy—but there was something holding him back.

He ran a hand through his hair, glancing at the young woman on the bed. If he was honest with himself, he knew exactly why he wanted to stay. He wasn't ready yet to say goodbye to Miss Winters. Perhaps another week or two wouldn't hurt. He could oversee the sale of the house and still plan to leave in a few weeks.

Miss Winters stood abruptly and sniffed, and he saw fresh tears about to spill onto her cheeks.

'I need a moment,' she said, crossing to the door and pulling it open. She was out into the corridor before he could stop her.

'Miss Winters,' he called, knowing that whatever he decided, he hadn't finished with her yet. Quickly he strode after her and caught her up just outside the door, gripping hold of her wrist. She stopped and turned towards him, and suddenly they both went very still.

George felt a surge of pent-up desire and an overwhelming urge to kiss her. He was consumed by the thought, unable to think about anything else. He looked down at her and saw the way her eyes flicked from his eyes to his lips and knew she was thinking the same.

Slowly he lowered his lips to hers and brushed a kiss against them. He was conscious of her past, of everything she had been through, and didn't want to do something unwanted, yet he felt her rise up on her toes to meet him, to kiss him back as if her life depended on it.

George groaned as she tangled her hands in his hair, all the longing flooding through him and out into that one kiss. He wanted to pull her close, to hold on to her forever, afraid that at any instant one of them would come to their senses and stop this madness.

For his part, George couldn't have stopped if he'd tried. Gently he eased her up against the wall so her back was pressed against the cool stone, and then he kissed her so she would forget everything but him. His fingers danced over her body, pulling her ever closer and caressing the few bits of bare skin he could find. Expertly he lifted one of her legs and slipped a hand under her petticoats, searching out the spot where her stockings ended and the warm skin began, loving the way she gasped in a mixture of surprise and pleasure. 'You taste so sweet,' he murmured into her neck as his lips trailed down below her ear to her collarbone. 'I want to taste every last inch of you.'

Kate let out a little breath of anticipation at the thought, as if ready to strip off here in the corridor and disregard the consequences.

They both froze as they heard the familiar sound of Mary's whistling followed by footsteps descending the stairs into the kitchen, guiltily jumping apart before they could be caught in such a compromising position.

They were not in view of the kitchen, but Mary could walk out at any moment. George felt his heart hammering in his chest, torn between the desire to carry on and damn the consequences, and his ever rising guilt at what he'd just let happen.

They waited as they listened to Mary bustle round and then heard her voice calling out to Marigold.

'I'll just go and find Miss Winters. I need to ask her about the dust covers in the yellow bedroom.'

George's eyes met Kate's and he saw the flare of panic he felt reflected in hers.

With a jerk she began moving, carefully smoothing down her dress and patting her hair to ensure everything was clipped where it was meant to be. Without looking at George, she summoned a bright and breezy smile and bustled into the kitchen before Mary could discover them in the corridor together.

# Chapter Fourteen

George picked up the piece of paper in front of him and tried to read it for the fourth time. It was growing dark outside and his eyes had to strain to see the words on the paper, but that wasn't the reason he couldn't concentrate.

Miss Winters. She was the distraction. Every time he tried to focus, all he could think of was the softness of her lips and how right she had felt in his arms. This attraction had been building for days, but now that it had been released, he doubted whether he could rein it back in.

With a groan he stood, remembering how she had kissed him back. There was no doubt in his mind she wanted it just as much as he did.

He'd gone down to her room to express how angry he was and ended up kissing her. It was not how he had envisioned his day going, and now he was plagued by contrasting feelings of desire and disgust at himself for letting such a thing happen.

'You're getting nothing done,' he murmured as he walked over to the window and looked out at the view down to the lake.

'Are you talking to yourself, my lord?' Miss Winters said as she entered the room carrying two candlesticks with lighted candles. He could tell by the slight wobble in her voice she was trying to act normal but struggling now that she had entered the room.

'I'm having a most unproductive afternoon, Miss Winters.'

'I thought you might like some light to work by.'

'That is very thoughtful.'

She turned to leave, and George had to resist the urge to reach out and grab her hand.

'Stay a moment, Miss Winters.'

'I really should see to dinner.'

'I'm not hungry. Sit with me.'

'A drink, then. I could bring you a cup of tea.'

'I don't want tea.'

She hesitated as if she were going to suggest something else and then chose a chair, perching on the very edge of a comfortable armchair opposite the one he was working in.

George sat down as well, wondering what he wanted to say now he had persuaded her to stay. Part of him knew he should apologise. He should ask that they forget the incident in the basement earlier and try to pretend nothing had happened. That was the most sensible course. Since their kiss, he had been wracked with guilt. His whole purpose in coming back had been to find the deed and prepare the house for a quick sale. He had planned to rid himself of anything that could remind him too much of the past, and yet here he was, considering staying longer.

'Are we alone in the house?'

Her eyes widened, and he realised what the question sounded like he was suggesting.

'I just mean do we have to worry about anyone overhearing us,' he added quickly.

'Mary and Marigold have gone home.'

'Good. I wanted to talk to you about what happened earlier.'

'We don't need to talk about it,' Miss Winters said, looking down at her hands.

'I think we do.'

The silence stretched out between them, Miss Winters resolutely not meeting his gaze.

He closed his eyes for a moment, allowing himself to consider what he wanted in that moment. For the first time in a long time, he didn't think of how he *should* feel or what would be the most respectful thing to do. He allowed his own wants and desires to come to the fore. It was liberating, letting go of the guilt of surviving that influenced so many of his decisions. He decided that for a short time, at least, he would try to live without the self-reproach he normally subjected himself to.

'I find myself obsessed with you,' he said softly. 'These last few days I have not been able to think of much else but kissing you, touching you, making love to you.'

'Lord Henderson...'

'Please, call me George. I do not want there to be this formality between us.'

'There needs to be a formality between us. I am your housekeeper, you my employer. I am a servant, you an earl.'

'We are both mere humans,' he said, and now she looked up at him. 'Tell me you don't feel it too. That pull.'

She opened her mouth but closed it again, unable to lie directly to him.

'I cannot offer you marriage, Miss Winters, but what I propose could be even more enjoyable for the both of us.' When she didn't say anything, he pushed on. 'I am still planning on leaving the country shortly, perhaps a month, maybe at most two, but I wonder whether in that time we give in to the desire we feel and spend the time together.'

'You want me to become your mistress?'

Her voice was low, but he detected a thrum of anger.

'I can't marry you, Miss Winters.' He repeated.

She stood and strode over to the window, looking out.

'Tell me you don't feel the attraction between us.'

'Of course I feel it.' The words exploded from her. 'I feel it every time we're close. Every time you walk into the room. Of course I want to kiss you, to touch you, to allow things to happen between us as if we were husband and wife. I lie in bed every night dreaming of you.' She took a shuddering breath, her chest heaving. 'That doesn't mean I can act on what I want. *Everything* has consequences. Consequences that one of us needs to consider.'

George regarded her in silence for a minute, knowing she was right. If they became lovers, there would be the temporary bliss of spending time with her, of making love to her, but he couldn't pretend it could happen without taking an emotional toll. And perhaps he had to consider it would be more for her. Of course there was the risk of ruination if anyone found out, but more than that, she had no real reason to trust him. She'd been hurt before by a man promising her everything would be fine.

'I can't stop thinking of you,' he said quietly. 'I am consumed by thoughts of you.'

He saw her eyes flicker to his and knew she felt the same.

'Why can't we choose happiness for once?' he said

quietly. 'For two years I have had nothing but misery. Every time I do something new, I am plagued by guilt. I question why I survived when Elizabeth and Clara did not. It is a cruel purgatory I am trapped in, alive but unable to enjoy any of the delights of living.'

Miss Winters took a step closer, and he could see she wanted to reach out for him, to comfort him, but she resisted.

'Choose happiness,' she said softly. 'Choose to start living again. Choose to let go of the guilt, to accept there was nothing you could have done to save your wives and that there is no way you can swap places with them.'

He nodded, knowing she was right.

'And if my happiness includes you?' he asked.

She scoffed and turned away. 'For a few short weeks. It is not worth it to me, my lord, no matter how much I might desire it. I must think of my future, for no one else will.'

Kate closed her bedroom door behind her and turned the key in the lock, resting her head back against the wood.

She couldn't believe how tempted she was by Lord Henderson's ridiculous proposition. She couldn't be his mistress, no matter how much her body craved his touch. It was an absurd idea, born of lust and attraction, and she had almost agreed to it because of her desire for the man.

Closing her eyes, she allowed the memory of their kiss to flood back to her. It had been wonderful and exquisite and everything she had imagined it might be, but it must be the only time. Her whole life had been ruined because she had listened to assurances made by a man who convinced her he cared for her. Lord Henderson wasn't like Arthur—she didn't think he would make empty promises—but she couldn't rely on it. Even with the best of intentions of keeping an affair secret, something was bound to leak out. The only way to ensure her reputation was not tarnished further was to stay away from Lord Henderson.

That was easier said than done.

She yearned to be touched, even just to be held. Here at Crosthwaite House, she'd had room for her emotional wounds to heal, but she knew she had locked herself away from the world. In the last six months, she had not let anyone get close, and suddenly she realised she was starved of intimacy.

'That is not a good enough reason to go around kissing your employer,' she said, moving away from the door and flopping onto the bed. In a few minutes she would rouse herself and head back to the kitchens to finish up the work of the day, but right now she needed to brood.

Desperately she wanted the happiness Lord Henderson told her he was offering, but she knew it was nothing more than a dream. Yes, she might enjoy the few short weeks they spent together, but what of her future? She didn't want to be a man's mistress, and it hurt her more than she liked to admit that Lord Henderson had even suggested it.

# Chapter Fifteen

'Forgive me,' Lord Henderson said as he came to find her that evening in the kitchen. It was dark outside, and the sun long since set. He walked into the kitchen with his hands held out in front of him, palms outstretched as if to show her he was not a threat. 'I allowed my desires to rule me, and I am sorry. I should not have asked you what I did earlier.'

Kate eyed him without saying anything, finishing the washing up and placing the last plate on the side to start draining.

'It was unspeakably rude. Can you forgive me?'

She stayed silent whilst she dried her hands and then turned back to face him.

'I know what you have been through,' he said quietly. 'Only a cad would suggest what I did, and I will regret it forever.'

Slowly she nodded. He looked suitably forlorn, and she didn't doubt the sincerity of his words.

'I forgive you,' she said. 'Do you forgive me for taking the deed?'

'I do.'

She felt a rush of relief, although so much was still

unsaid. She didn't know what his plans were, how long he was going to stay in Thornthwaite.

'Have you time to take the air this evening?' he asked.

She nodded, and he waited whilst she fetched her cloak from her room. Then they went up the stairs side by side. It was dark outside, but the sky was clear and the moon bright enough to illuminate the path ahead of them. They wound their way around the house first, in silence, both lost in thought.

'What will you do?' Kate asked eventually. 'Now you have the deed?'

'I still plan on returning to Italy,' Lord Henderson said quietly. He seemed subdued tonight, and Kate felt her heart sink. She had to refuse his proposition, but she didn't want him to leave. 'But I have not decided on a timeline yet.'

He glanced at the house, and she saw the uncertainty in his eyes, as if he was considering what he felt for his old family home. Suddenly he winced and stumbled but righted himself quickly, passing a hand over his brow.

'Is something amiss?' Kate asked with concern.

Shaking his head, Lord Henderson said, 'No, I am fine. A little warm, that is all.'

Kate looked at him closer and frowned. He did look flushed, even though the night air was cool and she needed to pull her cloak closer around her to guard her body from the fresh breeze.

They continued walking for a moment, and then Lord Henderson gave a shudder. Kate stopped and waited for him to stop too. When he turned to face her with a frown, she raised a hand to his brow.

'You're burning up.'

'It is nothing.'

'Your wound. When did you last check it?'

'With everything that has happened...' he said and trailed off.

'How long?'

'Perhaps a couple of days.'

Taking his hand Kate felt a rush of panic as she pulled him back towards the house. His skin was burning hot even on his hands, and she could see now there was an unhealthy sheen across his forehead.

'It was healing fine,' he protested as they entered the house and made their way to his study. Kate settled him into a comfortable chair and took a moment to light a few candles, ensuring the room was illuminated enough for her to see clearly. Then, with shaking hands, she helped him off with his shirt and eyed the bandage underneath. It was clean and dry on the outside, and Kate felt a swell of hope that was soon crushed as she began to take the dressing off.

The skin around the wound was puckered and red, and the flesh looked angry and inflamed. When she gently applied some pressure Lord Henderson grimaced and stifled a cry, and Kate saw the wound bulge under the stitches.

'It's infected,' she said, biting her lip. 'We need to get the doctor.'

For the first time, she wished they weren't alone here. She longed for someone to turn to, someone to send for the doctor whilst she ensured Lord Henderson was comfortable, but it was just her.

'Let's get you upstairs to bed first,' she said, glad he was still able to walk, knowing she would never be able to support any more than a quarter of his weight.

Together they walked upstairs, moving slowly, and she could see it took much of Lord Henderson's energy to make it up to his bedroom. Ensuring she was gentle, she helped him into bed and arranged the covers over him.

'I will fetch you some water and then go for the doctor.'

'You can't ride in the dark.'

'I must.'

'Miss Winters,' he said, trying to sound stern and pushing himself up in bed.

'Lie down,' she instructed him and gave him a look that wasn't to be argued with.

'Wait until morning,' he said, closing his eyes.

She leaned over him, plumped the pillows, and without another word slipped from the room.

George slept fitfully, remembering snatches of his dreams and finding it hard to distinguish dream from reality.

Sometime in the middle of the night, he was aware of Miss Winters returning and a cool hand on his brow. He felt himself relax and slip into a deeper sleep then, his body grateful.

Kate stood over Lord Henderson with a clean kitchen knife and grimaced. She'd ridden for the doctor in the dark, struggling to saddle Odysseus on her own, struggling to mount and even struggling to find her way in the darkness, but she had done it, only to find he had been called away and likely wouldn't be back for hours. His wife had listened to Kate in her panic and promised to send the medical man as soon as possible, but as Kate was leaving, she had gripped hold of Kate's arm and leaned in close.

*Best to let the purification out*, that's what she'd said. The woman had assisted her husband for years, and

Kate knew the villagers respected her advice almost as much as the doctor's, so here she was, standing over her employer with a knife and wondering if she could cut into his skin.

Kate put a hand to his brow and winced at how hot it was. Then she moved to the other side of the bed to get in a better position to cut the stitches that held the wound together. She had a cloth ready and some water to wash the wound.

'Lord Henderson,' she said quietly, placing a hand on his bare shoulder. He groaned but did not open his eyes. 'I'm going to touch your wound, Lord Henderson.'

Kate waited a moment longer for him to respond. Then, before she could lose her nerve, she took the knife, gripped the knotted end of one stitch, and sliced through it. Lord Henderson screamed, and Kate jumped off the bed as if she'd been burnt. A small amount of pus and blood seeped from the wound and as Lord Henderson quietened, Kate carefully mopped it up.

The next stitch elicited much the same reaction, as did the next. She quickly learned to push on through, her heart pounding and her tears threatening to blur her vision. Only when the wound was fully open did she sit back for a second.

She waited until he had settled and then began cleaning the area, adding pressure on the surrounding skin gently but firmly until she could be sure there was nothing more to come.

It was the early hour of the morning by time Kate had cleared everything away, wrapped his wound and collapsed into a chair by Lord Henderson's bedside. She slept fitfully, always with one ear listening for the doctor's rap on the door.

When he did finally arrive, the sun was almost up,

and Kate had spent an uncomfortable few hours in the upright chair.

'How is he?'

'He won't wake,' Kate said, ushering the doctor upstairs. 'Not properly. He opens his eyes every now and then, but it's like he's not really there.' She pressed her lips together, telling herself she wouldn't become outwardly emotional. 'It's happened so fast. Only a few hours ago he was walking around, having a normal conversation.'

The doctor nodded seriously. 'It can be that way. Let me look at him.'

Kate stood back whilst the older man checked over his patient, finding herself crossing her fingers behind her back, wondering if this little action might bring her luck. When he had finished, the doctor guided her out of the room, pulling the door closed behind him.

'Lord Henderson's heart rate is elevated, and his breathing is fast. His body is trying hard to fight this festering wound, but he is struggling. Keep him cool, ensure he drinks a little water, and pray for him, Miss Winters. There is little I can do for him now.'

The doctor went to walk away and then turned. 'You will need help. Do you want me to deliver a message to anyone?'

Kate hesitated and then nodded, knowing the doctor was right.

'Could you get a message to Marigold Lee and Mary Warrington? Let them know I will need them to live in for a few days if they are able.'

'Very well, Miss Winters. I will be back to check on him tomorrow. Send for me if you need me sooner.'

Kate went downstairs to show the doctor out, but once the door had shut behind him, she hurried back to Lord Henderson's bedside and took up her place beside him.

It was a long and lonely vigil. After a few hours, Marigold and Mary appeared, both carrying small bags filled with what they needed to allow them to stay at Crosthwaite House for a few days.

'How is he?' Marigold asked as she poked her head into the room.

'Not well, Marigold. I can't keep him cool, and I can't rouse him enough to drink.' Kate heard the note of hysteria in her voice.

Marigold hesitated on the threshold and then entered the room, pulling Kate into an embrace.

'He's a strong man. I'm sure he'll pull through.'

'You're right, Marigold. Of course you're right.'

'I'll bring you a nice cup of tea and some breakfast. I know you haven't eaten a thing.'

Kate wasn't sure she could eat with the ball of worry lodged in her stomach, but she nodded all the same. Tea would hopefully settle her nerves a little.

The day passed slowly, and Kate barely left Lord Henderson's bedside. He slept most of the time, occasionally waking to mumble something incoherent and sit up for a few sips of water before collapsing back onto the pillows and drifting off into unconsciousness again. Kate tried to do her best to follow the doctor's advice and keep him cool and well hydrated, but it felt like a battle she was losing.

It was comforting to have Mary and Marigold in the house for an evening, and they both offered to sit with Lord Henderson for a while so Kate could have a break, but she felt an awful premonition that if she left he might take a turn for the worse. So she remained, dishevelled and exhausted, but determined to stick it out beside him for as long as was needed.

In the middle of the night, she was dozing in the chair beside his bed when something woke her up. There was no other noise in the house, and as she sat forwards, still disorientated in the darkness, she realised the speed in his breaths. He was breathing quickly, almost panting, in his sleep. Kate laid a hand to his brow, shuddering in shock as she felt the burning heat of his skin.

Instinctively she knew this was his body mounting a final fight, that it was using all of its reserve to try and banish the illness from his body. She also knew that if he failed now, he would have no energy left to fight any more.

She placed a fresh cloth on his forehead after dipping it in water, to try and help cool him, repeating the process again and again. Then she sat on the edge of her chair and took his hand.

She didn't want to lose him. The idea of a world without him in it made her heart burn with pain. They may not have known each other for long, but she did know she cared for Lord Henderson, more than she had any right to. She thought of their argument, of his wild proposition that they give in to their desires.

Lowering her lips to his ear, Kate dropped her voice to a soft whisper.

'Please fight this,' she said. 'Don't give up. I don't want to lose you.'

Silently she sat back in her chair and made a promise to herself that if he pulled through this, she would reconsider his proposition. Perhaps she had been thinking about this all wrong. She had been focussed on the past, of how one mistake had changed the course of her entire life. Instead she needed to think about what would

make her happy, right now, not in five years' time or
ten. Lord Henderson's freak accident and subsequent
illness brought into focus how no one knew what the
future was going to hold.

The morning seemed a long time coming, but when
Marigold knocked softly on the door, Kate breathed a
sigh of relief. Lord Henderson had survived the night,
and his breathing had settled into a more reasonable pat-
tern. She even thought he was a fraction cooler when
she checked his temperature with the back of her hand.

'How is he?' Marigold asked, bustling round to tidy
up.

'I was worried he wouldn't survive the night,' Kate
said quietly, 'but he's fighting hard.'

'Good. Let's hope he wakes this morning and is able
to take some water to help build his strength.'

# Chapter Sixteen

'What is this?'

George cocked one eyebrow and looked from the dress to Miss Winters.

'It's a dress,' he said slowly.

'I can see it is a dress. What is it doing here?'

'It's for you.'

'I can't wear that.'

'Why not?

She looked at him as if he had gone completely mad. 'I'm a housekeeper.'

'I assure you there is no unwritten rule that house-keepers have to wear ugly dresses.'

She visibly bristled. 'My dress is not ugly.'

'Not on you it isn't, but it lacks...' he searched for the right word '...structure, or any sort of shape.'

Miss Winters's hand reached out, and her fingers brushed over the soft fabric of the dress. It was nothing ostentatious. The neckline was demure, and the colour muted. It would not make her stand out if she walked down the street. He had been careful about that, knowing what objections she might raise.

'Is there any harm in trying it on?'

'I do not see why you have bought me a dress.'

They were in one of the many downstairs reception rooms, a cosy room he had always been particularly fond of. It had calming blue wallpaper and comfortable furniture as well as an uninterrupted view of the lake beyond the gardens. Realising that convincing her could take a while, George took a seat, relaxing back into the armchair and regarding the woman in front of him.

'I am reliably informed you sat by my bedside for three days straight, sponging my forehead and supplying me with sips of water.'

Miss Winters lowered her eyes from his as if remembering that awful time.

'Since I have regained consciousness, you have read to me, discussed everything from politics to gardening, and ensured I was suitably entertained so I would not rush back onto my feet when my body needed time to heal.' He smiled softly. 'In the weeks I have been recovering, you have accompanied me on my walks each day, ensuring I did not stumble as I have grown stronger, and kept my spirits lifted with those wry little comments of yours.'

'I did not want you to rush things and relapse.'

'I now feel fully recovered. The doctor tells me even the wound is healing well. I know I am here today in some part because of you, Miss Winters.'

'My name is Kate,' she said quietly, her eyes lifting to meet his.

'Kate,' he said, feeling the weight of the moment in his chest. 'I wanted to get you something small to say thank you, and I saw you admiring this fabric when we visited the village last week.'

He grimaced. It had been a difficult trip, tiring whilst

he was still recovering, but Kate had made it as easy as it could have been.

'Try it on. Indulge me.'

He really thought she was going to refuse again, but after a moment she nodded.

'I will try it on. I doubt it will fit anyway.'

George was confident he had got her sizing right, but he smiled and inclined his head anyway. Once she had tried it on, he doubted she would want to go back to the grey sack of a dress she had been wearing.

His eyes widened as she looked down at the dress, and picked it up before she moved over to the screen that was positioned in the corner of the room. He had fully expected her to disappear downstairs to her bedroom to try it on, and his pulse quickened at the idea of her stripping off in the room with him.

'You are getting changed in here?'

Kate gave him a look he found difficult to interpret and then slipped behind the screen. For a moment George was so stunned he couldn't have moved even if a herd of stampeding cows were heading his way. Then he sprang to his feet and took two steps towards the screen before pausing, unsure what he was doing. Kate had been warm towards him these last couple of weeks. She had helped him with his recovery, and he felt she had genuinely enjoyed spending time in his company. For his part, he knew his attitude had shifted. The illness had made him slow down, halt his plans to leave immediately, and consider his next actions a little more carefully.

Of course there had been the simmering attraction between them, a few tense moments when their bodies brushed together accidentally, but nothing so overt as the look Kate had given him before she slipped behind the screen.

'I can help you with the fastenings of your dress,' he called.

'I manage every evening just fine,' she said from behind the screen.

'I wouldn't want you to strain yourself.'

'Your concern is noted, my lord.'

He was unable to stop himself from grinning, picturing her slipping out of her dress and stepping into the new one.

She said nothing. There was a long period of silence broken only by the rustling of material. George closed his eyes, knowing it was dangerous to imagine Kate in a state of undress. His imagination was liable to run away with itself, and at the moment he had no idea what her intentions were.

'I need some help,' she said, and George was striding forwards before his mind had properly registered the words.

As he stepped behind the screen, he took in the discarded old grey dress, and undergarments, and then his eyes came up to look at Kate. She was standing with her back to him, holding the dress in position with one hand. Immediately he could see the fit was close to perfect, and the dress was the right shape to complement every part of her body without being overly revealing.

'You need to lace it,' she said, looking over her shoulder.

Despite his lack of interest in women over the last few years, George had plenty of experience in helping women with the fastenings of their clothes, both during his marriages and before. Nevertheless, his fingers felt clumsy and stiff as he grasped hold of the ties that needed to be pulled tighter to secure the dress.

He felt Kate stiffen as his hand brushed against the bare skin of her upper back and lingered for a second before he returned to the task of securing the dress.

'There, all done,' he said, stepping away.

Kate followed him out into the room, regarding herself in the mirror.

'What do you think?'

'I may have to admit it is a little improvement on my grey dress.'

'A little?'

She shrugged. 'It is beautiful, but that does not matter. I cannot wear it. What would Mary and Marigold say? Or anyone who came to visit from the village?'

He cocked his head to one side, considering it. He had thought it was safe, a demure dress that did not need to signify any greater feeling between master and housekeeper than gratitude for her help and devotion these last couple of weeks, but he knew he had to defer to Kate on matters of propriety. He wasn't the one who would endure the suspicious looks or malicious gossip.

'I can return it if you wish.'

'No,' Kate said quickly, running her hands over the luxurious material. She looked like she surprised herself with the single word. Then she took a deep, shuddering breath and stepped closer to him, standing up on tiptoe and brushing a kiss against his cheek.

George was too stunned to react. Ever since their confrontation in his study, where he had asked her to become his mistress and she had vehemently explained why it was not only an awful idea but also an insulting one, he had been careful to behave respectfully towards her.

His desire surged at the contact, and he wanted to gather her in his arms. Before he could, she exited the room in a rustle of material, leaving him wondering what on earth had just happened.

Kate spent most of the evening trying to avoid George, mentally torturing herself over what she should do. The last few weeks she had spent in his company had been wonderful. Slow leisurely walks, games of chess, conversations that stretched long into the night. The illness and his reliance on her the days after his incapacitation had revealed a softer side to George, a side she couldn't help but feel herself falling for. The desire was still there, stronger than ever, but now it was paired with a deep longing whenever she had to spend time away from him.

Last night in bed, Kate had reminded herself of the promise she had made whilst George was in the grips of the fever that had nearly claimed his life. She lay there, unable to sleep, gripped by the idea of spending a few short weeks as lovers.

When he had first proposed it, she had felt hurt, insulted even, by the idea. For the past year she had worked on rebuilding her self-confidence, her self-belief, and part of that was believing she was worth no less because of her indiscretion with Arthur. When she had pointed this out to George, he had backed off and since treated her with nothing but respect. The longing remained, burning underneath it all, but he hadn't even mentioned the idea again.

Kate, though, was consumed by it. She thought back to that terrible night when George had been so ill and remembered the feeling of missing out. She knew any dalliance between them could only be temporary. Despite the emotional journey he had been on since returning to England, Kate knew George wasn't ready for anything more permanent yet. However, she wanted something to take with her in her heart when the time came to leave Crosthwaite House.

She knew there was a risk of ruin, a risk to her reputation, but she also knew she would regret it if she didn't listen to her heart and make the most of her time with George, however short it might be.

Decisively she stood and hurried upstairs, bursting into the study without even knocking. George looked up in surprise and smiled at her warmly.

'I was just thinking of you,' he said in a way that made her melt a little inside.

'You were?'

'If I am honest, I haven't been able to stop thinking of you all evening.'

'Do you remember what we talked about here a few weeks ago? That night you told me you desired me?' she asked abruptly, knowing she had to get the words out quickly before she lost her nerve.

'Of course. I apologise aga…'

She cut him off with a shake of her head. 'I've changed my mind,' she said, feeling unable to catch her breath.

'You've changed your mind?'

'Yes.'

'What do you mean?'

'I mean I would be open to…' She coughed, feeling her cheeks flush and wondering what on earth she was doing. Closing her eyes and shaking her head, she knew she could not say it out loud. She might want this, want *him*, more than she had ever wanted anything before, but she had been brought up to think decent young ladies did not go around propositioning earls. After taking a shuddering breath, she tried to force out something, anything, but nothing would come, so instead she turned on her heel and dashed back downstairs, leaving a bewildered George sitting in his study.

A few minutes later he followed, knocking softly on her locked door, but Kate had already buried her head under her pillow, wondering if she would ever be able to face him again.

# Chapter Seventeen

The morning was bright and beautiful, and Kate wasn't surprised when George appeared in the kitchen early. She had heard him going out on horseback soon after sunrise and had wondered when he would be back. She hoped he might let her forget her announcement the night before, and even as she thought of it, her cheeks grew hot.

'Will you join me for a picnic today?' George asked, as if nothing out of the ordinary had happened the previous evening.

'There is much to do here, my lord.'

'George,' he corrected her gently.

She glanced up and saw the warmth in his eyes.

'I have a confession to make,' he said. 'This morning I rode to the village and left a message for Mary and Marigold to take the day off. As a thank you for their extra work whilst I was unwell.'

'They're not coming to the house today?'

'No. We have the place to ourselves all day.' The way he said it sent little shivers of excitement down Kate's spine, and she felt her pulse quicken in anticipation.

'Now, I would very much like to take you out for a picnic to one of my favourite spots, and I insist I will prepare everything. It will take me a while, so for the next hour, go and occupy yourself somewhere else.'

'You're throwing me out of the kitchen.'

'Yes. Go and read a book or write some letters. Anything as long as you do not come back in here until I have finished.'

'I could help.'

'Go,' he said, smiling, and Kate found herself ushered away.

An hour later, she ambled through the hall, feeling a little lost in the house she had called home for the past six months. Three times she had crept to the top of the kitchen stairs to try to sneak a peek at what he was doing, and all three times he had quickly spotted her and marched her away.

So here she was, wandering around the ground floor rooms, unable to focus long enough to do anything more useful.

Choosing the sunny window seat, she flopped down and took a moment to consider her position. Last night she had tossed and turned, wondering what might happen next. George might ignore her proposition, but she doubted it, given he was downstairs preparing for them to spend a day together. If she went to Lord Henderson and asked him to stop this seduction, she knew he would. The man might be used to getting his own way, but he was not a cad. She needed to decide quickly if this was truly what she wanted. With a deep breath, she willed herself to let go of the past, to stop focussing on the distant future, and instead live for what gave her happiness today. Too long she had been caught up in what *had* happened and what *might* happen, and she didn't want that for herself any longer.

'You look like the subject of a painting in an art gallery sitting there with your leg dangling off the window seat,' Lord Henderson said, appearing in the doorway carrying a basket.

'What have you been doing?'

'Preparing lunch.'

'You've made a whole picnic?'

'Don't look so surprised. I might have been born into a life of privilege, but I can do a few things for myself.'

'I am impressed.'

'Perhaps wait until you've tasted the lunch first. Are you ready?'

She hesitated. If she was going to say anything, now was the time. Lord Henderson was holding out his hand, waiting for her to take it. She knew once she had laced her fingers through his, she would have crossed a line, given her consent to be swept along in whatever today might bring.

Deciding that for just a few hours she would dismiss all her misgivings and enjoy herself, Kate stood and took his hand.

They walked out of the house, away from the lake, and Kate realised that although she had explored most of the grounds of Crosthwaite House, instinct had always made her step towards the water, rather than taking the little hidden path that wound through the trees.

The day was warm with the sun already high in the sky and hints that summer might be on its way. Wildflowers bloomed on the forest floor, and birds sang high in the trees.

'Where are we going?'

'To a secluded little corner of the grounds.'

Crosthwaite estate and the surrounding grounds were not big enough to be called an estate, but the land attached to the house was certainly vast enough to get lost in. The path through the trees petered out, but Lord Henderson seemed confident in his navigation and took her on a route over fallen tree trunks and stepping stones until they came out into the open.

The view behind them was glorious. They had climbed a little from the house, and through the trees you could catch a glimpse of the water and mountains beyond. What caught Kate's attention, though, was the beautiful scene in front of her.

A little stream was winding its way down the side of the hill before tumbling into a shallow pool. At the other end of the pool, the stream started up again and continued its journey down to the lake proper.

'Beautiful, isn't it?' Lord Henderson said.

'Do you really want to leave this?' The question slipped out before Kate could stop it. She didn't want to ruin the day, to plunge Lord Henderson into a spell of melancholy as he thought about the sad memories associated with Crosthwaite House.

'No,' he said slowly, shaking his head, and for an instant Kate's heart soared. 'I don't want to leave it, but I think it is for the best. A fresh start.'

Now wasn't the time to argue, so she gave him a smile she hoped wasn't too forced.

Lord Henderson took his time choosing a comfortable spot and laying out the picnic blanket, moving the rocks that were underneath and smoothing down the soft fabric until he was happy.

'This way we'll have somewhere comfortable to sit when we get out.'

'Get out?'

'Of the water.'

Kate's eyes flicked across to the shallow pool.

'You mean for us to paddle?'

'Not paddle. Swim.'

Unbidden images of Lord Henderson stripping off and striding into the clear water sprang to her mind, and Kate allowed them to linger for just a moment before dismissing them.

'It will be cold.'

'The air temperature is lovely and warm. I am sure we will survive.'

'I don't have anything to swim in.'

Lord Henderson grinned and leaned in closer. '*That* is a matter of opinion.'

'You suggest we swim naked?'

'Have you ever tried it?'

Kate shook her head. She had swum before, dipping into the sea near her home on particularly hot days in childhood, but always she had kept a layer or two on, even as a child.

'The you have to. It is glorious.'

Kate eyed the water dubiously.

'The key is to run in with no hesitation. None of this dipping a toe or two.'

'You want me to strip naked and run into a freezing pool of water.'

'You make it sound so unappealing. Do you trust me?'

She nodded. She realised she did. Of course there were nagging doubts in her mind, the little voice that questioned her sanity, but she had resolved that for a few days, at least, she was going to only think about the present, not the past or the future.

'Then I promise you will enjoy it. Shall I help you with your clothes?'

'You have to go first.'

'Naturally.'

To her surprise he started to pull at his clothes,

shrugging off his jacket and then trying to manoeuvred his shirt over his head. The wound on his shoulder must have been healing well, for he hadn't needed to ask her to help him dress this morning, and he had changed the dressing for one that was much smaller.

When he had only his trousers remaining, he spun her round and began to unfasten her dress, loosening it but not attempting to lift it off her. He was happy for her to go at her own speed.

Before she knew what was happening, Lord Henderson must have stripped off his trousers and started striding towards the pond. She spun, watching him, unable to take her eyes off him. His confidence was enviable. No one, not even Arthur during their trysts, had seen her completely naked for years, not since her nursemaid in childhood. Lord Henderson walked with the assurance of a man who has shared his life, and his bedroom, with women and always found them appreciative of his body.

'I can feel your eyes on me, Miss Winters.'

Still she did not turn, watching as he entered the water, not once hesitating in the coldness.

'You never told me not to look.'

Even from a good few feet away she saw his raised eyebrow and felt herself blush.

'The water is glorious,' he said. 'Why don't you join me.'

Kate hesitated, knowing this was another of those moments of no return. If she stripped and walked into the pool.

Closing her eyes, she tried to picture the options, tried to think rationally, but it was as if for the last few days she had been on a moving platform, being drawn steadily towards this final destination. Deep down she had always known where this was going to end, and she hadn't taken a single step to stop it.

'Four weeks,' she whispered to herself. What was the harm in enjoying herself for four weeks? No one ever needed to know. When Lord Henderson left for Italy, she could start up a respectable new life far from any rumour or scandal, and she would have the memory of this intimacy to sustain her in her loneliest hours.

With his eyes on her, she slipped her dress from her shoulders and allowed it to drop to her ankles, then stepped out of it, leaving the garment where it fell. Underneath she had her stays and chemise, as well as her petticoat and stockings on her lower half. Quickly she unlaced the stays and wriggled out of her petticoat.

The chemise came down to just above her knees. It was made of thin cotton, almost see-through in the bright sunlight, and Kate could feel Lord Henderson's gaze trying to pierce through the thin layer. She would never admit it out loud, but she quite liked the feel of his eyes on her, willing her to strip off.

Slowly she bent over and rolled one stocking down her leg, suppressing a smile at the groan Lord Henderson uttered from his position in the water.

'I never knew you were such a minx, Miss Winters.'

Without responding, she moved on to the other stocking, taking her time to remove the garment.

'Now, you have to promise not to look,' she called.

'Cross my heart.'

'You're still looking.'

'It's hard to turn away.'

'You're a man of honour, Lord Henderson. Don't break your word now.'

Ever so slowly he turned around. She waited for a few seconds to ensure he was not going to turn back, and lifted the chemise off over her head. The air was warm, but still she felt a slight chill on her skin, unaccustomed as she was to being naked outside like this. It felt thrilling, to have nothing on, and a little dangerous. They were on private land, but it wasn't as if the grounds were surrounded by ten-foot-high walls.

After picking her way over the grass, she dipped a toe in the water. She knew she could not hesitate too long, for Lord Henderson's patience would not be infinite. Despite her bravado, she did want to be submerged before he turned around. Even though she was aware of where this interlude was leading, she didn't quite feel brave enough to stand there, elevated in front of him, completely naked to his gaze.

The water was clear and cold, and Kate had to steel herself to walk further into the pool. It was shallow here, although in the centre it must become deeper as Lord Henderson was submerged up to his neck.

When the water was up to her knees, she took a deep breath and then waded further in, the air catching in her chest as the water hit her abdomen and then her breasts. It was refreshing and chilling all in one, and she gave a little involuntary squeal as the water splashed over her.

'I take it by your cry it is safe to turn around.'

'It's safe.'

He turned, his eyes flicking over her, taking in the droplets of water on her face and hair and then down further to the abstract image of her naked body, half obscured by the refraction of the water.

'I wasn't sure if you would come in,' he said with a little smile. 'You surprise me a little every day, Miss Winters.'

'I wouldn't want to be boring.'

'No one could accuse you of that.'

He moved closer, as yet not trying to touch her even though she desperately wished he would.

Here in the middle of the pool, she could touch the bottom, but only just. She had to tilt her chin to keep it above the water. Lord Henderson stood easily, even bending his knees a little to bob around.

'Last chance,' he said quietly.

'Last chance for what?'

'To tell me to leave you alone.'

She knew he was right. In a few minutes there would be no going back, no changing what was about to happen. Right now she could walk away, step out of this pool and get dressed, return to Crosthwaite House and pretend nothing had happened. If she stayed, there would be no chance of that.

Knowing she had to be bold, to take what she craved, Kate reached out and put one hand around the back of Lord Henderson's neck, gently pulling him towards her.

'Last chance for you as well,' she said.

'*Nothing* could pull me away from you right now.'

He kissed her, his lips soft but insistent, and in her eagerness, Kate lost her footing, sliding under the water for an instant. She felt his arms loop around her, pulling her body to him, and instinctively she hopped up from the bottom of the pool and looped her legs around his waist. His hand dropped down under the water, holding her up and caressing the skin of her buttocks.

'Hello,' he said as he broke the kiss for a moment.

'Hello.'

'Have I told you you're beautiful?'

With gentle fingers, he tucked a stray strand of hair behind her ear. She shook her head. People had called her pretty before, and when she looked in the mirror, she liked certain aspects of her appearance, but no one had ever looked at her like this.

'You are beautiful,' he said, pulling her even closer. Kate felt her breasts brush against his chest, bolts of pleasure and anticipation shooting through her. She was torn between wanting him to claim her now, here in the pool, to slake some of the tension she felt brewing inside her, and wanting him to take his time, to tease her, to build the anticipation.

Ever so slowly his hand began moving under her, pulling her closer, caressing the skin on her thigh. The sensation was dulled underwater, even though it felt exquisite to Kate. She wasn't sure if she would be able to stay still if he was touching her out of the water.

Without warning he picked her up higher, pulling her legs so she was fully wrapped around his waist, and then stood to his full height and carried her out of the pool.

The air was biting on her wet skin, and Kate shivered. The movement from water to land made her hesitate and wonder if she was doing the right thing. There was no doubt her body wanted it, that instinctively her hips were moving to push against his, that every time he brushed against her it set her skin on fire, but in that moment Kate felt a little ripple of doubt.

Pushing it away, she told herself this was different. She had no expectations of Lord Henderson, not like she'd had of Arthur. He hadn't promised her love, just to slake this desire they both were feeling.

Carefully he laid her down on the blanket, and Kate looked up at him. He was dripping wet and gorgeous. Then his lips were on hers, and she couldn't think of anything but his kiss, his touch.

Slowly her body warmed, fuelled by the expert

caresses from the man above her. He trailed a hand over her breasts, across her abdomen, teasing her and skipping to the sensitive skin of her thigh, before he brushed his fingers against her most sensitive place. As he stroked and circled, Kate felt something surge inside her and she finally let go of the last of her resistance. She wanted to give all of herself to him, unreservedly, and she was determined she would.

Her breath came in short bursts, her neck arched as his fingers caressed her, and she felt a wonderful release pulse through her body. She cried out as wave after wave of pleasure consumed her, her body seeming to float off the ground.

Before she could recover, she felt his hardness press against her, and then he was inside her. Reflexively her hips came to meet his and she pulled him closer, begging him to go faster, to never stop.

Again and again their bodies came together until Kate let out a cry as the tension burst and she was lost to another climax. Almost immediately after, whilst she was still dazed and uncertain, she felt Lord Henderson pull out, and from the corner of her eye she saw him finish on the ground, rather than inside her.

For a long moment, Kate was too exhausted and overwhelmed to move, but she was glad when Lord Henderson came and lay beside her, pulling her in to his body. She had warmed from their cool dip in the pool and no longer felt the biting chill of the air as she had when her skin was still wet, but she welcomed the heat of his body against hers.

At first they didn't speak. Lord Henderson held her close to him and every so often kissed the skin on her upper back, but he didn't feel the need to fill the silence. For her part, Kate was wary of the emotions that could flood over her now they were quiet and still. To her surprise she did not feel any regret, not like she had that first time she'd given herself to Arthur. Then she'd cried after they had hurriedly made love.

Now she knew her relationship to the earl had changed, but she couldn't regret what had happened between them. He had made it very clear he was leaving in a few weeks, so it wasn't as though she was looking at preserving any long-term relationship.

The thought made her feel a pang of sadness. Along with the desire she felt for Lord Henderson, she realised she really liked him too. He was the first person for months who saw the real her underneath the image she had created for herself.

Rolling over to face him, she wrapped one arm around his body, wondering what would change now that they had been intimate. He had suggested she become his lover for the next few weeks, but nothing was settled, nothing was certain. She wasn't even sure what she wanted from him.

She hated the flicker of hope that had ignited inside her, that little voice questioning, *what if*? She had vowed never to be reliant on a man again for her security or happiness, never to trust their word when they promised her the world, but a rebellious part of her was bursting with impossible dreams.

'You're frowning,' Lord Henderson said, bringing a hand up to stroke the skin between her eyebrows until the muscles of her face relaxed.

Kate made an effort to smile, hoping it looked genuine. She *was* happy. She just wished she could see exactly what the future held.

'Is something wrong?'

There was no way she was going to tell him she

thought she might be falling for him, so she bit her lip and looked up into his eyes.

'When you finished...' she said, trailing off and feeling the heat rise in her cheeks.

He completed the thought for her. 'I didn't finish inside you.'

She nodded.

With a gentle smile, he kissed her nose and then stroked her hair. 'I don't want you to get pregnant,' he said simply.

'Of course.'

'Not just you, Kate, although that would be disastrous. I refuse to get any woman pregnant ever again.'

She understood why. Both of his wives had died whilst they were pregnant with his child. In a way she was sure he felt some warped sense of responsibility. It made perfect sense that he would not want to get anyone else pregnant, let alone a woman he was not planning on tying himself to.

It all made sense, but Kate couldn't help the faint pang of rejection she felt. It was irrational, ridiculous really, but still she felt it.

He held her for a while longer and must have noticed when she shivered slightly, for a moment later he sat up and reached for her dress.

'You're cold and I am being selfish, holding you here naked for my own pleasure,' he said with an irresistible smile. He kissed her, taking his time, and then pulled away, reaching for their clothes.

Kate turned away to dress, suddenly overcome with modesty, and when she turned back, she found George's eyes on her.

'I know I suggested we dress,' he said, moving towards her and taking her hand. 'But I wonder if I can persuade you to choose pleasure over lunch.'

## *Chapter Eighteen*

They were sitting together enjoying the early evening sun that shone through the wide windows of the library when the messenger arrived. George rose first, motioning for Kate to remain seated, and went to retrieve the message.

He waited until he was back in the library to open the envelope and read the short note inside.

'What is it?'

'A letter from Mr Sorrell. He has ensured everything is in place for when I find a buyer for the house. All the paperwork is in order.'

'Oh,' Kate said and tried to summon a smile. He could see how the idea of the future weighed on Kate when she allowed herself to think about it.

She would be all right. Kate Winters was a survivor. That much was clear in the way she had built this life for herself after fleeing her old one. Many young women who had known nothing of the world except their sheltered upbringing in their father's house would not have thrived the way she had.

Still, he did feel a lot of guilt. In a few weeks he would be pushing her out into the unknown. Her next employer might be a man like Lord Willcox, someone who thought his servants were his property and it was his right to do whatever he wanted with them.

'Come here,' he said, motioning for her to stop lingering in the doorway. He set the property deed on the desk, ensuring it wasn't somewhere it could be swept away or caught up with anything else, and waited for her to approach.

She stood in front of him for a few seconds as he took her hands, and then with a little *oof* of surprise, she fell into his lap as he pulled her down.

'You're fretting over what comes next,' he said quietly, raising his fingers to play with the wispy strands of hair at the nape of her neck. They were unbelievably soft, and he knew she liked it by the way she leaned her head into his shoulder.

For a long while Kate didn't say anything, and he felt quite content not pushing the issue. She would talk if she wanted, when she wanted.

'I will not deny I think of Crosthwaite House as my home,' she said eventually. 'To you my room might seem basic and sparse, but it is mine. It is something I have worked for, something I have earned for the first time in my life.'

'I can see how that matters.'

She sighed and leaned her head back fully on his shoulder. He liked the weight of her on him, the way her body relaxed as he stroked her, coaxing her to let go of the tension she carried.

'I will find another position,' she said, closing her eyes. 'I am sure of it. It is just the unknown I am dreading. That to and fro as you jostle for a position in a place, as people test you out, see what you tolerate and what you do not.'

To his mind it sounded terrible, and he admired her even more for choosing to make her own way in the world rather than take the small allowance her parents presented, with their disapproval and conditions attached.

He almost found himself offering her a place with him and had to quickly press his lips together. Their affair was a new foray out into the world for him. He was well aware he had withdrawn from life, from interacting with others, when Clara had died. Kate might have coaxed him back into it, but he couldn't fool himself this was anything more than a passionate, short-lived affair. No doubt he felt so easy, so positive about his time with Kate Winters *because* he knew it had an end point.

She twisted her neck to look at him and smiled softly.

'Don't worry about me,' she said. 'After Arthur broke my heart and my family ground the pieces into the dirt, I promised myself I would survive. And I will. I will thrive.'

'You are very beautiful when you look determined.'

'Thank you, I think.'

'You often look determined,' he said, kissing the soft skin of the back of her neck. 'It's one of the things I like about you the most.'

'Now Mr Sorrell has dealt with the legal side of matters, what does it mean?' she said, shifting on his lap, and he saw through the nonchalance she was trying to project.

'Nothing changes really. I still have to wait for Mr Sorrell to find a buyer for the house and sell the rest of the properties. It just means when there is someone interested, things will move more quickly.'

'That's good.' She shifted again and then slipped

from his lap, standing up and walking away, her hair falling over her face so he couldn't see her expression.

'I'll leave you in peace,' she said.

George jumped to his feet and crossed the room, catching her before she reached the door.

'How about a little trip out?' he asked, kissing her before she could answer. He found it difficult to resist kissing her whenever she was near.

'Like the trip yesterday, to the stream and the pool?'

He grinned. It had been an incredible trip. They'd made love three times in the open, each better than the last, and when they had walked home hand in hand, he had felt a contentment he hadn't felt for a very long time.

'Don't tempt me,' he murmured, nibbling at her ear. She let out a little moan, and he smiled. He loved finding out where her sensitive spots were. Instinctively she turned her head away from him, giving him greater access. 'No, I have something to show you, something I want your opinion on.'

'That sounds intriguing.'

'It would mean a short ride out, if you can bear to join me on horseback again.'

This time he would be able to wrap his arms around her as he had wanted to before.

'It will be getting dark soon. What if someone sees us? Won't they find it strange we are out riding together so late?'

'I know all the quiet paths, and if anyone does approach, I promise I'll dive off into the bushes to protect your reputation.'

'What if there are no bushes?'

'Then I will concoct a story so believable people will accept it without question.'

'How can I have any objection to that?' she murmured.

'Good. Let me know when you are ready to leave.'

She slipped from his arms, and he felt bereft. Watching her walk away, he was suddenly struck by how hard it would be to let her go at the end of their time together.

'You'll tire of one another,' he said quietly to himself, not really believing it would be true. He had thought his desire for his pretty housekeeper would diminish once they had made love, but instead he found he wanted her even more. The decision to give herself to him had not come lightly—he was aware of that—but when she had made up her mind to become his lover, she had not held any part of herself back.

They still had weeks of one another's company. Perhaps he would find she snored loudly in her sleep or had any number of annoying habits.

Kate marvelled at the ease with which George helped her up onto Odysseus. The night before, she had checked under his bandage to find the wound on his chest was healing well and the edges of the cut had come together nicely. There was no sign of infection, and she thought in a few days he might not even need the bandage anymore. George was moving more freely now, using the arm more and more.

He pulled himself up behind her and promptly wrapped an arm around her waist.

Kate felt a flush of pleasure. She had worried he might lose interest in her, that the day and night they had spent together, making love again and again, might make him tire of her.

So far his attention had not waned. Every interaction they had, he took the opportunity to touch her, to kiss her, until Kate was caught up in this heady, intoxicating web of desire.

'Be warned I am ready to push you into the under-growth if we do see anyone out and about at all,' Kate said, leaning her head back on his shoulder.

'That is heartless, Miss Winters.'

'A girl has to put her reputation above everything else.'

She let out a muffled cry as he kissed her neck, sur-prising her.

'I will sacrifice myself and my expensive trousers and vow to jump into even the thickest brambles if it means saving you from the gossip of the locals.'

They eschewed the roads, taking first a narrow path that ran parallel to the lake and then skirting round the edge of a few rock-strewn fields, sharing the space with the sheep that eyed them warily as they rode past.

Kate found it hard to keep track of time when she was spending it with George, but they must have rid-den for about twenty minutes when he pulled the reins to slow Odysseus before dismounting.

Kate followed him down and waited whilst George tied Odysseus's reins to a handy branch, and then he laced his fingers through hers.

'The village is just over there,' he said, indicating an area beyond the trees. 'It is perhaps a ten-minute walk.'

Kate could see where they were now and realised they had taken quite a circuitous path to get to where they were. She supposed George had chosen a route along which they were less likely to meet anyone.

'Come over here,' he said, leading her down an over-grown path. At the end of it was the back of a small cottage, and they had to skirt around the wall of the garden to reach the front.

It was currently uninhabited with grimy windows and a roof that looked like it might let the rain in, but overall the building looked sound. There was a large garden to the side and the back, and Kate realised the enclosed area on the other side of the road probably belonged to the cottage as well.

'I know it doesn't look like much at the moment,' George said, regarding the building with a critical eye. 'But it wouldn't take much to get it up to a habitable standard, and then a little more investment to make it homely. It is in a good position, only a short walk from the village, and it has some land to grow vegetables or something around it.'

Kate nodded, wondering where this was going. It seemed like he was trying hard to impress on her the good points of this cottage in need of some love.

'It has its own private access to the lake and even more of a garden around the other side.'

'It is a lovely cottage, or it could be with some work,' Kate said.

George fell quiet and nodded, then looked at her expectantly. 'What do you think?'

For one bizarre moment Kate thought he was offering her the cottage. Perhaps as payment for services rendered, or as a little refuge against the world he might drop into once every so often.

She opened her mouth, not knowing what she would say, but he continued, oblivious to her discomfort.

'I thought a lot about what you were telling me about Mrs Lemington, that the best way to show my appreciation would be to do something to protect her daughter's future. I think this could be the solution. It is a property I own, but not tied directly to Crosthwaite House. It does not need to be sold with the house.'

'You wish to make a gift of it to Mrs Smith?' Kate said, knowing her voice sounded a little hollow.

'Yes. She might choose to live here, or to rent it out. Or even sell it. Whatever would give her the greatest security. I would make it habitable first, of course, clear the garden as well.'

Kate took her time in answering, trying to suppress the mixture of disappointment and relief that flooded through her. She didn't *want* to be kept out here by George, visited every few months like a dirty little secret. She even told herself she didn't want a gift from him like this, a place to live in peace with no expectations or demands attached.

'I think that is a very kind and thoughtful idea,' Kate said eventually. 'I am sure it will put any worries Mrs Lemington has about her daughter's future to rest.'

George nodded in agreement and smiled as he looked at the cottage. She was struck how much he wanted her to like the idea and realised that he couldn't have had anyone to share his thoughts with for a very long time.

She felt bad about making this about her and forced down the roiling emotions that were building inside her, telling herself to look at the idea objectively.

'You will do the repairs first?'

'Certainly.'

'Then you must make your intentions known as soon as possible. Mrs Lemington grows frailer by the day, and I think it would be nice for her to know that her daughter's future is safe.'

'Good idea,' George said, stepping in closer and looping an arm round her waist. Even though he had only been touching her like that for a day, it felt a familiar gesture, intimate whilst not pressing for anything more right then.

Together they picked their way inside the cottage, and Kate could see it was in relatively good condition.

It wouldn't take much to fix the roof and put in a few new windows, perhaps paint some of the interior walls and fix any loose bricks on the chimney.

After they had completed their inspection, they meandered slowly back to the house, walking hand in hand and leading Odysseus by his reins. Kate knew she was quiet, but she couldn't seem to summon idle chatter. Her thoughts were too all-consuming.

# Chapter Nineteen

George watched as Kate slipped from the house and headed towards the lake, enjoying the lithe way she moved and how her skirts billowed out behind her. It was late in the afternoon, the time he knew she liked to make her way down to the lake to dip her toes in the water.

Part of him wanted to follow her. It was an urge he'd experienced all day, to seek her out, to join her whatever she was doing. Even if it were something mundane like making the tea they had enjoyed mid-morning or cutting a few flowers from the garden for the table.

She'd been quiet this afternoon, and he couldn't quite work out why. One thing he liked about Kate was her openness. Even though she tried to keep a calm facade no matter what, always something of her true thoughts peeked through, and she gave away what she was really thinking.

After their trip to the cottage he was planning on giving to Mrs Lemington's daughter, she had been silent and contemplative, and he couldn't figure out why.

Standing, he decided the easiest thing to do would be to ask her. Kate was honest. Either she would tell him or instruct him it was none of his concern, but there was nothing to lose from asking her.

He had made it almost to the front door when he heard a clattering of hooves outside, which made him pause.

Catching a glimpse of the visitor's face, George threw open the door and strode out. The man outside looked momentarily surprised, but as he saw it was George, he grinned broadly.

'Henderson, you rascal, why didn't you send word you were back?'

George ignored the question, instead walking up to his old friend and clapping him into a hug.

'Let me see to your horse,' he said, taking the reins and starting to walk the horse around to the side of the house.

'I know you like to keep a skeleton staff, but do you not have a boy for that?'

'No.'

'No one?' Henry Wolfburn shook his head in mock despair and followed his friend round to the stables.

'What are you doing here?' George asked, genuinely pleased to see the man. The last time he had seen him had been the day of Clara's funeral.

'I heard a rumour you were back. I had some business in Carlisle and I thought I would check to see if the gossip was true. I knew out of all your properties I would find you here if you were in England.'

'Good lord, it is good to see you. How is everyone? Margaret? The children?'

'Fine. Bess and Leonard seemed to grow a foot every day, and Margaret is healthy and happy.' He paused, waiting for George to enter the stable before together they started to remove the saddle and harness from his horse. 'How are you?' It was a loaded question, heavy with concern.

'I'm...' The words stuck in his throat along with a big ball of guilt and regret. He shrugged instead.

'Everyone misses you,' Wolfburn said quietly. 'You're family, Henderson. You always will be. My mother talks about you incessantly, and we all worry about you.'

George nodded, unable to put into words why he kept away. Deep down he knew he wasn't responsible for Clara's death, and that her brother would never blame him for it. It was a tragedy, but a natural one. Thousands of women died in childbirth each year, and never would he dream of blaming their husbands. Still, he felt responsible. It had been his child she was carrying, and she had been his wife to care for.

He started rubbing Wolfburn's horse down, allowing the repetitive motion to soothe away some of the tension he was carrying. When the horse had been provided with water and straw and was happily settled in a stall beside Odysseus, George led his friend back to the house.

'Come in, get settled. I can fetch you some tea if you're desperate, or I am sure my housekeeper will be back soon.'

Wolfburn followed him in, and George saw him looking at the house with an appraising eye. It had always been a favourite of anyone who visited, and he felt a pang of sadness to be losing it.

'I hear rumours you are selling.'

'You seem to hear a lot of rumours.'

'They haven't been wrong so far.'

George nodded as he led the way into the library. It was his preferred room in the house and the perfect place to sit and talk to guests whilst enjoying an uninterrupted view of the lake.

'I am selling. I'm selling everything.'

'Everything?' Wolfburn's voice was low, his words slow as if he thought he was talking to a man on the edge.

'All my properties in England.'

'That's drastic.'

George shrugged. 'I have no use of them. I am going to move permanently to Italy, or at least for a while. Then I might try Spain or somewhere else hot.'

'Where no one knows you.'

Ignoring the last comment, he glanced out at the view, trying to relax. Wolfburn was one of his oldest friends as well as being Clara's brother. They had met at school and been inseparable throughout their time at Eton.

There was the sound of the front door opening and closing, and with a start George thought of Kate. Soon it would be time for the two maids to return to the village, and then Wolfburn would see what a peculiar situation he had here with his housekeeper.

'Does the water ever warm up?' she called from the hall, oblivious to the fact George was not alone. 'I wager it is the warmest day since I arrived here and yet my toes still feel as though they are about to fall off.'

She breezed into the library before he could call out, and when her eyes settled on Wolfburn she stiffened, standing unmoving like a statue for a long moment.

'Wolfburn, this is my housekeeper, Miss Winters. Miss Winters, this is my old friend Lord Henry Wolfburn.'

'Pleased to meet you, my lord,' she said, dipping her

eyes demurely. 'I am sorry I was out when you arrived. Can I get you some refreshments?'

'That would be lovely, Miss Winters.'

She backed out of the room and disappeared, George letting out a silent sigh of relief. She couldn't know Wolfburn was Clara's brother, but he should have known he would be able to rely on her to be discreet.

'What happened to Mrs Lemington?' Wolfburn murmured, his eyes still on the door where Kate had disappeared.

'She took ill after her husband died, and she has gone to stay with her daughter in Keswick.'

'Shame. Send her my regards, I have fond memories of her from our childhood.'

'I will.'

'I am relieved you are not here alone. There were whispers you let your staff go and were fending for yourself.'

'As you can see, they are entirely unfounded. I have Miss Winters.'

'And other staff, I assume.'

'There are two young women for the village who come each day.'

Wolfburn fell silent for a moment and then stood, pacing across the library. 'You look well, George, physically at least. I was worried I would turn up and find you a husk.'

'I have been looking after myself. I swim in the sea each morning in Italy, and they have big rocky mountains to climb in the heat.'

'We are worried about you.'

'We?'

'The family. Mama, Margaret, even Elena.'

George smiled at this. Elena was Clara's little sister.

The last time he had seen her, she had been in that awkward phase between childhood and adulthood, wanting to join the adults but not quite ready to leave her childhood behind. She'd been nervous about her debut, reluctant to think about marriage, but downright resistant to her brother's suggestion of delaying her introduction to society for a while.

'You have nothing to worry about.'

'Of course we do. You disappeared. Right after the funeral. You left and no one heard from you for months on end.'

'I am sorry for that.'

'We understand, of course we do. I haven't come to seek an apology. Good lord, man, you have nothing to apologise for. We all know how much you loved Clara.'

George stood, running a hand through his hair and then walking over to the window.

'When we buried Clara I was a mess,' he said slowly, realising the best way to reassure his friend he hadn't gone mad was to explain. 'I needed to get away from everything that reminded me of her, all the people and places we would never see together again. I was hurting so much. I wanted to be somewhere I knew I would not bump into a passing acquaintance who might enquire as to Clara's health, and I would have to tell them the news. I couldn't bear it. I ran away.'

'With good cause,' Wolfburn murmured.

'It hasn't been easy over the years, and I do still miss her, but I am not running away now.' He shrugged. 'I enjoy my life in Italy. It is where I want to live.'

'You've always loved it here. Yet you're selling the house.'

'It was going to be my family home. Filled with my wife and my children and laughter and noise.'

Wolfburn nodded soberly. 'I understand. I honestly do. I wonder, though, if you might regret it in a year's time. What about when you fall in love and decide to marry? Won't you want a family home then?'

'I think I have given marriage a good enough go,' George said quietly. 'There will not be a third time.'

'You're thirty-two years old, Henderson. With a little luck you could live another forty or fifty years. How can you say today how you might feel in the future?'

'It is only a house.'

Their debate was interrupted as Miss Winters entered carrying a tray with cups and a teapot. Quietly she set it down, pouring out the tea without meeting his eye. She handed a cup to Lord Wolfburn before passing George his. Even then she kept her eyes downcast, and her manner was distant. Perhaps a little too distant, for he saw Wolfburn glance at her and frown as if he didn't quite believe her act.

'It is your home,' Wolfburn corrected him quietly. 'You may have other houses, other estates, but Crosthwaite House has always been your home.'

'Not anymore,' he said with a shrug.

Miss Winters retreated to the door and slipped away, and his eyes couldn't help but follow her. There was something hypnotic about her. Even in a situation when he should be focussed elsewhere, he couldn't keep his gaze from her.

'Then I have a proposition for you.'

Raising an eyebrow, he took a sip of tea and motioned for his friend to continue.

'Let us buy it from you.'

He almost choked on the tea, spluttering as he tried to catch his breath.

'Why would you want to buy it?'

'It's a beautiful house.'

'You have a beautiful house. You have three.'

It was Wolfburn's turn to shrug. 'Perhaps I want one more.'

'You could choose any house in the country. Why this one, with all the associated memories?'

'Memories are not bad things, at least not for everyone,' Wolfburn said softly. 'Clara was happy here. *I* was happy here when I came to visit in the holidays when we were at school.'

'What does Margaret think?'

Wolfburn had great respect for his wife and wouldn't make a decision like this without her.

'She agrees it is for the best.'

'For the best?'

'Better than a stranger buying the house.'

George looked at his friend silently. Wondering if he would admit the motivation behind it.

Wolfburn sighed. 'Indulge me. What does it matter to you who buys it? I will give you whatever price you are asking.' He paused and waited for George to meet his eye. 'Then in a few years, when you are ready to come back to England, it will not be lost forever.'

'You would buy it for the sole purpose of holding it safe for me, *if* I ever choose to return.'

'Yes.'

'I am not planning on changing my mind.'

'Then I have a beautiful new property that one day I can pass on to my children.'

'This is madness, Henry. Absolute madness.'

'Is it? When you think about it? You get to sell to a friend with no concern of legal wrangling or someone pulling out. If you never come back to England, I keep the house and enjoy owning a place my darling Clara spent some of her happiest days. If one day you decide you wish to come home, then you can either buy it back from me or not.'

'You've always been too bloody reasonable,' George muttered, straightening the curtain and looking down to the lake. If he was truthful, he would miss this view. He would miss everything about Crosthwaite House.

'Think about it. I am going to beg a bed for the night, but tomorrow I need to get home to Margaret and the children. Give me your answer tomorrow or send a message in the next few days. Don't sell this place to strangers.'

'I promise you I will consider your offer. Now, let me talk to Miss Winters to see what we can rustle up for dinner and let her know to prepare a room for the night.'

George left his friend alone in the library, pausing before he headed down the stairs to the kitchen. It was good to see Wolfburn again. He had expected a pang of distress at seeing the brother of his late wife. There were certain physical similarities between the siblings, but instead of crushing grief, he felt happy to see his friend, nothing more.

Kate was flitting around the kitchen, her head bent, pretending she didn't notice him enter.

'I am sorry for the surprise guest,' he said, moving towards her. He should feel awkward touching her, holding her, with Clara's brother just upstairs, but he had an overwhelming urge to pull her close.

'I will do my best with the few supplies we have for dinner,' she said, her demeanour stony.

'I had no idea he was going to turn up.'

'I will take his things up to one of the guest bedrooms. Do you have a preference as to where he goes?'

'No,' George said, hating the distance that was stretching out between them. 'Kate…'

'I think you'd better stick to calling me Miss Winters whilst Lord Wolfburn is here.'

'Kate,' he said resolutely, placing his hands on the work surface so his fingertips were touching hers. 'This doesn't change anything. It is one night, that is all. Then I get you all to myself again.'

Unable to stop himself, he stepped closer so he was standing behind her and kissed her neck, loving the way she shivered and leaned back into him.

'I feel like a dirty little secret.'

'No. You're not that, not at all.'

She turned her head, and he could see the tears in her eyes. 'But I am.'

'I am not ashamed of you, Kate,' he said quietly. 'Good lord, every man in England would be jealous that I got to spend my time with such a beautiful and interesting young woman. The reason we are keeping this secret is for your reputation, your future.'

He saw her consider this for a moment. Then she closed her eyes and allowed her body to sink against his, but still he could feel the tension there. They hadn't discussed why she had agreed to their affair. George had instinctively shied away from the topic, knowing the answer would be complicated, messy. She had been so adamant the first time he had proposed they become lovers, so aghast at his suggestion, and on reflection he had seen what an insult it had been. He'd treated her like a fallen women, worthy of less because she had already lost her virtue.

After his illness and recovery, when she had made it clear she did desire to engage in an affair with him, he had been careful to ensure it was what she really wanted. He didn't wish for her to feel pressured or regret their time together, but once she had reassured him she wanted what he was offering, he hadn't probed any further.

'One night?' she murmured.

'One night. Then tomorrow I am all yours, and you are all mine.'

She turned around and raised herself up on tiptoe, kissing him fleetingly on the lips.

'Get back to your friend. I will see to dinner.'

# Chapter Twenty

Kate cleared away the plates, moving quietly so as not to interrupt the conversation at the table. She enjoyed seeing George with his friend, talking and laughing, and she felt like a long buried part of him had been released tonight. A part that didn't feel guilty about being happy, that could revel in old memories without being sucked into them.

'Stay a moment, Miss Winters,' Lord Wolfburn said as she came to collect the last of the dishes.

'I wouldn't want to intrude, my lord.'

'I insist. Dinner was delicious, and I want to thank you for your hospitality, especially in building such a menu at short notice. Have you spent much time in the kitchen? Perhaps as a kitchen maid or cook's assistant?'

'I have picked up a little here and there,' she said, trying to be as vague as possible.

To give herself something to do, she gathered the whiskey glasses and set them on the table in front of the two men, then fetched the decanter of whiskey.

'Would you like a glass?' George said, to the surprise of both Kate and Lord Wolfburn.

Remembering the awful headache and nausea she

had experienced after her last alcoholic drink, she shook her head. Never again did she want to feel as though her skull was going to explode or the world was tilting around her.

'Tell me about yourself, Miss Winters,' Lord Wolfburn said, sitting back in his chair and swirling the amber liquid that George had poured him round in his glass.

'There isn't much to tell, my lord.'

'You didn't grow up around here? Your accent is from the south, I think?'

'My family are from Sussex.'

'How did you end up here?'

Kate flicked a glance at George, but he was sitting back in his chair, relaxed. She supposed it didn't much matter what she told Lord Wolfburn. It wasn't as though she would ever see the man again.

'I've always wanted to travel, to see some of the world. I am aware a woman in my circumstances will never get the opportunity to see Egypt or India, or even Italy like Lord Henderson, but I did not want to spend my life never having left the borders of Sussex.'

'You do not find it a strain to be away from your family?'

'Of course,' Kate said, casting her eyes down. It was difficult being away from her family. There wasn't a day that passed when she didn't wish things had turned out differently, but she was wise enough to understand there was no going back now. Her sister did not know about Kate's affair with her fiancé, now husband, but she would be devastated if she found out. Her parents had shown no compassion, no understanding that Kate might have made a foolish mistake, but that she was hurting and needed love, not contempt. Perhaps one day she might be able to return, to see if there was anything to salvage of their relationships, but it would not be any day soon.

'Do you plan to stay in the area once Crosthwaite House is sold?'

'I think Thornthwaite is the most beautiful place I have been.' She smiled. 'But I am well aware I will need to go where there is work.'

'You are very pragmatic, Miss Winters. You always were lucky, Henderson. Only you could go out of the country for years on end, never even know you had a new housekeeper, and come home to find your home in perfect order and running without needing any input from you.'

George shrugged. 'What can I say? I am blessed to have found Miss Winters.'

Kate's head snapped around, convinced that there was a double meaning in his words and wondering if Lord Wolfburn would pick up on it.

George was sitting serenely, smiling at the room in general.

'Now, I know it is early,' Lord Wolfburn said, before draining his glass of whiskey, 'and I promised scintillating conversation, but I find my eyes drooping. I am exhausted after the long ride this morning. I hope you will forgive me, Henderson. I think I need to go to bed.'

'Of course.'

'Let me show you to your room Lord Wolfburn,' Kate said, rising immediately.

'Thank you, Miss Winters. Good night, Henderson.'

They left the study, Kate picking up one of the candlesticks with a flickering candle in it, using it to light the way.

'You're in the green bedroom,' she said as they started upstairs.

'Thank you, Miss Winters. I wonder if I might be familiar and extend my thanks.'

'You do not need to thank me, my lord.'

'I think I do.'

Kate looked around, unsure of his meaning. The green room was close to the top of the stairs, and she paused outside the door, waiting for him to elaborate.

'When I heard Lord Henderson had come home to sell Crosthwaite House, I dreaded to think what sort of state he would be in. I expected to arrive to find a man physically and emotionally wrecked. Instead I discover he has finally started to heal.'

'I do not think I have any part in that, my lord. Time...'

'Time is a wonderful healer, I agree, Miss Winters, but I think you have reminded him what it is like to have a home, to be cared for. A person needs that. For too long Henderson has locked himself away and refused the kindness of others.'

'He has been here only a short time,' Kate said, still not convinced she had played a role like Lord Wolfburn was suggesting.

'I have friends in southern Italy. They have dropped in to check on Lord Henderson for me from time to time over the last few years. He has a beautiful villa with sea views, but he was just existing there.' Lord Wolfburn sighed, lowering his voice. 'The man has lost two wives and has now convinced himself that the future he had planned is no longer within his reach. My sister Clara was a wonderful, generous woman, and the last thing she would want would be him wallowing.'

Kate inclined her head, seeing the glint of tears in the man's eyes at the thought of his sister.

'I came here thinking Henderson would still be the mess he was whilst living in Italy, but I am hopeful he has started to see there is life beyond his grief.' Lord Wolfburn looked at her with sincerity in his eyes. 'I do not know what you share with him, but whatever it is, I thank you for playing your part in bringing my friend back from the brink.'

Before Kate could speak, Lord Wolfburn bade her good-night and disappeared into the room, closing the door firmly behind him. She stood still for a long while, trying to take in everything the man had said. It wasn't difficult to believe George had been lost even up until recently. He had been stuck in a cycle of grief, unable to break free. Perhaps she had played a small part in helping him along the difficult road of returning to something resembling a more normal existence.

'Thank you for this evening,' George said as she returned downstairs to find him in the study.

Kate hesitated, then closed the door behind her, walking straight to the chair where George was sitting and lowering herself into his lap. She kissed him, long and hard, pleased to feel him reacting to her by pulling her closer.

'We shouldn't,' he murmured, glancing at the door but making no move to manoeuvre her off of him.

'Your friend is very astute. If he doesn't know for sure we are lovers, he strongly suspects.'

'He said that to you?'

'He implied it.'

George closed his eyes, and Kate kissed the furrow between his brows.

'Don't frown my love,' she whispered, stroking his

hair. 'Lord Wolfburn cares only for your happiness, and he is under the impression that I make you happy.'

'You do make me happy.'

'Then do not worry he will judge you.'

'He is my late wife's brother.'

'And he is your friend. A very pragmatic friend at that.'

'What do you mean?'

'He wants you to be happy more than he wants you to hold on to your grief for Clara.'

'He said that? He always was sensible,' George murmured, shaking his head. 'And a good friend. He sent a mutual acquaintance to check up on me whilst I was in Ischia.'

'I gathered,' Kate said with a faint smile. She wondered what George had been like when he had first arrived in Italy, and what he would be like when he went back. She didn't enjoy thinking of him alone in his villa, eschewing company and stewing in his grief. Perhaps this trip home would help him to start socialising again, to see he could enjoy the company of others without being overwhelmed by guilt.

'What an odd afternoon,' George said.

'How do you mean odd?'

'Wolfburn has offered to buy Crosthwaite House.'

'He wants to buy it?'

George nodded. 'Not to live here, but to keep hold of it, in the family as it were, in case I change my mind at some point.'

'That is a very kind thing to do,' Kate said softly.

'I am not going to change my mind.'

'How do you know?'

He looked at her as if he hadn't expected the challenge.

'I know my own thoughts.'

'I'm not suggesting that you do not.' She fished around for the right words, grasping at them for a good half a minute before she felt ready to continue. 'Tell me how you felt when you lost your wife, George.'

'Devastated,' he said decisively. 'Crushed.'

'And when you think of it now, how do you feel?'

'The same,' he said, and then trailed off, realisation dawning. 'Not the same,' he corrected himself.

'How do you feel now?'

'I feel some sadness if something reminds me of her, regret that she will not be able to experience things we had planned.'

'But you feel different now to how you did then?'

'Yes.'

'I do not pretend to be an expert on grief,' Kate said quietly, holding George's gaze as she spoke, 'but I wonder if you might feel differently in another two years, or in twenty.'

'You sound like Wolfburn,' George said, shaking his head.

'These last couple of weeks I have seen how much this house means to you. I would hate for you to sell it and regret it.'

For a long moment, George was silent, and then he looked up at her before kissing her tenderly. When he pulled away, she saw the emotion in his eyes.

'Do you know I expected every room, every view, every place on the estate to be haunted, to stir up painful memories wherever I stepped?'

'Is that the case?'

He shook his head. 'No. Of course I remember Clara here, and some of those memories are tinged with sadness, but there are hundreds of other happy memories.

From childhood, adolescence, from the time I spent here with both my wives and as a single man.'

Kate remained silent, taking a moment to assess why she was pushing this. She would never forgive herself if she realised she was pursuing this for her own agenda, her own gain. She thought keeping Crosthwaite House would be the best thing for George, but she had to make sure that opinion was not influenced by her own desire for him to keep the property.

'Only you can decide what is best for you,' Kate said, 'but I wonder if Lord Wolfburn has given you a way to do what feels right, without having to worry about regretting it for the rest of your life.'

George closed his eyes and pulled her close, engulfing her in his arms and holding her silently for a long time.

'Everything feels clear when I am with you,' he said quietly.

She kissed him softly, brushing her lips against his and enjoying the feeling of being held completely. For a fleeting moment she realised this would be what her life could be like with a husband, someone to share those difficult moments with along with the good. She was struck how much she wanted this, and slowly it dawned on her how much she wanted George to be the man who made this her reality.

Breaking away, she stood, and after a moment turned so he wouldn't see the emotion in her eyes. She knew George could not give her what she wanted. His grief was not what was holding him back, rather a sense of guilt about carrying on with his life. Right now he was able to manage an affair, a short-lived liaison, but his actions showed he was not ready for anything more.

Kate pressed her lips together and started to clear the

glasses and whiskey bottle, wanting to have something to do, to keep busy. Perhaps if they had met another time in another way, they might have had a chance, but not now. Now all he could offer her was a few short weeks of pleasure before disappearing from her life completely. The prospect of never seeing him again made her heart ache, and she knew it would break her when the time came.

'Come upstairs with me,' he said, standing and gripping her hand. He must have seen the hesitation in her eyes, and he smiled tenderly. 'I don't think either of us wants to be alone tonight. On my honour, we can just lie together.'

'On your honour?'

'However much I am tempted…' he murmured.

'I have to clear the kitchen.'

'Leave it until tomorrow. Mary and Marigold can help in the morning.'

Kate hesitated and then nodded. If a few short weeks were all she was going to get, she might as well make the most of them.

## Chapter Twenty-One

Kate was quiet this morning, introspective, and even the funnier of his jokes were getting little more than a half-hearted smile. They had waved Wolfburn off after breakfast, and George had promised to consider his friend's offer.

'Let's go out,' he said, gripping her hand.

'Where to?' Kate said, checking over her shoulder as if to verify neither of the maids were in the vicinity.

'Does it matter? I think better in the fresh air.'

'Is there something you need to think about?'

'There is something I wish to ask you.'

'Now I am intrigued. Don't keep it a secret.'

'Come on. I know the perfect place.'

The day was warm with sunny skies, although there were a few clouds dotting the blue. George pulled on his jacket before they left, and Kate went to her room to fetch a shawl, but it felt good to step outside without a heavy coat.

Hand in hand they strolled through the grounds towards the lake. Kate had definitely relaxed with him the last couple of days. She was no longer worried about a local popping up and seeing them together, undisturbed as they had been for a while.

He realised how good it felt just to *be* with her. They didn't need to be doing anything special. Everyday activities were better with Kate by his side.

Quickly he stopped that train of thought. This little arrangement of theirs might be working out better than he could have ever imagined, but that didn't mean he needed to propose something more permanent. Even if the attraction between them showed no sign of diminishing and he liked her more every single day, he knew one day soon he would have to say goodbye.

'You're frowning,' Kate said, looking at him with concern.

'The sun is in my eyes.'

'The sun is behind us.'

He turned his head and saw she was right. 'I have very sensitive eyes.'

'So sensitive they look out the back of your head as well.'

'Minx. If you must know, I was frowning because I was thinking about when our time together comes to an end.'

If he didn't know her mannerisms well he wouldn't have noticed the slight stiffening of her posture or the carefully controlled expression that came over her face.

'Why were you thinking about it?'

For a long moment he didn't answer, not because he was trying to delay but because he hadn't ever finished the thought before. What did he want with Kate Winters after these next few weeks?

'I will miss you,' he said quietly. 'And not just your beautiful lips and delicious kisses.'

'You make it sound like I am not much more than a pair of lips to you.'

He grinned. 'You are so much more than that. I will miss your lovely round bottom and the way your breasts move when you're on top of me. I will miss...'

'Stop it,' she said, swatting him with a hand. 'Nice to see I am reduced to the merely physical when you think about my attributes.'

'Oh you are so much more than that, Miss Winters.'

He felt a flare of warmth for Kate and knew he couldn't ask her what he had been planning. It was too dangerous, too easily misinterpreted. What he wanted was for Kate to stay with him longer. Foolishly, when the idea had first occurred he'd thought of asking her, but he knew it was something he needed to think through first.

They were skirting around the edge of a group of trees and within a few minutes reached the edge of the lake.

'This way,' he said, pulling her along the bank to where a small jetty stuck out into the water. Halfway along, a rowing boat was tied to a post, bobbing gently in the water.

'Are we going out on the lake?'

'Yes. Unless you don't like boats.'

'Who doesn't like boats?' Kate said, crouching down and starting to untie the rope.

He hopped down into the little boat and arranged the oars, then helped her step from the jetty. The boat rocked as they moved around, and George took the opportunity to hold Kate tight, telling himself he didn't want her falling in.

'Do you grope everyone you take out on the lake?'

'No. It is a special service reserved only for you.'

He used the oars to push off the jetty, then let the boat glide away from the edge before he started to dip the wooden blades into the water. In his youth he was always out on the lake and had rowed for miles. Although it had been a while, soon his muscles remembered what was expected, and he got into a rhythm.

'Did you used to go out on the sea when you lived in Sussex?'

Kate was leaning back in the boat, making herself comfortable. He loved watching her like this, relaxed and not worrying about what the rest of the world might think of her.

'Not really. We would paddle a lot. It is one of my fondest memories as a child, being on the beach with my sister and running in and out of the sea.'

'Do you miss her?'

Kate looked out over the edge of the boat for a while, her eyes fixed on a distant spot.

'Yes,' she said eventually. 'More than I ever thought.'

'You weren't close growing up?'

'There are four years between us, which isn't all that many, but it meant we were at different stages of our lives all the time. I was still wanting to play with dolls whilst she was learning to play the piano, then I was finally old enough to play the piano and she was learning how to run a household.' She sighed. 'I always wanted to be at her stage, to do what she was doing.'

He nodded silently, allowing her to talk. Much of her past was still a mystery to him, even though he had pieced together some of it from the little things she had told him.

'Then Caroline was invited to go on a grand European tour with my mother's aunt, and just as we were getting to an age where we could have become confidantes, friends even, she left.' Kate grimaced, glancing over at him. 'And then I became entangled with her fiancé, which is never going to endear me to her.'

'She isn't aware of the liaison, though?'

'No. It was felt it would be best not to tell her. I almost did hundreds of times, but I could never find the right words.'

'So you lost your sister along with everything else?'

'I can hardly complain. It is entirely my fault.'

'Surely you don't believe that.'

Kate shrugged. 'I had an affair with the man my sister was promised to marry. I can tell myself they had never met, they weren't in love, that it was nothing more than a business arrangement, but the truth is they were betrothed and I disrespected that.'

He could see how much she regretted what she had done, and not just because it had all turned out badly.

'You think of this as a just punishment, don't you?'

'What do you mean?'

'This banishment, being cut off from your family, sent away to fend for yourself.'

Kate was silent for a long moment and then looked up, raw emotion in her eyes. 'I think we all have this sense of self, an image of the sort of person we believe ourselves to be. I always believed I was a good person, a person who would make the right decisions. That idea was shattered when I realised what I had done. I betrayed my sister, betrayed my beliefs, for the honeyed words of a scoundrel.'

'It has shaken your perception of yourself.'

'It has. And yes, I do feel like I needed to be punished for my mistake.'

'Not like this,' George said gently. 'Not by your family abandoning you when you needed them the most.'

'I chose for it to be like this,' Kate said quietly. 'They wanted to send me to a distant relative for a year, perhaps two. Allow Caroline and Arthur to settle into their married life together, and then they would think of how best to dispose of me.'

'Dispose of you?'

'Marry me off, but I didn't want any of that.' She had tears in her eyes now and was blinking furiously. 'My family were never the warmest, the most loving, but until then I had thought they loved me. However, when my father found out what had happened, I saw I was nothing but an inconvenience, something that could no longer be seen as an asset, so instead was a liability.'

'That was when you decided to leave.'

'I was heartbroken and I hated myself for being so easily manipulated, but I knew if I stayed I would be forever reminded of my mistake, and it would be used to manipulate me into doing things I did not want. Instead I decided to make my own way, to seek my own fortune.'

'Was it the right decision?'

She paused for a long moment, and he could see it was something she hadn't really allowed herself to think about.

'Yes. It was,' she said eventually. 'Even though this isn't the life I dreamed of as a child, or what I expected as I grew up, I am glad I made the decision to step out on my own, to have the chance to make my own choices for once.'

'I understand what you mean when you say this is not the life you expected,' George said quietly. He marvelled at her resilience, at her ability to view what had happened this past year with such a level head. She accepted her own guilt—more than that, she took responsibility for it—yet she also acknowledged the need for her whole life not to be ruined by one reckless decision. 'I admire you, Kate. I admire your strength and your certainty.'

'I do not always feel certain.'

'Yet here you are making your own decisions again and again instead of being married off to a weak-chinned fool whose only interest in you is your father's money.'

Kate shuddered at the thought.

'I cannot move forwards like you have,' he said softly. 'I am stuck, held back by my constant ruminations of the life I could have had.'

'George,' Kate said, a tremor in her voice, 'I do not think that is true. Perhaps it was at first, for a year, or maybe eighteen months, and you got used to thinking in that way, but that is not all there is for you.'

If anyone else had said the same to him, he would have dismissed it immediately, but he made the effort to consider Kate's words.

'You told me there are too many bad memories here, too many places that remind you of the tragedies that have befallen your wives. Yet these last couple of weeks I have seen your face light up when you have rediscovered a hidden corner of the grounds or bumped into an old acquaintance from the village. I think you have enjoyed being back here, but perhaps you tell yourself you haven't, that it is too hard to be somewhere with so many memories, because that is what you *think* you should feel.'

'I mourn Clara and Elizabeth.'

Kate sat forwards, rocking the boat. 'I would never doubt your grief and your love for your wives.'

He fell silent. Something in what Kate said had struck him and gripped hold, his mind unable to shake it off. On occasion he did wonder if he felt sadness because he thought that was what he was meant to feel, rather than his true emotion.

'Grief is a messy thing, or so I am told,' Kate said. 'There is no timeline or map to find your way out, but I wonder if you have bought into this narrative of being stuck in a perpetual world of grief, unable to move on. If so, then that is what is holding you back.'

George let the oars rest on the water as he contemplated Kate's words. When he had planned the trip back to Crosthwaite House, he'd expected to be overwhelmed by grief and sadness, and he *had* been a little surprised when it hadn't happened. Of course he felt a pang of melancholy when he thought of the lives of his late wives, tragically cut short, but he did not feel the overwhelming sorrow that kept him from doing anything else.

'I wish there was a guide for the bereaved,' he murmured. 'Something to tell you when it is right for you to stop sleeping on just one side of the bed, when to clear out their old clothes, when it is acceptable to laugh again, live again.'

'You feel guilty if you think about moving on with your life, so you have fallen into this trap of existing without properly living.'

He looked at her, really studying her, wondering how she was so astute. Deep down he had known what he was doing, but he had never allowed himself to admit it. Kate Winters had known him for a mere few weeks, and she had figured it out almost immediately.

'When I lost Clara, I told myself I would never be happy again,' he said, looking back at the house he loved so much and the countryside that was so familiar. 'When you realise it isn't true, the guilt threatens to overwhelm you. I *do* enjoy things, yet I felt like it was a betrayal of her.'

Kate took his hand in her own.

'How have we made such a mess of things?' she asked.

'Not everything,' he said quietly. One thing shone brightly in his life. One right decision he had made was asking Kate to be a part of it, even just for a short time.

'Not everything.'

Kate looked at the man across from her and acknowledged what she had kept hidden for a while. She was falling in love with him. It was wonderful and heartbreaking at the same time. Whilst she was here building impossible dreams, unable to stop herself from imagining a future with George, he hadn't once even talked about extending their arrangement. Never had she imagined she would ever be anyone's mistress, but right now she would give anything for it not to end.

Closing her eyes, she realised it wasn't quite true. She didn't want to be his mistress indefinitely. What she wanted was impossible. A happy marriage to a man who loved her as much as she loved him.

'I'm sorry if I have been maudlin,' she said. The trip in the little boat so far had been much more emotional that either of them had planned, and she didn't want George to push her away because she was making him confront deeply buried truths.

He reached out his hand to her and squeezed her fingers, almost dropping an oar in the process.

## Chapter Twenty-Two

The sun was beaming through a gap in the curtains as Kate stirred, illuminating a strip of floor whilst the rest of the room remained in darkness. They were in the master bedroom, ensconced in George's very comfortable bed. Each evening she would accompany him to his bedroom and each morning slip away before Mary and Marigold arrived.

She propped herself up on her elbow and looked down at George as he lay beside her.

'I can feel you looking at me,' he murmured.

'I thought you were asleep.'

He opened one eye. 'I want to be.' Then he grinned and looped an arm around her waist, pulling her on top of him. 'On second thought, maybe I don't.'

'Go back to sleep,' Kate murmured as she moved her hips over his. He groaned and gripped her firmly, wide awake now.

Suddenly he paused, frowning.

'You're wearing that horrible nightgown,' he said, fingering the sensible cotton garment. 'Last night when we went to sleep, you were naked.'

'I got cold.'

'Are you cold now?'

She shook her head, and in an instant he lifted the nightgown off, throwing it onto the floor somewhere.

'That is much better.'

Leaning down, she kissed him, her breasts brushing against his chest as he ran his hands down her back. Over the course of the week, they had made love in dozens of positions in dozens of places. Some were planned and romantic, like the time he had prepared the bedroom with flickering candles and beverages so they could enjoy each other all evening long. Others were spontaneous and sometimes a little less conventional, like the time they had been overcome whilst they were preparing breakfast and he had laid her back on the kitchen table.

This was her favourite, though, waking up in the early morning with George holding her close, making love before either of them even got out of bed.

She slid down onto him, letting out a little moan of satisfaction before she started to move her hips. She loved how he looked at her when they were intimate, loved the way he touched her so tenderly. Now his hands rested on her hips, helping her match her rhythm to his as they came together again and again.

Kate let her head drop back as she felt her pulse quicken, and then suddenly she froze.

'What was that?' she asked.

'Just a door,' George said, starting to move under her again. Kate felt her body relax. It was just a door closing somewhere downstairs.

This time they both stiffened as there was another bang and then the sound of voices.

'Mary and Marigold,' Kate said, her expression aghast. Generally she woke early so had never had a problem with being out of his room and downstairs long before the maids arrived.

For a long moment, neither of them moved, not knowing what to do for the best. Kate wanted nothing more than to stay here, to make love to the man she loved and then spend the morning in his bed, but she knew that wasn't possible any longer.

'Don't go,' George said as she slipped off him.

'I have to.'

'It is unlikely they will come in here.'

'What is the first thing they do each morning if you are not up and about?'

'Come to my room to see if there is anything I need,' he said with a quiet groan.

They both looked at the door and listened for a moment. All was quiet for now, no doubt with the maids starting downstairs in the kitchen.

'They will expect me to be down there,' Kate said, feeling a wave of panic wash over her. She had been so worried about people finding out, and now it seemed likely that it would be her own carelessness that would jeopardise everything.

She stood, scrambling for her clothes, dropping things almost as fast as she could pick them up.

'Calm down,' George said, reaching out and taking hold of her wrist. 'Let's pause a moment to think things through.'

Kate couldn't think. She had visions of Mary and Marigold bursting through the door, finding her standing here naked with the handsome but forbidden earl. Of course the two maids wouldn't want to ruin Kate's reputation, and they would no doubt have the best of intentions to keep things secret, but one day something would slip out, and once again Kate would be forced to flee to save herself from a scandal.

George stood, taking her in his arms.

'Stop,' he said, a note of authority in his tone. 'Whatever it is you are thinking, just stop.'

'We need to…'

'Let me help you dress, and then we can think of what we need to do.'

Kate forced herself to breathe deeply and allowed George to help her with her clothes. Only once her dress was fastened and her hair at least passingly presentable did she feel some of the fear ebb from her.

'Let us see if we can sneak you up the main stairs to some of the disused servants' rooms. You can descend the back stairs, act surprised to find them in the kitchen, and tell them you were organising something or other for me up there.'

Quickly George pulled on a pair of trousers and a shirt, clearly planning to finish dressing later.

'Let's go,' he said.

Her hand was on the doorknob when she heard the unmistakable squabbling of the two young maids coming up the stairs.

'Why do you always get to decide what we do?'

'I am older, Mary, and therefore more responsible.'

'Older does not necessarily mean more responsible.'

'Well, in this case it does. Anyway, Miss Winters trusts me more.'

'She does not.'

'She thinks I am very capable.'

'She thinks I am very capable too.'

'They're coming,' Kate said, unable to move. She watched in horror as George started stripping off his clothes. 'What are you doing? Get dressed.'

'Hide,' he whispered urgently, smoothing down her side of the bed and then slipping under the covers. Kate realised what he was doing almost too late.

Desperately she looked around for somewhere to hide. The curtains were heavy but did not reach quite to the floor, so her feet would poke out if she hid behind there. There was a chair in the corner, and she could slip behind that, but it would be hard to tell if any of her dress was poking out.

Her eyes flicked to the door that joined the room with the small dressing area and wondered if she could get there in time. Quickly she dashed across the room, slipping inside and pulling the door almost closed behind her.

There was a quiet knock on the door before it opened a moment later, and Marigold bustled in, pausing when she saw George still asleep in bed. He pretended to stir and sat up, blinking.

'I'm ever so sorry for waking you, sir,' Marigold said, recovering first. 'Normally you're up and about at this time. Is there anything you need?'

'No thank you, Marigold.'

Kate watched through the crack as Marigold backed out of the room, closing the door behind her.

After thirty seconds had elapsed, Kate was still trembling, and she couldn't move from where she was hidden in the dressing room. From her position she stood and watched as George rose out of bed and came over to the door.

'It is safe,' he said quietly, opening the door and taking her hand. 'She suspects nothing.'

'That was too close.'

'Perhaps I should send them away for a week,' he

murmured into her ear, kissing her neck once he had finished speaking.

'No,' Kate said quickly. 'You can't do that. If you do, they will certainly suspect something is amiss.'

'How am I meant to stop myself from kissing you these next few weeks? A man cannot store up that much desire for a few measly hours of the night.'

'You are incorrigible, but I know you are capable of such restraint.'

He groaned and kissed her, slipping his arms around her and slowly manoeuvring her back towards the bed.

'I know what you are doing, Lord Henderson.'

'What am I doing?'

'You're trying to distract me so you can get me back into your bed and have your wicked way with me.'

'I'm trying a little persuasion, that's all.'

'I need to go. Marigold and Mary will start to think it is strange I have not appeared.'

'You will come to me tonight?'

She hesitated. How close they had come this morning to getting caught should make her more cautious, but Kate knew she didn't want to give up her nights with George when their time together was so limited already. Mary and Marigold would leave before sunset for their walk back to the village, and then it would be just the two of them in the house. She would open the curtains a little more so the sunlight did the job of waking her better than today.

'I'll come to you tonight.'

'Then I will be counting down the hours.'

Kate saw the desire in his eyes and knew she had to leave before he kissed her again. One more kiss, one touch, and she would find herself tumbling into bed with him and damn the consequences.

Quietly she slipped out, padding down the corridor and heading upstairs before making her way to the servant's stairs at the other end of the house. It was an elaborate ruse, but at least she was mildly out of breath when she emerged into the kitchen.

'Miss Winters, we were wondering where you were,' Marigold said, hurrying over and giving Kate a squeeze on her arm.

'I was upstairs sorting through a few of the old servants' rooms, making an inventory for Lord Henderson,' she said, brushing her skirt as if concerned about dust.

'I'll get on with the dusting in the downstairs rooms, Miss Winters, unless there is anything else you would like me to do?'

Kate shook her head and watched the young woman hurry away to collect everything she would need for the morning, letting out a sigh of relief that Marigold did not seem in the least bit suspicious.

George felt restless. All day he had spent prowling around the house, unable to settle. Everywhere he went, the two giggling maids seemed to be under his feet, always a few steps ahead so he couldn't accuse them of following him, but he yearned for the peace of the last week, and he yearned for Kate to be here sharing it with him.

'Stop scowling,' she had hissed at him as she passed him on the stairs that afternoon. He *had* been scowling. Unable to concentrate on the work that needed doing, he had slipped from his study, hoping to catch a few moments alone with Kate. He had spotted her on the stairs, and he'd moved quickly to intercept her, but before he could pull her into a dark corner, one of the maids had scurried out from a downstairs room into the hallway.

Thwarted, he had allowed Kate to walk past him, but not without the frustration starting to build.

Now he was watching the clock. He knew Kate always sent the two young girls home at least an hour before sunset. This meant they could walk the two miles to the village and have time to spare in case of any mishaps. Judging by the position of the sun in the sky, it must be nearly time for the maids to leave.

Tapping his fingers on the desk, he listened intently for any sound of movement as the minutes ticked by, almost jumping with joy as there was the unmistakable thump of the downstairs door swinging shut.

George leapt from his chair and strode to the front of the house, wanting to confirm both young women had left before he went and swooped Kate up into his arms. Two figures were walking away from the house, starting down the drive towards the village. He watched them for a moment, checking one wouldn't suddenly remember something left behind and turn back. Kate would never forgive him if he compromised her reputation at the last moment.

When he was certain the maids were well on their way home, he hurried down the stairs and made his way to the kitchen. He entered the room and wrapped his arms around Kate before she even knew he was there.

'My hands are covered in flour,' she laughed as he kissed her neck.

'I don't care. Today has been the longest day ever.'

'I think you will find it has had the same number of hours as every other day.'

'It's had at least double, if not triple the number of hours in it. I should know. I've been watching the clock.'

He spun her round so she was facing him, stepping back only to let her wipe her floury hands on her apron.

'I suppose we do have only a short time left together,' she murmured, standing up on tiptoe and brushing a kiss against his lips. 'We should make the most of it.'

George felt an icy stab of pain burst through his heart. He didn't want to think of the moment in a few weeks or a month when he would have to say goodbye to Kate. He'd been a fool to think his desire for her would be slaked by a short affair. Every moment he spent with her he became more infatuated. Every day he wanted to spend more and more time with her.

He kissed her, trying to obliterate the thought, lifting her up onto the edge of the kitchen table. She had her arms around his neck, and he marvelled at how much she had changed in a week. Not her personality, but how at ease she was with him now.

'Stay with me,' he blurted out, unsure where the words had come from. It certainly wasn't a conscious thought.

'What?'

George breathed deeply a few times and then repeated the suggestion. 'Stay with me.'

It might not have been a fully considered plan, but he realised it was what he wanted. Kate made him happy. This past week was the happiest he had felt in years. He might not be ready to move on and lead a conventional life, to settle down with a wife and risk having more children, but he was ready to stop shutting himself off from the world.

'Come back to Italy with me,' he murmured, kissing her ear and then her neck. He pulled away as he realised Kate had stiffened under his touch.

'You want me to be your mistress?'

He shrugged. 'You already are, aren't you?'

She shook her head. 'No. Well, yes, but not in the true sense.'

'What do you mean *the true sense*?'

'You said it yourself. We are lovers, we share a bed, we are intimate, but we do not go out in public together. There is an element of secrecy.'

'Many men keep their mistresses secret.' He held up a hand, unsure why he was arguing about the choice of language. 'It doesn't matter. Whatever you want to call it, come to Italy. Be with me.'

She looked at him warily and climbed down off the table, moving away. He sensed she needed a little time, and knew he had sprung the proposition on her. Happily he would give her a few minutes to think about it, as long as she came to the right decision in the end.

George stood still, allowing her to prowl around the kitchen, head bent as if she were a cat stalking a mouse. The proposition had surprised him too, but as the seconds ticked past, he was becoming more and more convinced it was the right thing to do. Already he felt the weight of the prospect of parting lifting from his shoulders. Even though his departure date was not yet confirmed, it had felt as though every day was measured, every minute they spent together tinged with a hint of desperation because it could soon be their last.

It was a fresh start he was seeking. That was his whole purpose in selling Crosthwaite House and the rest of his English properties. There was no reason Kate couldn't be part of that fresh start, enfolded into his life in Italy.

Now he felt a sort of relief, even though Kate had not quite yet agreed. Already he was imagining beautiful summer days. They could swim in the sea together and walk on the beach, then return home and tumble into bed. Their days would be relaxed and undemand-

ing, and he wouldn't feel the terrible loneliness he had
before returning to England.

'How would it work?' She was shaking her head as
if about to turn him down, and he felt a flash of panic.
He had never even considered she might say no.

'Nothing really would change. I would sell this place,
and then together we would travel to Italy. I think you'll
love Ischia, but if you don't, we can find somewhere
else.'

'For a year, maybe two?'

'Yes.'

'Then what?'

He paused, trying to work out why her voice was so
flat and emotionless.

'I don't know. When can we truly know what the
future holds?'

'I know,' she said, stopping her pacing and raising
her chin, looking at him defiantly. 'You'll get fed up
with me, and because I am your mistress and not your
wife, it will be all too easy to convince yourself you can
get rid of me.' She shook her head. 'I have no doubt you
will be gentle with it—you are a kind man, George—but
you will get rid of me all the same. Perhaps find me a
position somewhere with one of your friends or ensure
I have excellent references for a job you arrange, but I
will be discarded all the same.'

George opened his mouth to tell her she was wrong,
but she continued before he could speak.

'Do not deny it, George. It is the way of the world,'
she said, her voice softer now. 'I may have lost my virtue, but I am from a good family and my expectations
in life are set to include certain things. '

'I can't marry you, Kate.' The idea of being responsible for another person, another wife, made him come out in a cold sweat.

'I know.' There was a note of sadness in her voice, but she held his gaze, and he saw she understood. 'And I can't be your mistress.'

Trying to stop his hand from shaking, he ran it through his hair. Even though they had agreed this would be a liaison that lasted a few weeks only, it felt as though she was being ripped from him. He didn't want to think of how grey and dull his life would be without her in it.

'I need a moment,' she said, taking off her apron and dashing from the room before he could say anything else. He heard the door leading outside open and then close behind her, and then there was complete silence.

George sat down on one of the stools next to the table and let his head drop forwards. It was impossible. He understood Kate's reluctance to become his mistress. She was right. She *was* from a good family, brought up to expect certain things in life. This past year, she had stepped outside of those expectations, but that didn't mean she had eschewed them forever. She was still young, still able to find a husband and have a family once she had recovered from the pain of being betrayed by the first man she had loved. Of course she could expect to lead a more conventional life. She had told him once that the thing she had learned from her experience with Arthur and her family subsequently pushing her away was to harness her desire to take ownership of every decision. She had built herself up from the wreckage and refused to be a victim, and he could see her determination to be the one who made the decisions about her future.

That didn't stop him from wanting to take her with

him, though. The idea that after these few short weeks he might never see her again ripped through him like an arrow, the physical pain almost matching the emotional.

He could ask her to marry him. For a moment he toyed with the idea, allowing it to pulse and grow in his mind. It would solve so many problems. Kate would have the respectable life she ultimately wanted, and he would have *her*. The thought of being able to walk down the street hand in hand with nothing to hide was appealing, as was the idea of waking up to Kate every day, sharing his life with her.

Standing, he tried to shake off the image. That was exactly what he couldn't have. Twice he had been blessed with marriage to good women, and twice it had ended in disaster. He was not superstitious—he did not think he was cursed—but he was not going to risk losing another wife, another woman he loved.

'She will want children,' he murmured to himself. Of course she would. It was another part of the life she had been raised to expect. Despite her detour from the normal path, Kate would still fundamentally want the normal things young women were raised to want. She would want children, and that was something he could not give her. The guilt he felt from Elizabeth's and Clara's deaths was immense, partly because they had both been pregnant with his children when they died. If he had not got them pregnant, both of those beautiful, vibrant women might still be alive. He definitely could not risk that with Kate. He knew Kate was right. For her sake, she couldn't return with him to Italy. That didn't make it any easier to think of giving her up.

George couldn't keep still, and the kitchen wasn't big enough for pacing. Quickly he ran upstairs, taking them two at a time, and dashed out the front door. Kate would want privacy to consider things, but the grounds were vast—there would be somewhere he could walk without running into her.

With his head pounding, he chose a direction and started walking, barely noticing anything around him, trying to suppress the crushing despair he felt deep inside.

# Chapter Twenty-Three

Kate shivered, knowing she should head back to the house but unable to bring herself to move. It was fully dark now, the sky dotted with stars and a crescent moon shining brightly over the lake. She should have brought a shawl or her cloak, but she had left the house in such a hurry she had been unable to think of anything but getting out into the fresh air.

Now all her joints felt stiff from the cold and from sitting in one position too long.

'Come on,' she murmured to herself, standing and stretching.

Slowly she began to pick her way across the stony ground, only able to walk a little faster once she had reached the lawn. Up ahead of her, the house was in darkness. Normally there would be the flicker of a candle in a room or two, but today it was completely dark. She wondered what George was doing. There had been real anguish on his face today when she had said she couldn't accompany him to Italy. In time he would understand. He would see why she'd had to make that decision. Right now, however, he might be hurt that she had rejected him. To him, his offer probably seemed perfectly fine. He'd never had people give him judgemental looks, seen them whispering behind their hands. And he never would. Even if he paraded a string of mistresses in front of the *ton*, his sins would be forgiven because of his title, his wealth, and his gender. It would be the mistresses who would be ostracized and maligned.

Of course she had known this day was coming, this separation, but she had hoped they had a few more weeks. Her time with George had been wonderful. He had taught her to laugh again, to appreciate spending time in someone else's company. He had shown her she could enjoy her body without being ashamed, and he had made her believe she was worthy of pleasure and happiness.

'Time to move on,' she said to herself, knowing saying the words out loud would make it more real.

There were lots of reasons to stay. Crosthwaite House was safe and familiar, and if she stayed a few more weeks, she would be able to spend those weeks with George. Yet she knew it would not be the right choice for her. It was time to decide what she wanted from the next stage in her life and how she was going to achieve it.

The hour was not overly late as she slipped into the house, and she paused for a moment, smiling as she heard George stomping around upstairs. It would be easy to hurry to her room, to lock the door behind her, and pack her bag, but that would be the coward's way out, and she had never been a coward.

Instead she walked up the main staircase and made her way to the room of the man she loved.

'Can I come in?' The door was ajar, and she saw George's head snap her way as he heard her voice.

Silently he moved over to the threshold and opened the door wider, his eyes searching hers.

'Can I come in?' she repeated. This time he stepped back, allowing her to enter the room and catching her wrist as she walked past him.

'I was worried you had gone,' he said.

'I wouldn't leave without saying goodbye.'

'You are going to leave, then?'

She looked at him. More than anything, she realised she wanted him to say that he was wrong, he wanted her to stay, he wanted to marry her. She yearned for a declaration of his love, a reversal of everything he had said before. She wanted to hear how he couldn't survive without her, how he wanted them to be married as soon as possible.

George remained silent.

'I am going to leave,' she said eventually, feeling her heart contract and wither at the words. 'I think you understand it is for the best.'

'If it were for the best, why does it feel like this?'

She didn't have an answer for him and instead placed her hands on either side of his face and kissed him. At first he was stiff, not resistant, but as if it was taking a long time to understand all the emotions that were flooding through him. Then he seemed to snap and kissed her back, looping his arms around her and carrying her over to the bed.

Together they tumbled onto the bedcovers, a tangle of limbs as he kissed her as if he knew it was going to be the last time. Kate tried to hold back the tears. This was supposed to be a way to say goodbye, but she didn't want it to be ruined by sadness. Being here with George had been wonderful in so many ways. She felt more confident, more poised, and ready to go after what she wanted in life. *He* had shown her she was desirable, that she was someone he wanted to spend time with.

It had also focussed her mind, and now she knew what it was she wanted. She wanted freedom, but she also wanted a family. The freedom to choose a future for herself, not dictated by her parents or anyone else. She did want the conventional set-up of a husband and a brood of giggling children, but she was determined to keep her autonomy, to be able to decide whom she would marry and when.

Of course she wished it could be George. He made her happy, he made her laugh, he made her feel as though she were floating on air. She didn't believe he wasn't ready to marry again. He certainly had a lot of love in his heart. His guilt held him back, the guilt of continuing with his life whilst his two late wives did not get to continue with theirs, but one day hopefully he would be able to move past that and live the life he deserved.

They made love feverishly, both wanting to savour the moment, and then collapsed onto the bed, legs entwined and George's arms holding Kate close.

They were silent for a long time, neither wanting to be the one to break the magic, and after a while Kate heard the deepening of George's breathing as he drifted off to sleep. She waited a while longer, almost tempted to stay wrapped in his arms, but knowing she had to rise.

Gently she kissed him on the lips, tears streaming down her face as she pulled away, certain her heart would always carry a piece of him. Then she slipped from the room and made her way downstairs.

It was harder packing her bag than she thought it would be. She had accumulated a few more possessions than when she had first arrived here at Crosthwaite House, little trinkets that Mrs Lemington, Mary, and Marigold had given her as gifts at Christmas, an extra shawl for the cold winters up north, and her thick-soled boots to survive the snowy season in the Lake District. She folded everything away carefully, knowing that in the days and weeks that followed, she would be glad to have a few familiar things around her. More than the physical process of packing, it was the emotional response she found devastating. No longer would she dip her toes in the waters of the lake every day or laugh with Mary and Marigold as they went about their work. She wouldn't have her sanctuary to come to at night or her little routines that had made her feel happy these last few months.

It was just after two in the morning when she had finished packing, and she spent some time at the little desk in the corner of her room. She wrote a note each for Mary and Marigold, apologising for her departure and asking them to help Lord Henderson, and also telling them what a great difference their friendship had made in her life. She wrote a note for Mrs Lemington, knowing someone would see it was delivered, thanking her for taking in a lost young woman and giving her a place in the world. Finally she took out a sheet of paper and paused, wondering what to write to George. She thought of telling him to choose to live his life, or perhaps showing him what a difference he had made to hers. In the end she wrote just three words, sealing it in an envelope before putting his name on the front.

She didn't dare lie down. As luck would have it, there was a coach from Keswick one day a week that ran all the way to Carlisle. Even though it was heading in the wrong direction, she knew it was her best hope of finding a coach to take her south. It also meant she could leave immediately and not have to hang around in Keswick for a day or two. She wasn't sure if George would come after her, but she knew if he did, she would find it hard to resist renewed requests for her to accompany him to Italy. It wasn't the right thing for her to do, but she couldn't rely on her mind being rational when he was around.

There would be gossip when she left. An abrupt departure would spark people's interest, and there wasn't much she could do about it. Thankfully she would be far away before the rumours could start and wouldn't have to listen to them. It would prevent her from returning and finding a job locally, but it was something that was out of her control. It was better to leave and have her departure overshadowed by gossip than to stay and be tempted to give up her dreams for the future for the shorter-term pleasure of spending more time with George.

Before the sun had risen, she ensured her room was left neat and tidy, picked up her bag, and then quietly crept from the house. She hesitated on the threshold, wondering if she was making the biggest mistake of her life, and then forced herself to push on.

A little way down the drive, she stopped and turned back to face the house, tears streaming down her cheeks.

'Goodbye,' she whispered, and then resolutely turned and continued on her way.

## Chapter Twenty-Four

The room felt cold and empty when he woke, and instinctively he reached over to pull Kate closer to him. They might have been sharing a bed for only a little over a week, but he had grown used to her presence in the morning and enjoyed waking up with her beside him. His hand touched cold sheets and for a moment patted around, as if he expected her to be curled up in a ball somewhere on the bed.

Sitting up, he looked around with a sinking sensation in his stomach. Of course she might be downstairs, eager not to have a repeat of the previous morning when Mary and Marigold had almost discovered them in bed together, but somehow George knew that she had gone. The house felt empty, as if it had lost its vital energy.

Slumping back onto the pillows, he knew the right thing was to let her go. If he chased after her, probably with a bit of persistence he could persuade her to come to Italy with him, to be his mistress, but she had been right to refuse him. It was no life for her, not when what she really wanted was the security of a husband, a conventional family.

George dressed in a daze and spent the early part

of the morning unable to settle. He wandered through the house, feeling bereft and remembering all the good times he and Kate had shared here.

He felt some relief when Mary and Marigold arrived, filling the downstairs of the house with their chatter.

Descending the stairs to the kitchen, he paused on the threshold, not sure what he was going to tell the young maids. As he stepped into the room, they were reading a letter each and he realised with a pang of sadness that Kate must have written to explain things herself. Even now she was ensuring his house ran as smoothly as possible.

'Good morning sir,' Mary said, seeing him first and bobbing into a curtsy. Marigold followed her friend, but he could see she was preoccupied.

'I take it those letters are from Miss Winters?'

'Yes,' Marigold said, her eyes flicking back to the words. 'Has she really gone?'

'I am afraid so.' His voice stuck in his throat, and he had to take a couple of attempts to clear it before he could continue. 'Has she explained?'

Marigold nodded. 'She said she was needed back home. I'm going to miss her, sir.'

'We all are.'

He felt hot as if he had a fever and touched his hand to his brow, worried his recent illness might have returned, but it was cool under his palm. Thoughts seemed to be racing through his mind, jumping about and not running in any coherent order.

'What would you like us to do, sir?' Marigold said, a tremble in her voice.

'Miss Winters always assured me you two were very capable of running this house, and in her absence, I hope you will continue with your normal jobs. I will think on what is best to be done about a housekeeper, but until then, please carry on as normal.'

'Yes sir,' they said, bobbing up and down again.

He turned to leave, suddenly feeling like he couldn't breathe and desperate for some fresh air.

'There is a letter for you, sir,' Mary said, holding out a small envelope.

George could see his hand was shaking as he reached out for the envelope. He could imagine what would be inside. Kate would have written him a beautiful note insisting she did not blame him for how things ended and urging him to live a full and happy life. Perhaps there would be a little wisdom on letting go of his guilt and making a conscious decision about moving forwards.

Carefully he tucked it into his pocket. He would read the note, but not yet, not here. He wanted to be in private when he did so.

Heading upstairs, he thought he might take the letter outside and sit on one of the benches that looked out over the lawn with a view of the lake in the distance. Before he could even step outside, there was a clattering of hooves, and he watched as a carriage rolled up the drive, stopping just outside the front door. For one wild moment he thought it might be Kate, returned in a flood of emotion to tell him she had made a mistake, that she didn't want to leave, so he was disappointed when the carriage door opened.

Mr Sorrell jumped down and turned around to help an elderly lady whom George vaguely recognised. He had spent some time at the balls and events of the *ton* when he was younger, and most of the faces were familiar even if he struggled to put names to some of them.

'Mr Sorrell,' he greeted the man, a little more abrupt than usual. 'What brings you here today?'

'Good morning, Lord Henderson. So sorry to intrude. I have brought Mrs Forthbridge with me today. She is very keen to see the house, and I thought you would not mind.'

'I do not wish to see the house,' the elderly woman said, giving George an appraising stare. 'Is something wrong, Lord Henderson? You look terrible. Nothing contagious, I hope.'

'No,' he said without elaborating. Mrs Forthbridge nodded in satisfaction and then turned her attention to the house.

'This is perfect. Where do I sign?'

'You wish to buy the house?'

'Why else would I be here, Lord Henderson? I am not in the habit of bumping round the countryside in a most unsatisfactory carriage for the mere fun of it.'

He paused, assessing the older woman. More than anything he wanted to send her away, to bundle her back in the carriage and get her off his property. The letter from Kate felt hot in his pocket, and he itched to tear open the envelope and check to see he hadn't been mistaken about its contents.

'Please feel free to look wherever you please,' he said, turning away.

'Perhaps your housekeeper would be able to give Mrs Forthbridge a tour, seeing as she was so obliging before,' Mr Sorrell said.

'She's not here.'

'Ah.'

George sighed and motioned for the older woman to follow him in. The quickest way to be rid of her would be to show her round and then tell her he would consider her offer. She didn't look like she was going to be dissuaded any other way.

'Here you see the grand entrance hall. Off to the left is the drawing room,' George started, trying not to roll his eyes at how slowly Mrs Forthbridge walked. 'The room directly behind is the library.'

He paused as Mrs Forthright stepped inside the room, remembering how he and Kate had spent one evening sitting in the two armchairs, talking about their dreams.

'This next room I use as my study, and as you can see, there are beautiful views over the lake from these rooms at the back of the house.'

He thought of Kate helping him sort through his papers, the first time he had looked up and felt a surge of attraction as she had given him that little smile of hers.

'I'm sorry,' he said suddenly. 'I am going to have to ask you to leave.'

His mistake hit him squarely in the chest as he realised what he had lost, what he had chased away. He couldn't have this woman in his house. He couldn't have anyone in his house.

'Leave?' Mrs Forthbridge squawked.

'Yes, sorry for the inconvenience, but the house is no longer for sale.'

George ignored her indignant expression and ushered her out into the hall before managing to manoeuvre her through the door, to the surprise of Mr Sorrell standing outside.

'The house is no longer for sale,' he announced.

'You have accepted an offer, my lord?'

'No. I'm not selling.'

'Not selling?'

'That's right. Take Mrs Forthbridge home, Mr Sorrell, and I will send instruction soon.'

George did not wait for an answer, instead re-entering the house and closing the door firmly behind him. He retreated to his study and collapsed into an armchair, feeling a sense of relief wash over him.

'You did it,' he murmured, wishing Kate was here to see what she had helped him to do. He had been so preoccupied with thinking the place was haunted with painful memories that he hadn't realised they were slowly being infiltrated by good ones. Of course he would never forget the times he had spent here with Elizabeth or Clara, but as time went on, those memories would get less acute and new ones would fill the gaps, diluting them.

Kate had suffused Crosthwaite House with her warmth and her spirit and brought the house back to life along with him.

He felt an emptiness in the pit of his stomach as he reached into his jacket pocket and pulled out the letter Kate had written to him. He wanted to hear her voice, to ask for her counsel, to tell her he had listened to her advice and was no longer in a rush to sell his family home.

Carefully he ripped open the envelope, pulling out the sheet of paper within. He unfolded it and looked at the words, his heart skipping one beat and then another.

*I love you.*

It was all the note said. There was nothing else written on it, just those three little words. George closed his eyes, his whole body feeling as though it was folding in on itself, a giant weight crushing him.

He couldn't breathe, he couldn't stand, and for a long moment he thought he might be sick. Slowly he managed to suck some breaths in, filling his lungs and forcing his body to start functioning again.

'What have I done?' he muttered to himself, unable to believe he had been such a fool.

## Chapter Twenty-Five

Kate sat in the drawing room and fidgeted, her foot tapping on the plush carpet and her fingers screwing up the material of her dress. She felt as though she were fourteen again, summoned to see her parents for some minor infringement of their rules.

With great effort, she sat up straight and lifted her chin, forcing her foot to still on the ground and her fingers to sit demurely on her lap. Whatever happened, she would not let them see how much they hurt her.

The clock ticked by on the mantelpiece, a huge wooden box with a minute hand that always lagged behind where it should. She wondered if this was a deliberate tactic to unsettle her, and at the thought, a steely calm ran through her.

'Kate, what a surprise,' her mother said as she breezed into the room. As always, the older woman was perfectly turned out with not a hair out of place. She spent hours choosing just the right shade and material for her dresses and the perfect hairstyles to compliment the shape of her face.

'Mother,' Kate said, rising and accepting a fleeting kiss on the cheek.

'You should have sent word you were coming,' her father said as he entered the room. He didn't make any pretence at being pleased to see her. 'Your presence places us in an awkward position. People think you are in Devon.'

'Cornwall, dear,' Mrs Winters corrected him quietly.

'Devon, Cornwall, what's the difference?'

'I suspect a lot to the people who live there,' Kate murmured.

Kate sat down even though she had not been invited to, smoothing down her skirt in an attempt to hide her agitation. Rapidly she was regretting coming here. Already she felt fragile after her departure from Crosthwaite House, alone and heartbroken, and a visit to her parents was hardly going to be soothing for her damaged heart.

'How are you?' she enquired, trying to be as pleasant as possible.

'Fine, fine, we're fine,' her father said.

'And Caroline?'

She wasn't sure if she imagined a subtle glance that travelled from her father to her mother and back again, but they were quick to hide whatever they were thinking.

'Caroline is fine. Happily married.' Her father replied.

'Good.'

'Why are you here, Kate?' her father asked.

'You're coming home,' her mother said with a little sneer of satisfaction. Kate shuddered at the thought.

'No,' she said quietly.

'There will be conditions attached, rules you must abide to,' her father said.

'I'm not coming home.'

'Your father has a match lined up and waiting for you. You will accept, of course, and then this whole nasty business can be swept under the carpet.'

'I'm not coming home,' she repeated.

'A good man, wealthy and willing to overlook any little indiscretions.'

'Of course he's not as young as you might like, but that is inevitable.'

'I'm not coming home,' Kate said a third time, raising her voice and looking both her parents in the eye one after the other. 'I merely came to ask you for Caroline's address.'

'Why do you want her address?'

'This is nonsense,' her father said and stood. 'I am taking you upstairs now, and you will stay there until your wedding day. No arguments.'

Kate stood as well, the anger overwhelming her as her father approached. He was tall, and although not particularly well built, could easily overpower her.

'Do not lay a finger on me,' she said, her voice low and dangerous.

The tension pulsed between them, no one moving until the silence was broken by the sound of the front door opening and footsteps in the hall followed by the low murmur of voices.

'Kate.' Caroline burst into the drawing room, looking genuinely pleased to see her.

Caroline threw her arms around Kate's neck, and Kate burst into tears, feeling all the heightened emotion of the last few weeks come flooding out.

'This is not…' her father began, but he was drowned out by Caroline's excited chatter.

'I've missed you,' Caroline said, squeezing Kate's hands. 'Mother, Father, I know you have missed Kate as I have, but I am going to steal her away. I have so much to tell her.'

'I really don't think that is a good idea,' Mrs Winters said.

'Do not fret, Mama. I will bring her back safe and sound soon.'

Without waiting for any more debate, Caroline took Kate firmly by the hand and dragged her out of the drawing room, only stopping to allow the footman to open the front door for them.

They walked briskly at first, as if Caroline feared they might be followed, only slowing once they were a few streets away.

Kate glanced over at her sister and felt a flicker of panic. Her whole reason for returning was to talk to Caroline. In all the months she had been away, she had been able to come to terms with everything she had done, except how she had betrayed her sister. Kate wasn't sure how much she was going to reveal. If Caroline was happily married, Kate wasn't going to put her own need to apologise above her sister's wedded bliss.

'Where have you been?' Caroline asked once they were far enough away to feel safe. 'It's been a whole year.'

'In the Lake District.'

'Ha. I knew you weren't in Devon or Cornwall. Mother and Father couldn't even agree which county it was. What have you been doing?'

'I found work, as a housekeeper.'

Caroline looked incredulous and shook her head. 'You always were a bit mad, Kate Winters.'

'How are you?'

'Pregnant,' Caroline said and held up a hand to forestall any congratulations. 'Pregnant and miserable.'

'I hear it is not an easy time in a woman's life,' Kate said diplomatically.

'It isn't, but that's not why I'm miserable.'

'Why are you miserable?'

Caroline looked around as if she was expecting people to be listening and lowered her voice further.

'My husband is a scoundrel,' she said with venom, 'but I think you knew that already.'

Kate went very still. She felt the anger pulsing out of her sister and wondered if it was directed at her.

'What do you know, Caroline?'

'Everything, or at least enough.' She squeezed Kate's arm. 'He tried to blame you for everything, of course, but I was able to piece together enough of the truth.'

Kate remained silent, not quite sure what to say. They were in a small park, not much more than two patches of grass with some trees dotted around the edges, but it gave them a modicum of privacy. Caroline led them to a bench, and they sat side by side for a moment, neither talking.

'Is he an unkind husband?'

Caroline shook her head, 'He doesn't hurt me physically, but he has a sharp tongue and very set ideas on what my place is in relation to his.'

Kate nodded. She could see that. Arthur had seduced her with his smooth charm. It was embarrassing, really, how easily she had fallen for it, and what she had been persuaded to do against her better judgement.

'We've been married a little less than a year, Kate, and already he has had four affairs.' She sighed and rubbed the bridge of her nose with her thumb and forefinger. 'I actually wouldn't care that much if it kept him away from home, but he does love to try and hurt me with them.'

'I'm so sorry, Caroline.'

'It isn't your fault.'

'It is. If I'd told you about him…'

'We'd probably still be married. It isn't like any of us had much choice in the matter. What Father decides goes, remember.'

'You are not angry with me?'

Caroline looked at her long and hard before shaking her head. 'Not now. I *hated* you when I first found out. I blamed you for how Arthur treats me.' She scoffed. 'For a while I thought he was like this with me because he was in love with you and resented me.'

'He never loved me.'

'I know,' Caroline said more softly. 'I do. I have seen how he draws a person in and then slowly breaks her down, and I have seen the mess he leaves behind when you start to realise he isn't this perfect man.'

'I am sorry,' Kate said again, quietly. She felt this sense of relief to have the secret lifted from her shoulders. The guilt she would still carry, perhaps even more so now she knew how terrible her sister's marriage was, but at least Caroline was willing to forgive.

'Let us not waste any more time on my scoundrel of a husband. I want to hear everything that has happened to you since you left.'

They stood and started strolling again, enjoying the early summer sunshine as they walked and talked. It was cathartic to tell her sister all that had happened. She spoke of the first few months of desperation, trying to eke out her savings whilst learning to live independently. She told her of the feeling of satisfaction the first time she had earned her own money and the jobs she had tried before falling into the housekeeper role at Crosthwaite House. Caroline smiled as Kate described the peace she had found there in the middle of the countryside and then how that peace had been shattered by the arrival of a brooding but charming earl.

'You're in love with him, aren't you?'

Kate nodded silently. 'And he cares for me, but he cannot love me. His heart is still too twisted up with guilt and grief.'

'That is why you left?'

'Yes. I couldn't bear to be around him but not with him. It was too difficult.'

The streets were busier now, so they headed to the promenade, joining the couples and groups strolling along by the sea. Kate felt a sense of calm descend over her. She knew any relationship with her parents going forwards would be tumultuous given their views on her actions and thoughts on how she deserved to be treated, but it was good to make peace with Caroline. They may not have been close growing up, but their relationship as adults had never been given a chance, and Kate was appreciative of the opportunity to build something real with her sister.

'So, what now?' Caroline said.

'I don't know. I am not staying here. In fact, I doubt I will go back home even to say goodbye. Father seemed to think he was going to marry me off to an old friend of his. Before you turned up, he was ready to manhandle me upstairs and lock me in my room.'

Caroline screwed up her nose. 'He means to marry you to Mr Trewlany.'

'Old Mr Trewlany?'

'Yes. He's been talking about it for months.'

Kate shuddered at the thought. She wasn't sure if her father was doing it to punish her for her indiscretions or if in his mind it truly was a good match. Mr Trewlany was old enough to be her grandfather, but he was rich.

'Then I certainly won't be going back home. I came back to Sussex to see you, Caroline. I wanted to start to mend things between us. Of everything I have done, the one true regret I have is that I hurt you.'

Caroline squeezed her hand and smiled. 'I do not blame you, Kate. Although I am a little envious of your freedom.'

Kate stayed silent, wondering what she was going to do next. She'd had a lot of time to think about it on the journey down from the Lake District, but she hadn't been able to think past this meeting with Caroline, not rationally.

'You might consider approaching Aunt Francesca.' This was their mother's aunt, the one Caroline had spent time with on her grand tour of Europe. 'She wants a companion, someone to keep her company at home like I did on the trip to Europe. In her last letter, she bemoaned the lack of suitable applicants for the position.'

'She lives in Hampshire, does she not?'

'Yes. She tries to pretend she's an old battleaxe, but once you get to know her, she's kind and generous. I really think you would like her, Kate.'

'I am not sure she would approve of me.'

There was a gleam in Caroline's eye. 'She *hates* our father. Thinks he ruined Mother. She thinks Mother changed after marrying him. If you tell her of Father's plans to marry you off to old Mr Trewlany, I expect she would hire you on the spot.'

Kate considered this for a moment. She had spent much of her savings on the trip south. It would be good to have respectable employment, even if it was only a short-term arrangement whilst she decided what she wanted to do after a few months.

'I will go and see her.'

'Good. Now I have to go home before Arthur gets annoyed I have been gone too long.'

Kate nodded, knowing her sister's time was not her own anymore.

'I will write to you,' she said, taking Caroline's hand in her own. 'Please write back and tell me all your news. If Aunt Francesca does give me a position, Hampshire isn't too far away. Perhaps we can arrange a visit.'

'Take care of yourself, Kate,' Caroline said, pulling her sister into an embrace.

Caroline set off briskly along the promenade whilst Kate stood watching her leave. Only when her sister had disappeared into one of the wide streets that led away from the sea did she move. Tonight she would find accommodation in Eastbourne, and tomorrow she would look into transport to Hampshire.

For a moment she felt a sensation of melancholy settle over her. She was missing George. Every new thing she experienced she wished she could share with him. Her heart was aching, and she didn't know how to start to heal from something so momentous.

Looking out at the crashing waves, she wished he was here, enjoying this view with her. She wanted to be walking hand in hand down the promenade with him, talking about their hopes and dreams, scolding him for kissing her in public but secretly glad he still desired her so much he couldn't keep his hands to himself.

Shaking her head, she began to walk away. It was silly to torture herself like that. George had offered her what he could, and she had made her decision to walk away. There was no point in going back over events time and time again or wishing for a different outcome.

Blinking away the tears that threatened to fall, Kate took a deep breath of salty air and told herself to be brave. One day her heart would stop hurting, and she would be able to think of something other than her love for George.

## Chapter Twenty-Six

Looking up at the smart townhouse, George paused for a moment before knocking on the door. He had been surprised when the trail he was following led to Eastbourne. From everything Kate had said, he knew her parents had been less than supportive when they had discovered the mess she'd got into with Arthur.

He felt guilty for driving her back to somewhere she had been so unhappy and knew she did not have the options he did. When her money was gone, she either had to beg for charity from her parents or find employment elsewhere. He did not doubt any charity she received would come with strict conditions.

'Lord Henderson,' he said as the footman opened the door. 'I am looking for Miss Kate Winters.'

The house was grand in an ostentatious way, and the livery of the two footmen reflected this theme with plush material and shiny buttons. The two young men swapped a glance and then showed him inside, one disappearing to find someone to receive him.

The drawing room had so much gilding it made his eyes hurt, although the furniture was comfortable and sturdy. He sat, wondering if Kate was upstairs, imagining her contemplating the reason for his visit nervously.

It wasn't Kate who glided into the room a few minutes later, but an older woman who had a hint of auburn in her hair and a few freckles across her nose. That was where the similarities with her daughter ended.

'Lord Henderson,' she said with a broad smile that reminded him of a snake. 'It is an honour to receive you here in our humble home.'

'Thank you for your hospitality, Mrs Winters. I am sorry to be so abrupt, but I am looking for your daughter, Miss Kate Winters. It is a matter of some urgency.'

'May I enquire the nature of your acquaintance with my daughter? *We* have not been introduced before. I would certainly remember.'

'I know Miss Winters from her time up north,' he said, refusing to reveal any more. 'Is she here?'

Mrs Winters's tongue flicked out over her lips, and she hesitated before she spoke. George could see her trying to work out what he wanted with Kate, whether he was friend or foe.

'Kate is not here.'

'Do you know where she is?'

Mrs Winters didn't answer. It would seem strange to admit she did not know where her unmarried daughter was, yet she couldn't claim to be aware of her location and then refuse to share it with someone as influential as an earl.

'If you care to leave a note, I can see it gets to her,' Mrs Winters said eventually.

'Is there somewhere she would go?'

'I am sorry not to be able to help you further, Lord Henderson.'

'Perhaps your husband might know where she is.'

'My husband is out, unfortunately. If you leave your card and details of where you are staying, I will ask him to call on you when he returns.'

George knew he wasn't going to get anywhere here. Either Kate had been and gone and they did not know where, or she hadn't actually returned to Eastbourne to see her parents.

'I understand you have another daughter.'

'Yes, Mrs Caroline Evans.'

'Would you be so kind as to furnish me with her address so I may enquire there?'

'Kate would not…' Mrs Winters began and then trailed off, instead standing and going to the small writing desk in the corner of the room. She jotted down a name and address and handed the piece of paper to George. 'I am sorry I could not help you any more,' she said, still trying to ingratiate herself even though she had been nothing but obstructive.

George stood and took his leave, stopping outside the house to read the address.

He had to stop a few times to ask for directions, but soon he was standing in front of a well kept house that looked out over the sea. It was in a prime position with glorious views and a bracing sea breeze.

Again he was admitted to a well furnished drawing room and asked to wait for the lady of the house. His title was helpful for gaining an audience without a prior appointment. Not many people wanted to say no to an earl.

He was left waiting for a few minutes before he heard footsteps outside the door, and then a man entered.

The man was tall and handsome and self-assured in a way that made George's skin crawl. He knew immediately this was the infamous Arthur, the man who had convinced Kate she was in love, ruined her, and discarded her.

'Lord Henderson,' Arthur said, motioning for him to have a seat. 'It is a pleasure to meet you. What brings you to our little corner of the south coast?'

Superficially the man was pleasant and effusive, but George could see the coldness in his eyes. This was a man who did not mind whom he hurt to get what he wanted.

'I am looking for your sister-in-law, Miss Kate Winters.'

'Dear Kate. As a male relative, I am obliged, of course, to ask what your interest is in Miss Winters.'

George let the silence draw out between them. 'A personal matter,' he said eventually.

'We have been worried, wondering where she's been these last twelve months.' The man's eyes snapped up and searched George's, as if trying to work out what the connection was.

'Do you know where she is?'

'Alas, Lord Henderson, I have not seen dear Kate for a while. I can ask my wife, but she is out visiting friends at the moment.'

'I will be staying for a few days,' George said, standing up abruptly. There was something predatory in Arthur Evans's tone, and he felt a wave of revulsion pass through him. 'Your wife can reach me at this address if she has any information.'

He handed the man his calling card with his temporary address written on the back. Without waiting for him to say anything further, George strode from the room. Part of him wanted to haul Arthur Evans up against a wall and beat him senseless for what he had done to Kate, but Kate wouldn't thank him. She had to live with this man as part of her family, and George's interference would not be appreciated.

As he descended the couple of steps at the front of the house, the door opened behind him again, and a hand caught hold of his arm.

'I will meet you in five minutes in Devonshire Gardens,' the woman said. She was gone before George could reply.

She obviously did not want to be observed, so he put his head down and walked away as if nothing had happened, only stopping to ask for directions to Devonshire Gardens when he was a few streets away from the house.

'Lord Henderson, I presume,' the young woman said as she joined him on a bench in the gardens a few minutes later. 'I am Caroline Evans.'

'I am pleased to meet you, Mrs Evans.'

'I am sorry for the subterfuge. My husband…' She trailed off, not completing the thought. 'I do not have much time, but I assume you are looking for my sister.'

'I am. Have you seen her?'

'Yes. Yesterday she paid a visit to our parents' house, looking for me. We went for a stroll.'

'Is she here in Eastbourne still?'

'She planned to travel to Hampshire to visit our great-aunt. I do not know if she has left yet.'

'She meant to leave today?'

'If there is a coach. There is not much reason for her to stay here any longer,' Mrs Evans paused and then gave him a curious look. 'I hope you have realised you made a mistake.'

'Sorry?'

'In letting my sister go. She's in love with you.'

George closed his eyes and took a deep breath to

steady himself. He desperately hoped he wasn't too late to fix this.

'The coaches go from the centre of town, three streets up that way,' Mrs Evans said with a smile. 'Go. You may be able to catch her before she leaves.'

George stood, ready to run if he needed to. He took a moment to thank Kate's sister and then started off through the crowds.

He saw her from a street away, standing in one of her drab grey dresses with her hair neatly tucked away under her bonnet. Her back was to him and he couldn't really see her face, but he would have known it was her anywhere.

As he approached, a coach rumbled over the cobbles and stopped in front of a small crowd of people. One by one they started getting in the carriage, handing their baggage to the driver, who was stowing it on top. He was a few feet away when Kate passed her bag and took a step up into the carriage.

'Kate,' he called. Her posture stiffened, and he knew she had heard him. Slowly, as if unable to believe her ears, she turned to face him.

George continued forward until he was right next to the coach, ignoring the impatient sigh of the man standing behind Kate.

'Don't go,' he said, holding his hand up to her, hoping she would take it so he could help her down. If she rolled away in that carriage, he wasn't sure his heart would ever mend.

'Up or down, miss?' the impatient man behind her barked gruffly.

To George's relief, she took his hand and stepped down to the pavement.

'We're leaving, miss,' the driver said, motioning to her bag. 'Do you want your bag?'

Kate looked over her shoulder at the coach and the seat that should have been hers, then back at George, searching his face for some clue as to why he might be here.

'Give me half an hour,' he said quietly. 'If you still want to leave, I will personally deliver you to the next coach to Hampshire and pay your fare.'

'Please pass me my bag,' Kate said to the driver, thanking him when he unloaded it and handed it down.

George felt a flood of relief. She might not have forgiven him yet, but at least she was willing to hear him out.

# Chapter Twenty-Seven

They had walked a long way in their quest for privacy, most of it in silence. Kate had led him west, away from the town centre, along the promenade to the seafront gardens filled with flowers and then beyond to a spot where a lone bench sat on the incline of a hill, looking out over the sea.

'You are a long way from Thornthwaite,' Kate said as they settled back against the bench.

'As are you.'

'What are you doing here, George?'

He cleared his throat. The journey from the very north of the country to the very south had not been a quick one, and he'd had plenty of time to consider what he was going to say to Kate whilst he travelled, but he could hardly remember any of it. He was seized by a sudden panic, unable to think of anything but the awful realisation that if she turned him down, if she rejected him now, this would be the end of everything between them.

'I read your note,' he said quietly.

'Ah.' Kate looked out at the view, biting her lip.

'It gave me the kick I needed,' he said, reaching out for her hand.

She looked at him with confusion in her eyes.

'I have been the biggest fool, Kate. I do not know how you have managed to fall in love with me when I have been so blind, so obtuse.'

She turned her body towards him so their knees were touching. It was a bold move out here in the open, but there was no one walking by.

'Somehow I did anyway,' she murmured.

'These past couple of years, I have been locked in this prison of my own making. At first it was grief that was holding me back, but then it was this feeling of overwhelming guilt. I felt guilty when the grief became less, and I felt guilty for continuing my life when Clara and Elizabeth were not.'

Kate reached out and put a hand on his cheek. 'Do not blame yourself. Our minds do all sorts of strange things to try to protect us from our own emotions. Sometimes they get it wrong.'

'If I hadn't met you…' he continued before trailing off, shaking his head. If he hadn't met her, he would have been lost.

He closed his eyes for a moment and was surprised when Kate brushed a kiss across his lips. It was exactly what he needed, exactly the reminder of why he was here, and it gave him a flare of hope that he would be able to salvage the mess he had made.

For a long moment he allowed himself to enjoy the kiss and the affection he felt as he held her tight in his arms.

Kate's hands were shaking as she pulled away, ready to hear what George had to say. Of course she still loved him—there was no way her love for him could flicker and die in the space of a few short weeks—yet she felt as though her thoughts were jumbled and she could not work out what was for the best. She suspected he loved her, and perhaps that was what he had come to say, but it might still not be enough.

'I need to apologise,' he said softly. 'For the insulting offer to make you my mistress. I was blinded by my desire for you, and I felt like I would do anything to keep you in my life. Including insulting you in the worst way possible.'

It *had* felt like an insult. She understood why he hadn't been able to propose to her, at the obstacles that had held him back, but she had been hurt that he would think becoming his mistress was the life she deserved.

'I know what you would have had to give up if you'd agreed to travel to Italy with me, and I still cannot believe I asked it of you.'

She nodded, accepting his apology. At least he could see how it had hurt to be deemed not worthy of a conventional life and all the things young women dream their futures would be.

'I love you, Kate,' he said quietly, and she felt her heart soar. She wished they had not had to go through these last few weeks of torment to get here, but it was wonderful to hear that he loved her like she loved him. 'I love you with all my heart, and I hope you will consider becoming my wife.'

She let out a little gasp at the proposal, even though she had half expected it. He hardly would have ridden the length of the country to reiterate his last offer.

Quickly he held up a hand and rushed on, his words falling out of his mouth so fast now she had to concentrate to keep up.

'I want to give you everything, a loving husband, a partner in life, a home.'

'A family?'

George fell silent, and she searched his face for an answer.

'I can't lose you,' he whispered eventually.

'You won't lose me.'

It felt like the minutes ticked past slowly as he sat there, eyes closed, not saying anything, until eventually he nodded.

'I want a family with you. I want that life more than anything in the world, but I worry…'

She took his hand. 'We shall face those worries together.'

'Does that mean…?'

Kate nodded. 'Yes, I will marry you.'

He kissed her then, standing up from the bench and taking her in his arms. Right now he did not care who might see or what scandal they sparked. Right now all he cared about was kissing the woman in his arms, the woman he loved.

'I have some good news,' he said as he pulled away just a few inches, refusing to relinquish her completely.

'What?'

'I have the perfect family home for us to raise our children in.'

'Does it have beautiful views over a stunning lake?'

'It does.'

'And a very comfortable master bedroom?'

'So comfortable I would wager you will not want to leave it for a week, perhaps not even a month.'

'I like the sound of it already. You have decided not to sell it?'

'I have decided not to sell it. How could I when I cannot imagine living anywhere else with you?'

# *Epilogue*

Pacing backwards and forwards outside of the room was not what he wanted to be doing, but ten minutes earlier, Kate had thrown him out whilst her sister helped her change. It had been a long labour so far, and the summer heat made the room stuffy and uncomfortable. He didn't doubt Kate would enjoy the feel of some fresh nightclothes, but he hated not being in there with her.

Caroline opened the door and poked her head out into the hall.

'She's ready.'

George went to enter, and his sister-in-law caught him by the arm.

'I understand why you worry, but Kate is going to be fine.'

He nodded, unable to answer. Today was the culmination of nine months of worry.

'Come here,' Kate said as he re-entered the room. He went to her side, leaning over and kissing her gently on the lips. 'I missed you.'

'And I you, my love.'

She used his hand to manoeuvre herself into a more comfortable position and ignored the admonishing look from the doctor. The doctor was here at George's request. If it had been Kate's choice, she would have just had her sister and Mrs Smith, Mrs Lemington's daughter, who had journeyed from Keswick specially to help out. He had looked panicked at the lack of medical supervision, and Kate had agreed to a doctor being present to supervise as needed, even though she thought it unnecessary.

Kate pulled him to her, gripping his hand tight as another contraction took over her body. He watched her ride the pain, blowing out deep huffs of air.

'Not long now,' Mrs Smith said as she came over and rubbed Kate's back.

'I need to move.'

Kate struggled up onto her knees, throwing a warning glance at the doctor as he stepped forward as if he were about to protest. Mrs Smith helped her lean on the back of the bed, and as the next contraction came he heard Kate let out a deep groan, deeper than he had ever heard before.

'Baby is on its way,' Caroline said, smiling at her sister. 'Dig deep and find one last burst of effort. Soon you will be cuddling that son or daughter of yours.'

Kate stood on shaky legs, cradling the infant to her chest. It had been a long labour but a straightforward one, and now that she had her daughter in her arms, all the pain was worth it.

'Welcome to your home, little one,' she said, turning her body slightly as she showed her daughter the view from the window.

She felt George coming to stand behind her, slipping a gentle hand around her waist.

'We should give her a name,' George said.

Kate shrugged. She was in no rush. They had all the time in the world to settle into life with a baby, and she meant to make the most of it.

'Have I told you how incredibly proud I am of you?' George murmured as he kissed her neck.

'Only twenty or thirty times.'

'Well, I am proud.'

'And I am of you,' Kate said, turning to face him. He had been quiet this last month as the birth approached, and Kate had known no amount of reassurance from her was going to make him any less apprehensive.

'I did do a wonderful job of rubbing your back.'

'That is not what I mean.'

'I know,' he said quietly, kissing her on the top of her head.

Kate leaned into his arms and felt a wave of contentment wash over her. A year earlier she had been without a true home, alone in the world. Now she had a husband who loved her and a beautiful baby daughter. They lived in the house she felt was destined to be her home and were surrounded by people who cared.

'Aren't you two the picture of married bliss,' Caroline said as she entered the room with a tray of tea. Outside there were hushed voices and giggling, and Kate craned her neck to see Mary and Marigold waiting for a glimpse of the baby.

'You can come in,' she called.

'Oh, she's beautiful,' Marigold cooed, stroking the soft hair on top of the little girl's head.

'She's absolutely perfect.'

For a few minutes the maids made a fuss of Kate's baby daughter before slipping away. Mary and Marigold had been delighted when Kate returned with George and had not been all that astonished when they announced their impending marriage.

The two maids had agreed to stay on at Crosthwaite House, coming up from the village daily, and now that Kate and George's family was getting bigger, they had recruited a few other staff, but Kate had requested they all be locals from the village, people who were keen to go home each night. She liked having the house to themselves at night once everyone else had left, and it wasn't something she was eager to give up.

Caroline helped her get settled in bed, and George gently took hold of their baby daughter so she could have a sip of tea.

'I've been thinking about what you suggested,' Caroline said to George as she turned to leave. 'I would like to take you up on your offer.'

'That's amazing, Caroline,' George said, beaming.

'What offer is that?' Kate knew she had been preoccupied these last few days, but she hadn't heard anything being discussed.

'I wanted to finalise things first,' George said as he leaned over and kissed his daughter on the forehead. 'I know Caroline is unhappy in Eastbourne, and I know how much you miss her. I had the opportunity to buy a cottage in the village for a very good price. I have offered it to your sister if she would like it.'

'You have said yes?' Kate asked.

'If you are happy with the arrangement,' her sister said.

'I am ecstatic, Caroline.'

Kate felt the final piece of her happiness slot into place. Still she felt some guilt and regret over the situation with her sister, especially as her marriage had not improved in the past year. Arthur was openly living with one of his mistresses now, and Kate knew Caroline hated living in Eastbourne, where everyone knew of her affairs. A move up here with her daughter, leaving Arthur behind to do as he pleased, would be the fresh start she needed.

'I will leave you to rest, and tomorrow perhaps we can discuss the details.'

Caroline left, and Kate settled back onto the pillows, enjoying her tea.

'That was very thoughtful of you,' she told George. 'I know how you worry about her.'

'How about Maria?' Kate said suddenly, looking down at their baby daughter.

'Maria?'

'I like it, and she will fit in when we finally go on our honeymoon to Italy.'

They had been due to set off on their honeymoon six months earlier, just as Kate had realised she was pregnant. Knowing George's concerns over the pregnancy, they had decided to stay at home, but now their daughter was safely born, Kate was eager to see the country George loved so much.

'She looks like a Maria.'

'I think the name suits her perfectly. My lovely little Maria.'

Kate rested her head on her husband's shoulder, and together they stared down at their little baby. She could sense the happiness in her husband now that his apprehension had settled, and she wanted to capture this moment and hold it close forever.

'Right,' George said, sitting up. 'Shall we get you dressed? I think it's time for your paddle in the lake.'

Kate looked at him and shook her head. 'I know you

are joking,' she murmured quietly, 'but a promise is a promise, even to oneself.'

'You are not going down to the lake mere hours after you've given birth.'

'I know,' Kate said. 'I went this morning instead.'

'You were in labour this morning.'

'Caroline convinced me exercise was good for controlling the pain in early labour.'

'And you convinced her dipping your toes in the lake was a good idea?'

'I had my shoes off before she could stop me.'

'You are one of a kind, Lady Henderson,' George said, kissing her gently whilst trying not to disturb the baby in his arms.

* * * * *

*If you enjoyed this story, make sure to read*
*Laura Martin's Matchmade Marriages trilogy:*

The Marquess Meets His Match
A Pretend Match for the Viscount
A Match to Fool Society

*And why not check out one of her other great reads?*

The Captain's Impossible Match
One Snowy Night with Lord Hauxton
Her Best Friend, the Duke
The Brooding Earl's Proposition

# COMING NEXT MONTH FROM

## HISTORICAL

*All available in print and ebook via Reader Service and online*

### THE ART OF CATCHING A DUKE (Regency)
by Bronwyn Scott

Commissioned to paint the new ducal heir, Guinevere is drawn to Dev Bythesea. Raised in the maharaja's palace, he's unlike anyone she's ever known, but she's not the impeccable duchess Dev requires...

### A LAIRD FOR THE HIGHLAND LADY (Regency)
*Lairds of the Isles* • by Catherine Tinley

As a carefree second son, Max never considered marriage—until he meets Eilidh MacDonald... But is shaking off his decadent persona enough to win the flame-haired lady?

### CINDERELLA'S DEAL WITH THE COLONEL (Regency)
by Jenni Fletcher

Abigail's plan to confront the scoundrel whose scheming led to her ruin goes awry when his handsome younger brother Colonel Theodore Marshall offers her a job...

### LADY AMELIA'S SCANDALOUS SECRET (Victorian)
*Rebellious Young Ladies* • by Eva Shepherd

When debutante Lady Amelia is courted by self-made Leo Devenish, he has no idea she has a scandalous secret: she runs the magazine he's planning to take over!

### HER UNFORGETTABLE KNIGHT (Medieval)
*Protectors of the Crown* • by Melissa Oliver

Marguerite never expected to see Savaric, the knight she'd once loved, again. She's wary of trusting him, but how long can she resist their still-burning connection?

### CLAIMED BY THE VIKING CHIEF (Viking)
by Sarah Rodi

Wren despises everything Jarl Knud represents, yet as she uncovers the man beneath the fierce Viking chief, she's tempted to claim one forbidden night of passion!

---

# Get 3 FREE REWARDS!

**We'll send you 2 FREE Books <u>plus</u> a FREE Mystery Gift.**

**FREE**
Value Over
**$20**

Both the **Harlequin® Historical** and **Harlequin® Romance** series feature compelling novels filled with emotion and simmering romance.

---

**YES!** Please send me 2 FREE novels from the Harlequin Historical or Harlequin Romance series and my FREE Mystery Gift (gift is worth about $10 retail). After receiving them, if I don't wish to receive any more books, I can return the shipping statement marked "cancel." If I don't cancel, I will receive 6 brand-new Harlequin Historical books every month and be billed just $6.19 each in the U.S. or $6.74 each in Canada, a savings of at least 11% off the cover price, or 4 brand-new Harlequin Romance Larger-Print books every month and be billed just $6.09 each in the U.S. or $6.24 each in Canada, a savings of at least 13% off the cover price. It's quite a bargain! Shipping and handling is just 50¢ per book in the U.S. and $1.25 per book in Canada.* I understand that accepting the 2 free books and gift places me under no obligation to buy anything. I can always return a shipment and cancel at any time by calling the number below. The free books and gift are mine to keep no matter what I decide.

Choose one:  ☐ **Harlequin Historical**
(246/349 BPA GRNX)
☐ **Harlequin Romance Larger-Print**
(119/319 BPA GRNX)
☐ **Or Try Both!**
(246/349 & 119/319 BPA GRRD)

Name (please print)

Address                                                                                              Apt. #

City                                        State/Province                              Zip/Postal Code

**Email:** Please check this box ☐ if you would like to receive newsletters and promotional emails from Harlequin Enterprises ULC and its affiliates. You can unsubscribe anytime.

### Mail to the **Harlequin Reader Service:**
**IN U.S.A.:** P.O. Box 1341, Buffalo, NY 14240-8531
**IN CANADA:** P.O. Box 603, Fort Erie, Ontario L2A 5X3

**Want to try 2 free books from another series! Call 1-800-873-8635 or visit www.ReaderService.com.**

---